THE FIRST

BOOKS BY LISA M. GREEN

The Awakened Series

Dawn Rising
Darkness Awakening
Midnight Descending

Standalone Novels

The First

See the rest at *lisamgreen.com/books*

NEWSLETTER

Sign up for updates and information on new
releases at *lisamgreen.com/newsletter*

THE FIRST

A tale of myth, mystery...and a past long forgotten

LISA M. GREEN

TRIDENT PUBLISHING

ISBN: 9781952300097 (hardcover) / 9781952300103 (paperback)

This book is a work of fiction. Names, characters, places, and incidents are either products of the author's imagination or are used fictitiously. Any resemblance to actual persons, living or dead, or actual events is entirely coincidental.

First published in the United States of America in February 2014

Trident Publishing
Atlanta, Georgia
tridentpub.com
contact@tridentpub.com

Dedicated with all my love

To Jason,

my best friend, my mate, my muse, and my inspiration. Without your guidance and insistence, this story would never have been given life. I'm sorry I couldn't write about the dinosaurs.

To Autumn,

my light among the Shadows.

AUTHOR'S NOTE

This story is for all of those who believe in something so strongly that they have no question in themselves as to where their faith lies.

This story is also for those who don't know what to believe, or question what they believe, as the world pushes them down a little more each day.

For those who would find offense within the pages of my book, I deeply and sincerely apologize, as this is not my intention in the least. I would, however, remind them that this is a work of fiction. It is intended to entertain and provoke thought, and I would never claim that it is otherwise. You will begin to understand over the course of this novel how important it is to take it all with a grain of salt while keeping an open mind and an open heart. After all, it is just a story. But it's my story, and I hope you grow to love it as I do.

"You never know how much you really believe anything until its truth or falsehood becomes a matter of life and death to you."

– C.S. Lewis

~ PRELUDE ~

No one had prepared for this moment.

How could they? Eons of progress and here they were, chasing after a mythological wisp of smoke. Not a wisp. For there it was, and they were going to leave a legacy far beyond anything they could have hoped for. The biggest find in all of history.

Little did they know the power they were messing with in their naive ecstasy. The danger was far too great to risk, yet all they could see in their blindness was fame and notoriety on the horizon. But the sun was setting on their dreams, their hopes.

And their world.

The destruction was instantaneous … at first. An eruption of malice entered the world in a flash of lightning and thunder. The spread was rapid with nothing to contain its power. They should have known. They should have realized.

There are consequences for playing with fire.

CHAPTER 1

The fire's going out again.

Outstretched arms reaching, stretching, to the sides, the ground, the sky. *His* arms. Beckoning me forward, not forcefully, but urgently. Who is he? Is it a sign, a signal, a summons? I wish I knew what he wants, but, as usual, I will not find the answers I seek.

The fire's going out again!

Struggling through layers of unconsciousness, I drag myself onto an unwieldy elbow as I attempt to open my eyes. Total blackness looms before me. Well, that doesn't make any sense. There should be at least some light filtering through the windows by now. Oh, right. My eyes are still closed.

The... FIRE... is... going... OUT, Rinni! Get up and help me!

You see, I should have expected the current lingering pain in the small of my back. At least my eyes are open now. Mori has never understood how to be subtle.

Wait, did he say the fire…?

I'm on my feet in less than a second, all thoughts of the pain and Mori's rude boot to my back forgotten.

"Give me the rod, and you go get more wood! Grab the smaller stuff for now. Go, hurry!" I scream anxiously.

When faced with trouble or disaster, I'm usually fairly calm, but my concern has been growing as of late. The communal fire, when properly attended, should never go out. At least, it never has before as far back as anyone can remember. The stares I've been getting out in the village are beginning to make me think that people are blaming us. Mori and I. We've been tending the fire since we were old enough to do it on our own. Kirris and Whelsi were the previous Tenders, and they taught us everything there was to keeping the fire. Up until recently, not once in all of our years as Tenders has anything out of the ordinary happened. Except for that one time with Bhradon, but that wasn't my fault. Seriously, it really wasn't.

There is so much more to tending than just watching the fire to keep it at a steady blaze. Mori and I are two of four Tenders for our people. The other pair, Jinsa and Prastin, has been doing this a little longer than us, but only by a few years. We share the responsibilities of gathering the wood from the Healing Tree, keeping it stocked in the firehouse reticule, and, of course, tending and watching the fire to be certain nothing happens. We also share the burden of day versus night shifts so that all of us can enjoy time with family and friends. And the two (now three) instances of the fire practically burning out have just happened to be on *our* shift.

It's not that the fire wouldn't burn out if we just stopped supplying it with fodder. But the wood from the tree burns long and bright, so that even a slow, steady hand is enough to keep things blazing for a long time. One portion of kindling will last for days, and I had just placed a fresh ration on the fire when our shift began last night.

Mori returns with the firewood from the container out behind the house, and we begin to stack the wood in the fashion that our predecessors taught us. Not easy when you consider how enormous our communal fire is. But we know what we are doing, and soon the fire is slowly building back up, albeit much less and much lower than it should be.

Everyone knows what that look in Mori's eyes means. He has the uncanny ability to invoke shame and humility on almost anyone with just that look, even when they've done nothing wrong. Like myself, for instance.

"What?" My brain joins my ears in preparation for one of his lectures.

"Well, perhaps if someone wasn't so busy snoring. Not to mention dreaming of strange men...."

"I do *not* snore! It was my time for lie-down, so you should have been paying more attention. The fire doesn't just suddenly go out. And I don't dream about strange men!"

"Sure sounded like it to me: 'What's your name? Who are you? What do you want from me?' And it isn't the first time, Rinni. Of course, I'd imagine it was Bhradon, only I'm pretty sure the two of you have exchanged more than names by now—"

"What is going on? Did it go out again?" Julos, one of our Primaries, is standing in the doorway to the firehouse with a look of concern mixed with anger on his wrinkled face. I'll deal with Mori later.

I believe that contrition is the best approach at the moment.

"Good morning, Prime Julos. I humbly beg forgiveness on behalf of my brother and myself for allowing this to happen once again. However, we do not know why it happened, as the fire was being carefully tended at the time." Stop with the condescending looks, Mori. "Immediate and precise action was taken once the problem arose." Listen to me sounding so formal. Gani must be having a stronger influence on me than she realizes.

Julos is not amused or impressed, I see. "Quick action is all well and good, but why the need to begin with? There is no precedence for this sort of thing. You know that our entire livelihood depends upon that fire! I'm beginning to think that something devious is afoot...."

Now my amusement has fizzled and died, along with all sense of proper commune decorum. A tiny voice in my head is telling me I'm going to regret this momentarily, but it is, after all, a very tiny voice. "Primary, are you implying that Mori and I have somehow abandoned our people in thought and spirit by attempting to destroy them, in order...to what?" Surely that isn't my voice piercing the very air within the firehouse. I never get this angry. "For what, Julos? What possible reason would we have for destroying our own people and ourselves in the process?" Sobbing and shouting in an alternating rhythm that even I can barely understand.

Out of the corner of my eye, I see that Mori's contemptuous glare has softened into one of honest concern. I can tell that my outburst has made him uneasy, but my emotions have run completely off course, and I carry on with my bizarre orchestra of distressed hysterics. Luckily, Julos has maintained his composure and is rational enough to see the danger in allowing me to continue down this awkward path.

"Hush, my child." Somewhere deep down, my brain balks at his use of the word *child*. I am no more a child than Mori. Even though we are twins, people seem to forget this fact when regarding me as an established member of the community. We are both of bonding age, despite the fact that Mori seems far too interested in Gani's garden to find a mate. But I digress. To Julos, as well as the other Primaries, we must all seem as children. Yet his use of the word does not suggest age. I know this, but my experiences have left me sensitive to this sort of thing. One of the roles of the Primaries is to be as father-mother figures to the rest of us, guiding us as a parent would. They are our elders; therefore, we are their children in a sense.

He continues in a soft tone, softer than I've ever heard him use before. "Corinne, you and Morick are both dear to me, dear to us all." *Whatever that means.* He knows perfectly well how much his entire family *despises* me. "Your role is so very vital to our community. Never have I meant to insinuate that you would be capable of harming our people in any way. I am merely worried that something is behind all of this. What, I do not know. But many things have been developing lately that warrant explanation." At that, his words are cut off as an earsplitting alarm begins to sound.

Uh, oh. I know that sound.

CHAPTER 2

With incredible speed for a man of his age, Prime Julos bounds from the firehouse, just as Mori turns to me with a visage of apprehension that I've never seen him wear before. I'm still angry at him for his previous comments, but at the moment we are united by a common enemy, and there are more important things at stake.

"Do you think we should check on Gani?" he asks me with trepidation dripping from his voice.

"Yeah, it would probably be a good idea. Why don't you run back to the hut while I stay here to keep an eye on the fire?" My face dares him to make a snarky comment.

"Rinni, look. There's no point in all this. You were right. It was my responsibility to keep the fire going. But I swear to you that I was watching the whole time, and there was nothing I know of that I could have done to stop it. It just…disappeared into the ash." I wish he wouldn't do that. Here I was, planning on being mad at him for the rest of the day or perhaps longer, and he has to go and apologize. It's amazing how easily he does that.

"Don't waste time with all of that. I know. I've seen it too, remember? Just please go check on Gani and come right back. Hurry!"

I need to make sure that Bhradon is safe. My mind falters with a sudden sickening realization. *It's Seventh Day. Oh, please no... it's Seventh Day!*

As Mori runs from the firehouse, my mind is already imagining the worst. *Seventh Day... Bhradon would have been outside the gates last night on Sixth Day patrolling the western planting grounds. Would he be back by now? It could have happened anytime during the night!*

I can't do this. I have to check on him now.

Luckily, I run into Jinsa almost immediately. Actually, what I mean to say is I collide violently with her as I careen in a sideways track out of the door to the hut.

"Rinni, what are... why did you... hey, wait! Where are you going? Is Mori tending the fire?" she asks in a perplexing and slightly perturbed manner. Even at this harrowing moment, there is some amusement to be found in her attempts to show anger. Jinsa never truly gets mad at anyone.

I barely hear her words from further down the path as I had never stopped my forward motion, having quickly picked up a sprint again without missing more than a stride or two. "He went to check on Gani. Could you please handle the fire till he gets back? Bhradon was on patrol last night!"

There is no doubt in my mind that she understands what I mean by that statement. Everyone knows that Bhradon is my mate, whether they approve or not. *Please don't let it be him!*

Even as the thought enters my head, I know that it is a selfish one. But hoping that it is no one is fruitless, and I cannot imagine my life without him. We have been friends since I was very young and bonded in our hearts as I became old enough to understand and appreciate such subtleties. Our people, especially Gani, do not like the fact that he is older than I am. While we're both still considered young, Bhradon is forty-two years old, while I am only thirty-two. I say *only* because that is the way that many here see it. In their eyes, I am too young for him, too inexperienced in life by comparison, and frankly not good enough.

Bhradon has been one of the most sought-after males among our people for years, with mothers once parading their daughters in front of his parents' home as if they were the latest crop to be harvested. Not once would he even look at them. It was quite a disgusting display, if you ask me. But that was a few years ago. He has since passed the appropriate age when young girls entering the period of bonding at twenty-eight should be available as mates. Those females have long since bonded with others and started families of their own.

The talk in the village for some time was that he did not like women and preferred to be alone. But they were all blinded by their own desires. Deep down, they knew the truth. Bhradon loves *me*. He always will. He has waited all this time for me, and we *are* bonded now: in heart, body, and soul. I was far too young at the time for anything physical to be appropriate, but Bhradon is an *extremely* patient man. The Primaries would force everyone to acknowledge it officially if we asked, but I keep waiting for our people to open their eyes themselves and realize there are more important things at stake than their stubborn pride. Until then, he and I are both content to live apart and steal moments alone as often as we can. Obviously we would rather live together as mates, but Bhradon understands how important the acceptance of our friends and family is to me.

You should hear Gani going on about it. She's been a guardian to my brother and me since we were fairly young. After our parents died, she was the closest family we had. Gani is our great-mother, our mother's mother. Ganitha is her real name, but only Mori and I call her Gani. I guess it's our way of giving her a parental title that is all her own. At one hundred and thirty-four years old, you'd think she would tire of village gossip. She listens to the talk in town far too much if you ask me, but I don't think she means half of what she says.

A large crowd is gathered ahead of me in the distance as I rush onward to the gates, my long dark hair racing away from me, desperate to fly far away, bouncing with every bounding step, every tread that takes me closer and closer to the truth. Pushing aside as many people as I physically can in my haste, I distinctly notice the absence of my objective. I can usually feel on some level when he is near, but my heart is beating so fast that I cannot trust my own internal observations. Both anxious to see and terrified to look, I find myself panting breathlessly after my arduous dash from the firehouse. My pants and tunic cling to me, covered in sweat and desperation. And now that I'm here, my legs betray me when I attempt to move again. Does the root of fear somehow lie in the lower extremities?

My breath is quickening, and I can feel a panic attack coming on. *Oh no, not now!*

Well, of course now! When else have I had a better reason to panic? The salty liquid languishing on my upper lip is the first indicator to me that I am now openly crying. I don't cry very often, but I see all of my life before now rushing at me in a blaze of images, and they are all of Bhradon.

In the midst of my preemptive grief, strong arms envelop me in the gentlest of embraces. I look up.

"Shhh! What's all this about? No worries, beautiful! I'm here. You're here. That's all that matters. No need for tears." Half-smiling, he adds, "You keep that up, and you just might get too ugly and swollen for my taste."

I want to hug him, kiss him, hit him as hard as I can. How can he say something like that at a time like this? He knows, though. He knows exactly what I had been thinking this whole time. He does this so often I sometimes wonder if he can really read my mind. He knows I am having one of my panic attacks. And he is here, here with me. Alive, and here with me. I sigh loudly but end up sobbing in mute relief.

None of this changes the wail of the steam-powered sirens as they scream their message across the entire village: the Shadows have returned.

And someone is dead.

CHAPTER 3

No one is speaking. No one dares to move. The sirens are now silent.

There is no body. *Why is there no body?*

"Why is there no body?" I ask aloud, hoping Bhradon can shed light on the mystery.

"Othon set off the alarm, as far as I know. He's got Seventh Day morning patrol in the southern fields, so I assume that's where it happened." His voice belies his calm exterior.

Patrolling the outer planting grounds is the most dangerous job among my people. We have been forced to expand our farming beyond the gates in order to feed everyone, but we don't have enough resources to expand the gates that far into the Unknown. The only ones who even see these fields are those who plant, harvest, or patrol them. And Bhradon is one of those lucky ones.

Lucky to still be alive, that is. The Shadows come increasingly more often and closer to our very gates.

Patrols are split up among those who normally work or farm within the gates. Each of our seven days has a morning and a night patrol. These patrols are sent out in teams of two to keep watch over their appointed set of planting grounds. Keeping watch is a poor choice of words, as that does not really describe what they do. But it is what we call it. What would they be keeping watch for? The Shadows? That alone would be a waste of time, as no one can escape the Shadows once they find their target. No, they are there to water and tend the fields for the most part. The ground fights our every move to feed ourselves, and needs constant and pervasive attention morning and night in order to provide us with what we need.

The night patrol in the southern fields on Sixth Day is usually Jocabin and Winslir, but I see Jocabin standing not far off with a blank look on his face. I look to Bhradon, who also notices his presence among the crowd. Just as we are about to nudge our way through the throng to inquire about last night, two Primaries begin a course through the center of the people in single-file. Everyone naturally steps aside to allow them passage to the front, where most everyone seems to be focusing their attention since there is a very noticeable lack of a corpse. Prime Lahreni and Prime Feraldos are two of our eldest Primaries, and are deeply respected and venerated among all. They reach the front and turn to face everyone. Feraldos raises his hands to silence the already hushed crowd.

"Good people! It is with a heavy heart and a bitter sadness that we inform you of the death of another of our own, Winslir. His mate and their three children will need your help and guidance during this dreadful time. Please offer whatever you can in the name of love." Prime Lahreni's voice is as soothing as her presence.

However, something is very wrong. What does it all mean? I am tempted to speak up, but in fear I let the words die on my tongue. No one would listen to me, even if they were thinking the same thing.

Bhradon's voice rings strong and clear in the near dead silence. "Can someone explain what happened?"

My hero. *Or else he's reading my mind again.*

The two Primaries look over at us with bewilderment not attributable to the question they had just been asked. "What do you mean by that, Bhradon? You know what happened. It seems to be occurring more and more frequently, so you should be well aware of what has happened to poor Winslir, as with many others." Prime Feraldos is not as calm as his counterpart was only a moment ago.

"With all due respect, Prime, I am referring to the fact that he seems to be missing from his own burial gathering. You have to admit that seems a little strange to the rest of us. And I am wondering why we haven't heard anything of Jocabin's story, seeing as he is standing right over there. What's going on here?" The muscles around Bhradon's mouth have tightened into tiny knots. I catch myself staring at his mouth and realize that I am getting distracted.

Several others have begun to express their concerns as well by this point, and the Primaries are futilely attempting to quiet the maelstrom that has seemingly erupted in a matter of seconds. Out of the corner of my eye, I notice Jocabin being forcefully dragged from the proceedings by Prime Julos. As they head toward the small hill where the Hall of the Primaries is located, I place my hand on the side of Bhradon's face and turn it in their direction. I cannot read the look on his face, but he suddenly looks down at me and nods at the path leading to the building. Oddly enough, I feel myself smile at him as we begin to sneak away from the group at the gates. I like it that he never excludes me or tries to hide me from anything that is going on in town or in his life. We are partners, and we trust each other explicitly.

The fact that I place complete and total blame on him for the incident when the communal fire went out for the first time is beside the point.

The first thing we notice as we step into the Hall is that no one is within sight. This is odd because there is always at least one Prime in the main room of the Hall at all times. That's kind of a large part of their job: to be available and ready if someone comes in with a problem or dispute to discuss. They are our mentors, our judges, our leaders.

When I look to Bhradon for his response to this, he merely shrugs at me and points in the direction of the back rooms. We aren't normally allowed in the back rooms, so I find it odd that it seems Jocabin has been taken there at the present. Someone is definitely hiding something. But why? We have no secrets from one another, at least not any important ones. Everyone helps one another out, and people know each other's business usually because it's no secret. My relationship with Bhradon is slightly different only because it is such a delicate situation. It's not that we are hiding it. People just don't want to talk about it, so we don't.

Turning the corner, we are immediately bombarded with the frantic whispering of several voices. Several Primaries stand with their backs to us and Jocabin trapped in the corner. My shock quickly wears off but not before the hesitation costs me dearly.

A muscled arm pins me from behind. Unable to move my body, I try to spin my head around to get a glance at my attacker. This doesn't seem to be working to my advantage, as all I'm doing is twisting my neck painfully. The next thing I know, I'm staring at the tapestry adorning the wall *outside* the room we had just entered. Jumping up, I feel another arm grab me from behind, but this time I'm ready. I jab my elbow as hard as I can into what I hope is their stomach before they have time to react.

A low, muffled noise emits from the floor behind me. I turn around to face…Bhradon. Great.

Well, at least I got him back for the comment from earlier.

"Okay, admittedly I deserved that for my lack of forethought on that one. But I'm going to need a moment here." I decide that I do, in fact, feel bad. Really bad. And despite the humor of the situation, there is an enormous severity to what just happened. What *did* just happen anyways?

"What was that all about?" I question the air, the ceiling, the floor. *Anyone? No?* Fine.

"I'm fairly certain we've been thrown out of a very important meeting, Rinni. I recommend we leave as we've been so politely asked to do, and come back later when our audience has thinned out a bit." I love this man. I really, really do.

We make no secret of our exit from the Hall just to be sure that they hear us leaving and assume our prying was at an end. Oh, how little they know of us! Bhradon and I used to sneak into that very building (among others) as children just out of sheer curiosity. More than the inquisitiveness of two precocious children is at stake now.

Something very, very odd is going on.

The early morning air greets us with far too much cheeriness for such a somber set of circumstances. It's true that I perhaps don't feel a *personal* loss at the death of Winslir, but any death in our village evokes a sense of impending doom and empathetic sadness among just about everyone. But this is just plain wrong. What could have happened to him that the Primaries don't want us to know? And why are they hiding Jocabin? Did he do something bad? That doesn't really make sense because he would be tried and sentenced in the main room of the Hall, and anyone would be able to attend if they so desired. Besides, that sort of thing rarely ever happens. Most of the judgments handed out are concerned with petty disputes and domestic offenses. I'm certainly not trying to insinuate that my people are perfect, but they are—for the most part—good and decent people just trying to survive.

Determined to put on a sunny display to hide our ulterior motives, Bhradon picks me up once we reach the path leading back down the hill and carries me the rest of the way. Who am I to complain?

"Rinni…" His lips continue to move as if he wants to say more but no sound emerges as we journey soundlessly toward the village center. For a moment, I don't respond in the hope that he will finish his thought instead of hiding behind that stoic exterior of his. He never hides things from me, but he does have the reputation among the others as being very quiet and thoughtful. Little do they know that he is merely observing them—their words and actions bridging deep windows into their very cores—and storing those revelations away in the back of his mind. Bhradon has an astounding affinity for judging people's character and can therefore predict with almost uncanny certainty exactly how and when many of our people will act in certain situations.

Still nothing. *Why can't he talk to me?*

"What's wrong?" My trepidation is rising despite the pluckiness of the morning breeze as it brushes my face without fear of retaliation. Hold on a minute. What am I talking about? How exactly does one retaliate against the wind? Am I seriously losing my mind? Despite this self-analysis, there is a bizarre humor behind the idea, and I begin to imagine all sorts of ridiculous scenarios. I don't realize that I am snickering aloud until I look up, and those thoughts immediately die the second I look at his stricken face.

"What's wrong? What's *wrong?* How can you even *say* that, Corinne?" Using my birth name. Not a good sign. "After what just happened…this isn't funny! It's not funny at all. Winslir is… well, he's presumably dead, and Jocabin and the Primaries are hiding something. Or at least some of them are. I don't know. I don't know what to think right now. I don't know what to say. But I'm scared. This isn't the time for your odd sense of humor, Rinni. Something very strange is happening, and I'm convinced it has something to do with the Shadows. We have to get to Jocabin and find out what happened last night." He stops awkwardly and abruptly as he releases me to the ground directly beside the waterways that flow down through the middle of town from the Healing Tree.

Our entrance into the village center has attracted a few stares, but the overall lack of disdainful looks among our audience is a positive sign in my opinion. But that's not really what I should be focusing on right now. I've never seen Bhradon like this before. And he called me Corinne. He knows I hate that, especially from him.

"I'm…I'm sorry. I…I swear I wasn't laughing about any of this." Well, I can't exactly explain what I *was* laughing about without sounding like a complete idiot. Best to leave my skirmish of retribution against the offending breeze out of this.

Did I really just… never mind.

My sigh must be audible to half the center. So much for a light and cheery facade to hide the severity of the situation. Why aren't any of these people concerned about this morning's events? Always so involved in each other's lives, verbally investing themselves in every little detail. No secrets. Yet the second something is out of place, they turn a blind eye. Is there something I'm missing here?

"Bhradon, I'm scared too. What really scares me the most is how everyone else seems to be completely ignoring all of this. They saw, Bhradon. They saw the empty space where his body should have been. And they don't seem to care. That courtyard was filled with people who had questions, but they refused to voice them."

Why are they so complacent now when I know they have doubts still lingering in the back of their minds?

His response is silence, and I know that he is trying to formulate an answer to a question that has no easy answer. I understand that now is not the time. Here is not the place. Somewhere where we can be alone. Somewhere where our words are ours, and no one else can judge or condemn us.

The Healing Tree.

CHAPTER 4

Despite its importance in many of the village's day-to-day functions, the Healing Tree is rarely visited by most of our inhabitants.

The wood for the fire is harvested on a regular basis, as new branches sprout almost daily, but this is only done in the evenings when the heat of the day has somewhat abated. The leaves and bark are collected as needed by those who assist the Healers, usually an apprentice or two. Several kinds of medicinal—yet flavorful—teas are made from the leaves. We also use the roots, as well as leaves, to create a base and flavor for soups. I do so love when Gani makes cassava-bean soup, especially when she adds in extra pieces of root and lets them soak in for hours or even days. The spices from the roots are undeniably delicious and comforting. She always lets me fish out the pieces afterwards to save for the town builders. While the roots are not truly edible, the drained husks can be salvaged by the builders and made into all sorts of sealants and materials for patching and repairing things around town. Nothing is wasted here.

Though not as aesthetically pleasing as the flowering plants surrounding the clearing, the Healing Tree provides us with kastana nuts. They are delicious roasted over a cooking fire and provide a tasty diversion from our normal fare. In many ways, the sap is the best part, if only because we use it for so many different things. Like the mouthwatering berry pastries we sometimes get from the bakery. Or less delicious uses such as patching roofs.

The sheer size and magnitude of our tree makes all of this possible, especially since each portion reaped is replenished by nature just as quickly as it is again needed. Though the roots may grow back within a few days, we cannot afford to throw away what could be put to better use. With so many people to support, even a tree the size of the Healing Tree cannot provide everything all at once. The collections are made on a rotational basis. No one is wanting, but no one is wasting either. We are only able to survive because we respect this balance.

After a couple of slightly awkward moments of indiscretion in which my sense of personal decency was tested, Bhradon suggested, at the prompting of several prominent figures and not a few Primaries, that we discover more remote rendezvous locations. The tree was a perfect spot because most of the time no one is around, and it's easy to spot when someone is coming as the clearing is secluded and surrounded by tall flowering plants on all sides. The path up is entirely devoid of anything growing above knee-height. No surprises as long as you are keeping an eye out.

As we approach the barrier, Bhradon spreads an arm across a row of plants to clear a path for us to enter. I step first into the clearing. I stop. I stare. This…can't be right. Weird lighting? The sun hitting it in just the right—*wrong*—way so as to give an illusion of…what?

What am I seeing here?

"What…is this?" I'm assuming he's behind me now. Either that or a very large building just crashed into my back. Does he see what I'm seeing, or am I really losing my mind? Images of battling invisible natural elements drift back into my thoughts, and I suddenly realize that I am, in fact, losing my mind. The signs have been there all day. I've been dreaming of a man I've never met, I screamed hysterically at an old man for no reason, and I fought the forces of nature. All in a day's work, I say. Why didn't I notice this before? I breathe a sigh of relief as this is far better than the alternative. What's a little insanity compared to the survival of our entire population?

"No, sorry. Never mind. It's okay. Just having a mental breakdown is all. No cause for alarm." How does he put up with me? No, seriously. I really need to know. Maybe he's crazy too, and we just complement one another's craziness.

Turning around, I see the look of confusion on Bhradon's face. *Is that what I looked like a moment ago?* I wonder. Looking back at the tree, it's obvious he's staring at it. How can he not? The thing is massively huge and takes up your entire peripherals at close range.

He turns to look back at the way we've come, as if to verify to himself that we had indeed entered the right clearing. "This…the tree, Rinni! Don't you see the tree?" Well, of course I see it, silly. It's an enormous tree standing right in front of us.

I was seriously hoping for a mental breakdown there. No luck on that end, huh?

What I actually say is this: "Yes, but how could this be? Maybe we're experiencing some sort of shared delusion right now. Gani says that's happened before when people accidentally consume root that's gone bad. That has to be it! I'm sure we shared a meal yesterday, right?"

"We did, Rinni, but I don't think this is in our heads. For one thing, I feel perfectly normal. When that's happened in the past, people always said they felt strange and kind of dizzy. We have to tell someone now. How could this have happened since the last collection time? The tree was healthy the last time we were here, Rinni. That was... nine days ago? Right? No way would they have missed this. I mean, look at it!"

I am looking at it. In horror.

Now that I know I'm not imagining this, the reality is beginning to sink in like that building that rammed into my back earlier.

Where once there were a multitude of branches curling off in all directions, a marked difference can now be seen in the number of limbs reaching up and out to the sky. And the leaves. The leaves are in such a pitiful state, their brittle or withering brethren looking on in scorn at the ones that are still managing to survive. This latter group seems to be an alarming minority. Kastana nuts litter the ground in various states of decay, but so very few are actually growing on the tree.

The most frightening aspect of all is the Healing Tree itself. The crumbling exterior is noted by an extreme absence of large sections of bark that cannot be attributed to recent collection times. They don't take that much at one time, and it grows back. This isn't growing back. And what's there doesn't look very healthy at all. I can feel my knees shaking as the ground suddenly comes closer in friendly greeting.

Or maybe I fell.

I'm lifted up by strong hands, but my head is swimming and my stomach feels as though I may vomit. There's a mouth near my ear speaking words. Strange words. Shaking my head to clear away the dizziness, I try to focus on Bhradon's newfound language. He probably made it up, but I feel a sense of duty as his mate to listen to his nonsensical linguistic mutterings.

"Rinni, do you hear what I'm saying? We have to tell someone about this immediately!" Oh, good. My auditory faculties are back. *That's* what he was trying to say to me. My head must be clearing now. "Think about what this means, Rinni. The Primaries need to know…" He trails off mid-sentence as his mouth catches up to what his brain should already know. What even I know.

The Primaries are hiding something. And I don't just mean Jocabin. How can we trust them? *How can we not trust them?* Surely they know about this already. Surely someone knows. *The collectors would know. The apprentices would know.* Just exactly how far down does this hole go? And will we ever hit the bottom?

It's not the fall I fear; it's the crash at the end.

CHAPTER 5

We walk back down the hill in silence, neither of us able to formulate our thoughts or suspicions into audible words. How could we even think that so many people were hiding such a deadly secret from the whole of the community?

Preposterous notion indeed.

The liveliness within and around the village main does nothing to lighten my mood, even when I notice Jinsa's two-year-old son trying to "help" his father with retrieving the water for their daily needs. His tiny hands splash into the waterway with a plop as he tries to use them as a ladle, with naive hopes of reaching the bucket in time before the water dissipates from his outstretched fingers. The spectacle, on a normal day, would have me laughing until tears came into my eyes. If nothing else, my thoughts become darker as I begin to think of all that is at stake right now. Her children, my future children, all of us.

I suddenly realize that we never accomplished our original intent for seeking out the tree to begin with. So many strange occurrences. How do we decide what to do? Bhradon usually has all the right answers, but he is mute on the matters at present. Our feet lead us in a natural direction, straight to my house. Gani may not like Bhradon as my mate, but she adores him like a grandson. I admit it makes no sense, but that is how silly this whole thing is anyways.

Having no prescribed course of action to follow, I instinctively open the door and enter our kitchen. Gani has her back to us as she leans over our cooking fire and the large pot that is sitting on top of it. Berry cakes. I smell berry cakes! My stomach is rumbling before the thought can finish working itself out in my brain. I guess we still have to eat, right?

As we start to sit down at the table, Gani's voice rises to what would normally be an unnecessary pitch. Nothing, I repeat *nothing*, is unnecessary as long as Gani is the one doing it. Bracing myself for whatever lecture is about to come, I initially fail to notice the shadow attempting to blend into the furthest corner of the room.

Huh. Odd.

"Corinne," she begins in a loud and seemingly distraught voice. Only Gani (and apparently the Primaries) gets to call me by my birth name. Sort of a great-mother's right, you know? I figure I should let her continue before I inquire about our abnormally shy guest. "I have no idea *what* you have been up to this morning, considering the fact that the morning has barely begun, but I am far too old for whatever nonsense you are getting yourself into. And Bhradon, you ought to know better, old as you are. Whatever this is, it had better be gone from my kitchen before the sun is fully up." As she speaks, the shadow in the corner begins fidgeting with its robes. I know the feeling. Gani has a way of making you feel guilty, even when you aren't the one she's fussing at.

Only now do I notice that the shadow has transformed into an old man. And not just any old man.

"Prime Elfiro. Welcome to our home." His presence is strangely disconcerting. Do I really fear the Primaries? Could they actually be hiding something serious? Why would they do that? *And why are you here?*

"Why are you here?" Only too late do I notice the brusqueness in my tone. I was going for flippant. Oh, well. Down to business it is then.

"I wish to speak with you and your…friend. It is extremely important. Otherwise I would not have troubled your great-mother with my unscheduled visit."

"No trouble at all, Prime Elfiro." Now Gani decides to put on the charm. "I am merely concerned about the welfare and doings of my great-daughter. If there is a problem, please let me know, and I will handle it immediately." Her pointed stare in my direction is obviously meant to intimidate me. I love my Gani, but it is really hard to be frightened by a tiny old woman. Not that it's never happened.

The Primary asks if we can speak in private, so I usher him and Bhradon into the sleeping quarters that Mori and I share. The tension in the air is palpable as I motion for Elfiro to sit on Mori's bed. As Bhradon and I take a seat across from him on the opposite bed—*my bed*—the intimacy of that simple act is not lost on me. I cannot help but imagine what it would be like to share it with him. Bhradon, that is. Not Prime Elfiro. Gross.

Hesitantly, Elfiro looks at both of us with an audible sigh.

Outside, the sounds of the town in early morning motion fill my senses and distract me completely away from the scene before me. It's not that I don't care about all this craziness. It's just that I already know what he's going to say. Is he going to confess to some terrible scheme against the village? Of course not. He's going to tell us that what we saw was nothing and to just run along and play like good little children. And maybe that would have worked. When we were children.

"…and this is obviously just a big misunderstanding. The two of you know you aren't allowed in those rooms, especially you, Bhradon. You are far too old to be sneaking around the Hall like a rebellious child. And we were performing a sacred ceremony to help our poor Jocabin in this time of great distress. No one had any intention of doing you any harm. Our only intention was to keep you away in case you frightened him even further. My presence here is to remind you of your place in this town. Among all the elders that have not been appointed as Primaries, your great-mother Ganitha is one of the most respected among the people. Do not do anything further to incur her wrath… or ours." The thinly veiled threat does not go unnoticed by either of us as we stand stiffly to acknowledge the exit of the Primary. He stops briefly to toss a quick farewell to Gani, who looks back at us with confusion in her eyes. Well, at least I'm not the only one with a severe lack of clarity in this increasingly frustrating situation. Walking toward her and her stare, I feel the gravity of today's events hit me all in one fell swoop.

And suddenly I can't breathe. I can't think or draw a full breath, and I find myself standing outside in the morning sunlight. The air is strangely full of motion and intensity, a not altogether unwelcome sensation this time around. As I try to take in full breaths, I watch. Everyone has a role, and everyone fulfills that role. We do what we do, and we don't complain about it. Not because we have no choice but because it is our choice. We choose to live. We choose to survive. We choose to persevere through it all despite our small numbers. Whatever happened to the rest of this world, we are still here. That is not a gift to be squandered or taken lightly.

Out of the corner of my eye, Bhradon's tall frame strides over from the door to loom over me, blocking out a portion of the sun's blinding light. Slowly, I turn my head in his direction with what I hope is a serious look in light of everything.

"How…where did you go?" Perhaps I misheard. The silence stretches on for a moment as I try to contemplate some hidden meaning in his words.

"Well, right where I'm standing would be, presumably, the obvious answer. I didn't realize I'd been gone long enough to go anywhere else. This just…I needed some air. Everything feels incredibly wrong. Today feels like a dream. A very bad dream." The image of a man with outstretched arms beckoning to me suddenly fills my senses as I once again struggle for air.

The look on Bhradon's face does nothing to alleviate my distress. "No, Rinni. I mean how did you get out here so quickly? I turned to follow you, assuming you were going back into the kitchen to eat, and you weren't there. Gani said you were headed in her direction, but she turned back to the fire when Elfiro left."

"I needed some air, so I walked outside. I've been right outside the door in this very spot for the few blinks of an eye since I stepped out." Maybe we all just need some rest. My short-lived, if inconvenient, lie-down earlier was the only sleep I've had since our shift started yesterday at sunset. I've been around his home long enough to know that Bhradon never sleeps well, stirring frequently and mumbling to some invisible entity. He says he has a lot going on in his head but never chooses to elaborate. I don't count that as a secret. We all need our privacy within our own heads.

With a strange look in his eye as if I have suddenly grown an extra head, he decides to drop the topic in favor of more pressing matters. The decision is made to first pay a visit to some of the people who would have seen the Healing Tree recently. No need to approach the Primaries just yet until we can gather more information.

Plus, they don't know we know. Not yet.

As we head inside to grab a quick bite to eat before we venture out to the home of Milana, a long-time friend as well as an apprentice to the Healers, the sound of rapidly approaching footsteps signals the arrival of Mori. *Where has he been all this time?*

"And where have *you* been?" Did I just sound like Gani? I believe I did. Huh.

His scowl tells me my tone is still somewhat lacking in lighthearted friendliness. I will try to work on that. "If you must know, I ran back to the firehouse looking for *you* after checking on Gani, only to find Jinsa tending the fire. The still struggling fire I might add. Then I stayed until Prastin showed up so she wouldn't be alone." At this last statement, his cheeks flush a brilliant red. Sigh.

My brother is woefully inept when it comes to women. That is, when it comes to communicating with them or being in the same room. I remember one time years ago during Harvest Festival when some girl—I forget who—sidled up next to him with a sugarcane stem in her hand. She stood there for ages, and the two of them kept sneaking peaks at one another from the corners of their eyes. She suddenly reached over, placing the stem in his hand while grabbing his other hand. The poor girl proceeded in attempting to half-coax, half-drag him onto the dancing grounds. Did he smile and accept her offer? No. What he in fact did was much the opposite. After dropping his hand from hers, he quickly backed away, mumbling something no one could understand. The sad thing was that I wasn't the only one who witnessed it. He, of course, meant no harm. He just doesn't know how to talk to girls, so he runs away. And I do mean *runs* away.

With Mori, shyness is not just an understatement: it's an art.

And now he looks at me inquisitively as if he can see everything that is going on in my head, everything we have witnessed this morning. Being twins, we naturally have empathetic connections to one another. But sometimes the implications created from that bond are just creepy. No one likes to think that their thoughts may not be private.

Either way, there is no way to avoid telling him without him knowing something is up and following us anyways. Realizing that he is still gazing at me as he waits for an explanation, I open my mouth to explain the situation without sounding crazy.

I hope.

Thankfully, Bhradon saves the day again. If he told someone that the sky was yellow, they just might believe him. "Did you see what happened at the gate this morning?" he asks my brother.

"No, I ran all the way here then went back to help with the fire. I heard someone say it was Winslir. Why? What happened?"

"His body wasn't there." I admire Bhradon's ability to keep from shouting out about Jocabin and the tree all at once. That probably would have been my strategy.

The look of confusion on Mori's face is completely understandable. "Ok, so where was it?"

"We don't know. But Jocabin was there in the crowd, meaning he survived and might have information. The problem is that Prime Julos dragged him off to the Hall before we could ask him anything."

"So we go up to the Hall and ask, right?"

Bhradon's patience is wearing thin by the look of the lines forming around his eyes and between his brows. We need to get moving on this. I decide to speed the process up a bit. "Mori, we tried that, and they kicked us out." He starts to interrupt, but I'm already one step ahead of him. "Yes, we are definitely going back. Later, when we can be more…discrete. But right now we have a much bigger problem." I hesitate. The swirling emotions over the business with the Healing Tree are making it hard for me to form the words.

Bhradon jumps back in by explaining the details about the tree, and where we are headed. His face plastered with anxiety and a touch of anger, Mori nods his head forcefully.

"Right. Right." In the silence that follows, he continues to nod in an almost unconscious way. "So we go and figure this whole thing out." Mori's determination is contagious and surprisingly comforting. Though he tries to hide his irritation, I can still see he is frustrated by what happened in the firehouse this morning. Another issue we need to investigate. That fire is our life, and our livelihood rests on the ability to keep it going. The wood from the tree is everything to us. Without it, our village cannot survive. Without it, the fire dies and us with it. The tree is all we have without venturing farther out into the wilderness and risking many more lives than we already do.

The Shadows are never far away.

CHAPTER 6

Despite our need for haste, the enticing smells floating out from the bakery cause my mouth to salivate as we pass by on the way to Milana's house. Realizing I haven't eaten a proper meal since before our shift yesterday, I indulge in a moment of aromatic ecstasy as my olfactory nerves register the intense sensory experience. Apparently, the quick bite at home did nothing to satiate my appetite.

Berry pastry. Oh so divinely tempting.

No, we must push on. I am not thinking about the flaky pastry crust. I am certainly not thinking about the warm syrupy filling. My stomach growls traitorously in loud protest.

The two companions I'm lagging behind slow down to look at me only momentarily as I put on a show of innocence. No need to burden them with my remonstrations of hunger when there are more important factors at hand. I shrug my shoulders and press on.

On our left is the mill where the wheat crop is ground into flour for the bakery to use in breads and pastries. A massive building with large numbers of workers, the wheat mill is the broadest building in town and the largest of the three mills. The other two mills process the sugarcane and cotton, respectively. All three mills, as well as the bakery, are powered by steam emitted through pipes that lead away from the firehouse. The people rely on that fire in order for our society to remain functional. We survive because we have so much integration between the Healing Tree, the fire, and our daily lives. The loss of that connection would be catastrophic.

Milana lives across the town on the far side of the waterways, just east of the village center. The three channels begin to branch off just north of the center and continue down past the southern wall and the fields beyond. The firehouse lies directly west of the Great Bridge, which, incidentally, I used in my scramble to the gate earlier this morning. It is the only bridge that provides access across the river before it splits off into the channels. However, the bridges in the village center are the most traversed because of their location. One might imagine an extended bridge across the entire span of the three channels (which isn't very wide at that point because the split is just barely north of there). Instead, we have three separate bridges, one for each channel, called the Central Bridges. The Southern Bridges work the same way as the central ones, only they are much farther apart at that point. Living on the southwest end of town, we sometimes use the Southern Bridges. However, it is usually easier and more practical to head toward the village center.

As we cross the final stretch of the Central Bridges and continue east out of the village center, the Festival Grounds to our left catch my eye as I remember Mori's embarrassment from earlier. My poor brother. Forever doomed to celibacy and loneliness.

I've got to find him a mate.

The Festival Grounds are used infrequently, but the visual appeal of the place is always kept in order by the Grounds Keepers. These are the people whose role in our community is to maintain the land within and around the area, as well as around the Hall and other prominent places in the village. The only flowering plants we have are those surrounding the Healing Tree, so some of the workers tend to the plants, while others gather a portion of the flowers and use them to create small garden areas and beautiful garlands that drape around the wooden posts on the edge of the Festival Grounds. When the torches are lit during Harvest Festival or other holidays and celebrations, the effect is simply breathtaking. I almost envy the Grounds Keepers and their ability to create something so remarkably stunning. Though not a vital craft, it is truly a skill beyond comprehension. My comprehension, at least.

Our destination lies directly in front of us now, so I take the lead and step up to the door with the intention of signaling our presence. Before I even reach the threshold, a hand reaches out and grabs my arm, forcefully pulling me inside. Okay, this has to stop. Why do I keep being yanked and pulled around today?

This time, instead of being greeted by a wall hanging, I find Milana's face inches from mine before she suddenly pulls me into a very uncomfortably tight hug. As she finally pulls away, I notice out of the corner of my eye that Bhradon and Mori have entered just behind me, Bhradon with a quickly fading expression of apprehension and protectiveness. I can only imagine what he was thinking for a moment there. As for me, my heart is slowly receding back down from my throat. *What was that all about?*

"Milana, what was *that* about? You nearly frightened me to death!" My exasperation is, I hope, clearly evident on my face, if not in my tone. I'm not usually one for overly dramatic theatrics.

"Oh, Rinni! Please, please don't say anything! I can't…I don't want…please just promise you won't say anything!" Anxiety riddles every inch of Milana's face, and I can feel the hairs on the back of my neck standing up as I realize what she means.

She knows. Oh, she definitely knows.

Mori is cowering in the corner, presumably to put as much distance as possible between him and my best friend, despite the fact that we all grew up together. Bhradon steps forward and gently pushes her into the next room.

"Where is Norsyno? And the children?" His voice is almost a whisper, but the implied severity is still evident.

"Norsyno will be at the cotton mill until sunset, and the children are out playing somewhere." She pauses before continuing in an even quieter tone. "The Healers won't need me today."

"And why is that?" I breathlessly demand. I notice the disparity between the lightness of my speech and the raging emotions within my head. Only then do I realize that I'm shaking.

Because I already know the answer.

CHAPTER 7

"They told me not to say anything to anyone. That people would worry and that the town would lapse into chaos over nothing. It's nothing, they said. The Healers are helping the Primaries find a solution. This will all be back to normal soon. They promised." The look of pure conviction on her face breaks my heart in a million different ways. Poor, sweet Milana. So trusting. And here I am about to shatter her tightly held illusions of hope.

I clear my throat of these deep sentiments before I begin speaking. "You saw it, didn't you?" As I probe her for answers I already hold in my heart, I reach out to grasp her hand in mine. Her hand is icy, trembling, and pulsating with an intensely built-up range of emotions that I can only try to fathom. She is beyond scared. She is terrified. Yet she believes wholeheartedly in the ability of the Healers to fix what they are passing off as a minor problem, as opposed to the nightmare that it really is. As

I wait for her superfluous reply, I am beginning to see the bigger picture.

Her voice is scarcely a whisper as she speaks one word: "Yes."

"Then you know how serious this is. The Healers...what are they going to do? This is really, really bad! That tree is dying, Milana!" Screaming out these last words, I unconsciously slump down into a chair, staring at the earthen floor as if scrutinizing it for the answer we need.

I can feel rather than see Mori step up behind me. His presence is calming as he places his hands lightly on my shoulders. Feeling a sudden charge of energy, I whip my head around in time to see him look at Bhradon before he states, "Obviously we need to go speak to the Healers. Maybe they do have an answer. Maybe we can help."

Reaching back into my memory, I stop when I stumble across Milana's first words when we arrived. *How did she know our purpose in coming here?*

"Milana," I turn my head slowly in her direction. "How did you know why we were here?"

Embarrassment floods her cheeks with a rosy flush. "I saw the two of you head up toward the clearing earlier. I was standing outside the house with one of the children when I noticed you walking that way. I knew where you were headed." Her blush is attempting to extend beyond the confines of her face. "I...I know you go there sometimes. Together. And I knew you'd see. That you'd realize I had seen it, too. I've been waiting for you to show up."

She stammers as she plunges forward in a stream of whispered cries: "Please, Rinni! Please don't say anything. They'll know I told you. The Healers will be so angry! Just let them handle this."

Pity almost overwhelms me as I stare into her teary eyes. "We have no desire to get you into any trouble, Milana. As you said, we saw it with our own eyes. That's all they have to know." Looking back over my shoulder to the two most important men in my life, I struggle to put on what I hope is a convincing smile. "The Healers won't be any help to us in solving this. They don't know any more than we do, I fear. I suspect the Primaries are hiding something. And I mean more than just this. I can't be certain, but I have a feeling—a very strong feeling—that there is more to this than just the Healing Tree. We need to speak with Jocabin. Somehow."

Bhradon nods in affirmation of my words. "Rinni's right. They won't tell us anything even if we ask. So we need to pursue the only course of action that we can right now. Jocabin is probably still in the Hall, making this a very tricky situation. Normally, I would feel very uncomfortable sneaking around like this, but..." He stops and looks me dead in the eye for what seems an eternity. "...our lives and our futures may be at stake here. And I won't stand by while it happens."

The three of us head toward the door as Milana looks about frantically as if she's lost something. I stop just before the entrance to her home to embrace her. I put my arms around her and whisper every comforting word I can think of into my friend's ear. I can only hope it's enough.

The sun is now directly above us as morning wanes and midday burns its scorching mark onto everything within reach. The air is now almost unbearably hot as we march back toward the village center. Suddenly, as I'm staring at the ground in an attempt to avoid the blaring brightness in the sky, my slumped head bumps into the back of Mori's frozen form. I look up, perplexed by his sudden stillness, just in time to glimpse the source of his immobility.

Cyndene. Why, oh why does he do this?

I breathe a sigh as loud as I am physically capable of mustering, hoping she actually heard me. Mori turns to me with a look of reproach on his face. I shrug. He knows how I feel about her. Or more accurately, how she feels about me. How her entire family treats me. They are one of the chief difficulties when it comes to Bhradon and me. All because he refused her sister Saraben as a mate. And now they treat me as if I've done something horrible to them, even though Saraben has had a mate for years and has two small children with him. Refusing to move on, they still give me a withering look whenever our paths cross. Perhaps I shouldn't be having these thoughts today. After all, Cyndene and Saraben have just lost their brother. Did I mention that Winslir is—*was*—Cyndene's older brother? As the middle sibling of the three, he was the closest in age to Mori and I. Saraben is closer to Bhradon's age, but Cyndene is the baby. Barely of age to find a mate, she still exudes an immaturity that expresses itself in callous words and flippant remarks that are completely unnecessary. Prime Julos is their great-father, so she and her family have always held one of the privileged distinctions in our society. Hoorah for me.

And she is heading straight for us. Great.

Mori has now become a solid block of flesh and refuses to go any further. If he has a thing for her, he is definitely a glutton for punishment. Maybe he has a death wish. Either way, he is blocking my path and my attempts to avoid the tiny fiery-eyed girl bouncing toward us with an obvious purpose. I sigh again in case she missed my earlier one and await the inevitable.

Her mere presence in our midst has Mori visibly sweating and panting slightly. I desperately need to find him a mate. Someone with a sense of human decency. There's not a single tear in her eyes. Winslir wasn't a friend of mine, but even I feel badly about his death. At least enough to pay my respects to his family, cruel as they may be.

"I am so sorry for your loss, Cyndene. Your brother will be missed by us all."

Her eyes hold a gleam of bemusement as she searches my face. "Right. I'm sure you're heartbroken. Meanwhile, my family is suffering this loss while no one does anything about it." Her face now seemingly inches from mine, she leans in even closer to whisper in harsh undertones: "I know you know something. Something about my brother. Something no one is telling us. And I want to know what." She steps back from me and looks Mori up and down like a sack of grain. "What's with him?"

I look over and see that Mori is now leaning against the bridge railing, with his head held over the side looking down at the swirling waters. Even this girl turns him into goo.

There's no point in addressing her accusations. We don't know any more about Winslir's death than we did this morning. "He just needs to eat something. We're all fairly weak, so if you'll excuse us, we'd like to get home and have a proper meal. Again, so sorry for your loss. If there is anything that our family can do for yours, just let us know." I let that last part slip out without thinking. Hmmm. *Oh well.* I can be the bigger person here. Certainly under these circumstances, surely?

Cyndene's frustration is physically apparent as her eyes widen and her fists tighten at her sides. As I begin to walk toward home again, she puts her finger to my chest to halt my forward progress.

This girl really has some nerve.

"Don't think you are fooling anyone, *Corinne*. I know you and your little *companion* found something today. I watched both of you follow my great-father into the Hall, and I saw your faces after you came back out. You *saw* something. And believe me when I say that I will find out what that is. My brother's wife and children are alone now because of this whole mess." Anger flashes across her eyes as she speaks, but she then turns quickly away as if nothing happened. "I've got my eye on you," she shouts back over her shoulder.

Bhradon, I see, has strategically placed himself away from the center of the storm. If it was a male denizen in my face like that, I'm certain I'd be witnessing a tragic drowning right now.

Females. I don't blame him.

After Mori restructures his breathing patterns, we head home to get something to eat. I cannot think properly when I'm starving. Gani, as usual, has a multitude of foods ready for our consuming pleasure. I smile at her as we stuff ourselves with soup, bread…and berry pastries. I almost feel bad for indulging when so much is going on around us, but there is nothing we can do until nightfall. My smile fades as fear and dread mix with anxiety and nausea.

Nightfall can't come soon enough.

INTERLUDE
~ A ~

The sickly sweet stench of sweat permeating through the air between the trees. Running, running. Bare feet on the cool earth. The ground is always cooler underneath the trees. The trees are everywhere. It's always cool, except now. Except now as they run for their lives.

What a strange concept, he muses to himself, acknowledging the irony.

Don't think don't think don't think—

Just run. Run fast. Run faster. Faster or they'll find us. Catch us. Kill us. *Or worse.* There is no going back.

We are in this together.

CHAPTER 8

Funny thing about sneaking around in the dark…

Yeah, there's *nothing* funny about sneaking around in the dark.

Every shadow condemns us, pointing accusing fingers in our direction as we slowly creep along in silent apprehension. Apprehension of what lies before us, the air pregnant with the anticipation of discovery. Of answers. Of the truth. Hoping to find those answers, to unearth the real truth. Afraid of finding we are right, hoping we are wrong.

Hoping there is nothing to find.

All the pleasantries of daylight are forced into stark blackness as we approach the rear of the Hall. The enormous roof awning looms overhead, blocking out any residual light from the waning moon. Lurking shades threaten from every corner, gnawing at my determination. Why did it seem so much less sinister when we were youths? Courage is wasted on the young it would seem.

Turning sharply just yards before reaching the wall of the building, we head instead to the adjacent hut. In the exposed clearing between the structures, the moonlight reflects off Mori's confused expression. I smile to myself, reaching out to push him along as my brother vainly gestures toward the Hall. He cranes his neck around repeatedly in an attempt to express his questions. His mouth flops open and shut, open and shut, all without any actual sounds or words. But I continue to nudge him forward gently without giving him the opportunity to break the silence and get us caught.

Bhradon is already creeping into the back door of the unoccupied building as if he had lived there every day of his life. And we did on occasion, when we were younger and less cautious. The house may be vacant, but not empty. In truth, it's a storage shed. The building is only used during the day, so at this time of night there is no danger of being discovered as long as we are quiet.

This storage shed also houses a secret, a vastly lucrative secret.

We discovered it more than twenty years ago when Bhradon decided we should scavenge for a midnight snack after traipsing around the northern part of town with Milana and Rhionnon. Rhionnon is Bhradon's longtime friend, and once upon a time, we were sure he'd pick Milana as a mate. Sadly, he had other interests, but that night the two of them followed us all the way to the back of the storage shed. Until they got scared and took off together back toward the middle of town. Bhradon, being far more mature at eighteen than my young impressionable self was at eight (despite the fact that we age far more rapidly up until puberty than we do after), stepped up to the door and walked right in as if he owned the place. Just like tonight. Just like every time over the past twenty years. In fairness, it's been quite a while since we've done this, but nothing has changed. That night, all those years ago, he and I quickly swept through the small building in hopes of finding something delightfully interesting. What we found was so much more. A gateway into another world.

Or, you know, the next building.

Tucked away in the farthest back corner, partially hidden under several sacks of grain, is a small circular door almost the same color as the earthen floor. A door leading to a ladder and a tunnel black as night. On the other end, another ladder with another door, a door leading up from the ground in one of the back rooms of the Hall. How it got there or what it's normally used for are still unanswered questions. It's not as if we could ask and avoid admitting to sneaking in. I mean, we never took anything other than the occasional piece of fruit, but children are expected to be in their beds at night. And to stay out of forbidden buildings.

Forbidden fruit always tastes sweeter.

As Bhradon peels back the cover to the secret door, I watch the words die on Mori's lips when he sees what we are doing. Oh, right. We never actually told Mori about the underground passage. He was a bit of a tattletale back then. Not on purpose. He just couldn't keep his mouth closed about anything if Gani so much as looked at him.

Lucky for us, Mori can usually keep his thoughts to himself now, though I do see him casting sidelong glances in our direction throughout the journey to the other side. Once we climb up the ladder into the Hall, however, his stupefaction turns quickly into anger once realization dawns.

"The Hall? We're in the *Hall*? Are you out of your mind, Rinni? Anything beyond the main room is a sacred area. How could you let your friend here drag us…" Bhradon's shadow dancing in the torchlight is an overpowering presence in the room, and not just physically. He towers over Mori's smaller frame.

"If you want to turn around and head back to your nice warm bed, you go right ahead. And keep hoping you continue to have a warm bed to sleep in. If the Shadows are growing bolder, when they come to grace your doorstep and take Gani or Rinni away, will you be able to forgive your apathy?"

"Um, no, I just… it's just that this is so, so wrong. We shouldn't be here. We're not supposed to be here."

"Neither should Jocabin."

"Point taken."

Enough of this. I have to interject before they get us in trouble. "Perhaps we should save any conversations for later when we aren't in serious danger of being caught sneaking into the building we're not supposed to be in?"

They glance at one another and nod in my direction. Bhradon heads to the door leading into the antechamber beyond. Stopping to peek around both sides of the entrance, he then motions us forward. Torches line one side of the narrow set of hallways, flickering with a secret knowledge, a hidden breeze, the fire dancing as if to beckon us further into the depths, further into our quest for answers.

We're heading down the left vestibule, in a far more remote area of the Hall than we've ever been during any of our brief excursions, when the sound of fevered cries erupts from the darkness.

Someone, at least, is here.

My instinct leads me to follow a side passage down a very long hallway with two identical doors at the end. Again, I feel a pull toward the door on the right, a feeling I cannot describe but know I must follow. Turning the knob slowly, I lightly push into the door with my shoulder and look back to make sure the rest of the group is behind me in case this all ends badly.

Badly doesn't even begin to describe it.

CHAPTER 9

First, there is the issue of Cyndene. The issue being why she is standing behind Mori and Bhradon as if she'd been invited to this little party all along.

What a sneaky little creature she is. And persistent at that.

Second, now that I've managed to push the door open, I'm not exactly sure what I'm looking at. *Why is he doing that?*

"What are you doing?" I let the words escape my mouth before my brain has a chance to completely register the situation: namely the fact that we are supposed to be on a covert mission, and I just blew our cover to anyone within earshot.

In the middle of the room lies Jocabin on the floor, covered in blankets and a sheen of sweat as if he'd been tending the fire for days on end. He is thrashing around wildly in a seeming attempt to ward off an unseen entity, the thought of which begins to make my skin crawl. Right now, my mind is ready to believe just about anything with the way things seem to be progressing.

At the sound of my outburst, he leaps from his pallet on the ground and grabs me violently into the room. *Not again.* Immediately, my instinct is to defend myself, as he is obviously not in his right mind and could conceivably be a danger to both me and himself if given the opportunity. I swing out with my other arm with the intent to push him forcefully away from me, but Jocabin is surprisingly strong for a man who looks like he's at death's door. His wide, remarkably focused eyes stab me with their intensity, freezing my action mid-swing and forcing me to gaze back into them against my will. I can see the desperation in the depths of those dark pools, but I also register something else there. *Terror.*

Not just fear. Pure unadulterated panic. And suddenly I think I know why.

Without pausing to consider my actions, I grab Jocabin by the shoulder with my one free arm and pull him so close to me that our noses are nearly touching as I look him straight in the eye. All of this has occurred in such a short amount of time that everyone else has barely entered the room behind me at this point. Strangely enough, the two men don't seem fazed in the slightest by the sudden appearance of Cyndene. I barely notice all this in the rush of adrenaline and curiosity that is overwhelming my senses.

In a voice more conducive to the nature of this undertaking, I address the thought by asking him the question that must be asked: "Jocabin, what did you see out there?" My voice carries the query on the wispy tendril of a breath, stopping dead center of the space and hovering over us with its pregnant silence.

He looks around behind me before reaching around to close the door quietly. I notice that he continues intermittently staring at the door even while his eyes flit back and forth between my friends and me. When they land on Cyndene, his demeanor completely unravels, and his face contorts into a twisted visage suddenly full of an immeasurable amount of pain. Throwing himself on the ground at her feet, Jocabin is overcome with grief as he grovels below her stunned form. She looks at me first, then to the others, but no one seems to want to intervene in this particularly naked display of emotion on the part of what is obviously a very ill man.

When the moment passes and still no one moves, I walk over and place my hand on his shoulder. Leaping into the air, he makes a high guttural noise and shrinks into the corner with the blanket over his head. The others are still staring at the bizarre display, but Mori slowly walks over to the terrified figure and gently pulls off the blanket. At first Jocabin tries to fight the intrusion, but eventually he relinquishes his cloth prison and stares into Mori's eyes much like he did to me.

Only this time he begins to speak. His voice is high-pitched but soft, and he continues to glance at the door from time to time.

"They know. Yes, they do. I heard. I saw. They know everything." At this, his voice falters, and instead of the focus from before, I see his eyes glaze over and take him somewhere else.

"Who? Who did you see?" Mori tries to help him sit up, but the effort seems too much for Jocabin. Instead, he leans onto Mori in an effort to keep staring at different points around the room at intervals.

"Not who. Not who. What. They're what. They're here. They

know. And there's nothing we can do about it because they're asking questions, and now they know." The prickling of the hairs up and down my body signals the onset of a chill that begins in my chest and radiates outward.

"What are they? And what do they know? Jocabin?" This time Bhradon chimes in, and I can hear the fear in his voice.

"The Shadows. They know everything. They know we're here. And they know how to get in. I heard them, I tell you. I heard them, and I heard what they said. Well, what one of them said."

A feeble attempt to take deep breaths does nothing to stop my brain from bashing itself against the inside of my skull in an attempt to get out. Is he saying that the Shadows...*spoke?* Of course, this is nonsense. Shadows don't speak. They can't speak. They don't think or communicate, at least not in the same way as we do. They are creatures of the night who only thrive on violently killing our people and leaving their bodies behind when they are done. They can't *know* anything.

I hesitate before I voice my thought this time. I don't want to upset him or send him into another frantic bit of hysterics by telling him that he's wrong or suggesting he's not quite in his right mind, which is apparently the case. Instead I decide to simply say, "Are you sure you *heard* them? Was it some sort of noise that they were making? How would they know how to get in, Jocabin?" The gates are secure, and the fires on the outer rim keep the Shadows at bay for all but those who venture too far past the gate.

"But he'll tell them. He has to. No one could blame him for that. They'll ask, and he'll tell. No doubt about that. It wasn't noise, I tell you. It was words. I heard it when they took..." His words break off this time in a choking sob of tears as he looks straight at Cyndene. Her eyes haven't left his face this entire time.

"My brother? Are you saying they *took* him?" Feral features transform her face into something not unlike ugliness. A wild, animalistic ferocity in her eyes that harbors unmitigated malice, if not for him or us then for the creatures who have destroyed her family.

But the Shadows never *take* anyone. Why would they? They've never before shown an interest in eating the flesh of their victims. Shredding, yes. But never consuming. The idea of being stolen away by a Shadow is the stuff of nursery tales, occasionally told by some well-intentioned mother or great-mother looking to put a healthy dose of fear into older children. Nothing prevents a sense of morbid curiosity like the thought of being ripped to shreds by a horrible monstrosity, to be alone and dying in the vast unknown wilderness, apart from anyone or anything familiar.

So why does he think the Shadows took Winslir? Maybe he is confused by the absence of Winslir's body as well. I can imagine this is overwhelming for someone who has been through something so dangerous.

Wait. I think I'm missing something here.

How is it even possible that he lived after all that? The Shadows never leave survivors. Ever. The thought alone implies some semblance of sentience on their part. And I just sounded like our addled friend here.

Before I can bring up this point into the conversation, Cyndene is nose-to-nose with Jocabin with that same fiery look in her eyes. He elapses into a vacant stare despite her uncomfortable closeness, the filmy glaze of his eyes belying the lucidity of only a moment ago. With a hiss, she asks, "Where is my brother? What did they do to Winslir?"

For a moment, I believe that he isn't going to answer her,

that he's lost in his own delirium. Perhaps he'd been given some medicinal substances to ease his obvious anxiety and mental state. But the moment she mentions her brother's name, his face turns ashen and begins to sweat anew. Shaking his head vigorously, he hugs himself around his mid-section, mumbling incoherent strings of words. One catches my attention.

Alive.

CHAPTER 10

Again, I find myself stooping down to speak with this poor creature who will probably never be the same again by the looks of things. Sitting myself down on the floor next to him and his blanket, I begin to softly stroke his back and hum a melody our mother used to sing to Mori and me when we were little. A choking feeling of nostalgia envelops my entire being, desperately seeking for a solace from these ghastly times that now face us. Normally I don't miss my mother too much since we were young when she and my father died. But sometimes—just sometimes—I wonder what my life would be like had they not left the compound that night.

Jocabin's mutterings cease suddenly, and he leans his head back against the wall of the room. The room itself is exceptionally small, especially for five people, the dark stone walls threatening to close in on us, and I abruptly realize that this is the first time

I've even noticed anything about my surroundings. My mind traces its way back to the task at hand, aware that we could be discovered at any moment. It's a miracle we haven't already. Perhaps a new tactic is best.

"Where are the Primaries?" I ask him in hopes that he will be able to pick up a normal speech pattern with a change of topic.

"The Primaries are around. Not too far. Not too close or else they would have heard you before when you yelled at me. That's why I grabbed you into the room. So they wouldn't hear, wouldn't come looking for you. Or me."

"You don't want them looking for you? Don't they know you're here?" Bhradon chimes in with his best attempt to follow my lead.

"Yes, they know. They put me here. But every time they come back, they keep making me think and talk, and I can't. Can't do it anymore. You're trying to make me think about it, too. I know why though. You want to know what happened to him. They just want to know what I heard. I told them I didn't hear much. Just what I said. That one said 'with the others.' Then it said the word 'alive.' And that's all I know, all I heard. Maybe it said more, but I didn't hear it. Didn't seem like they were big on communicating, just that they could. Some at least. But that's all it said. And they took him. So now he'll tell, and they'll know."

This is far more than my brain can handle at this point. Cyndene, however, seems to light up at the mention of her brother.

"So you're saying they didn't kill him?" Her pleading insistence is easy to pity in this moment.

"No, I'm sure they killed him by now. They always do. But they took him, and he was alive then. Stupid, stupid boy...." His loud sobbing is going to get all of us in serious trouble.

"Please just tell us what happened. How did you escape?" Thankfully, Mori jumps in to intervene before Cyndene can react to the previous statement.

"Didn't. Didn't escape. They didn't see me because I was still on patrol nearer to the gate. I told Winslir not to run off. I told him to either hold it or go where we were. But he didn't listen. Figured he was shy or something, though before I guess he always just waited until our patrol route was closer to the trees. Then we could watch each other's backs at the edge of the woods. No, he took off toward the wilderness! Made way too much noise for my comfort level. Still, I never thought it would really happen. I don't know why. It happens often enough to make you think it should. But I took off after him when he reached the trees. I couldn't let him do that. It was too late though. Too late. Before I even reached the darkness, I could hear them slinking around, and my blood froze. So I…" His voice trails off as a look of pure anguish crosses his face for a fleeting moment. "So I just stood there. Wasn't anything I could have done, but I stood there and couldn't run. Couldn't run for help, couldn't run away. It wouldn't have mattered, but I didn't."

The need to comfort, to console, him through all of the pain and sadness he has experienced over the last day overwhelms me. I can't even imagine the pain, the fear, the desperation.

The guilt.

It must be incredibly hard for Winslir's little sister to hear all of this. She won't see this pitiable man's sorrow, and she won't recognize the regret in his red watery eyes. Her brother is…well, he has to be dead, right? And I think of Mori and how much I'd miss him if he were gone. Even more so because we have a closer bond as twins. Mori means everything to me, and I can't imagine my life without him and Bhradon in it. A rogue tear escapes to roll unabashedly down my cheek, almost as if to scold me for my ill feelings toward Cyndene.

Well.

She doesn't. Doesn't see. Doesn't recognize. But who can blame her in this moment? Still, the three of us pull her away when the telltale signs of heated rage flash across her flushed face. Anger is not typically associated with our normal tendencies when a loved one is gone. Death is usually a very long time coming and is almost welcomed at the end by the one who is passing. Those who are left behind grieve in their own way, but we have come to accept this as a natural part of who we are. No one ever speaks of what happens after, a taboo discussion among our people, so I've always assumed the next step is eternal rest. That almost sounds nice, especially when you've lived almost two hundred years or more, and life has nothing left to offer you but more toil. A nice long nap.

But when the Shadows slaughter someone, the sacrifice of one of our own is much harder to bear. Unexpected and premature, the death is a reminder that not everything in life is pleasant and full of longevity. Those are the moments when we take the time to appreciate the life we have left and the joys that we share. Without those reminders, perhaps we would lapse into a thankless apathy. Perhaps not.

But still, Cyndene's anger is apparent, and no one can fault her. However, we cannot allow her to take her emotions out on Jocabin. None of this is his fault, no matter how much he tortures himself into mindless insanity. Remorse is written all over his face and is eating him alive from the inside out. But there is nothing he could have done. He is absolutely right about that.

We need to question Jocabin further but not while Cyndene is present. I'm not sure when she even joined up with us. Or how.

The rest of us say our goodbyes and back out of the room, leaving him to his tearful mutterings and paranoid delusions. Cyndene starts to fight Bhradon's grip on her forearm, but in the end, she allows him to pull her slowly out of the room. She takes one long final look at the last man to see her brother alive and bows her head in grief. The wrath turns to tears in an instant, drowning out any words we might offer in this moment.

The issue now is getting her out before the Primaries hear her or come calling on their unwilling visitor. We head back through the labyrinth of hallways until we reach the room with the secret passage. Crawling down one at a time, we head straight back to the outside world.

I really don't know what to do at this point. I look over at Bhradon, who is staring back at me with a look of utter helplessness. Females. I guess that's my cue to handle the grief-stricken girl, despite the fact that he *knows* how she feels about me. Sometimes being the bigger person is easier simply because you have no choice. Plus I really do feel sorry for her at this point. Her pain is real. Her sorrow is real. Her unusual vulnerability in this moment is strange, but very real.

Placing my arm around her shaking form and wrapping myself tight against her, I lead Cyndene away from the men. They are heading home. I have other plans it seems.

At first, she balks at the sudden contact, or perhaps simply because I'm the one touching her, but almost immediately, she relents and sags against me. Weaving my way through town, I lead her in the direction of her home with the intent of dropping her off at the door with a wave and a smile. Perhaps a word or two of empty encouragement. For what can one say in these moments that will lessen the sadness and the loss?

When we reach her door, Cyndene turns to look at me. And I am taken aback by the transformation she has undergone. Her visage has a softer air about it, so very different from her usual scowls and sneers. I wait expectantly, assuming she wants to comment on Jocabin's words from earlier.

How wrong I am.

"I'm sorry I snuck up on you like that," she begins. "When I told you earlier that I was keeping an eye on you…well, I meant it. I know it sounded rude and all, but I really didn't mean it that way. Not completely. I was just so upset about Winslir, and I felt like no one cared. No one batted an eye at the whole situation, as strange as it was. I don't understand how everyone can be so heartless. Or blind. But you…*you* were asking questions. I heard the two of you at the gate. I can't even call it a burial gathering. There was no burial. No body. His body…" At that, fresh tears spring anew and flow swiftly down her face. Her sobbing begins to increase again, and I'm afraid she's going to awaken someone inside the house. Trying to explain why I'm standing outside their door with Cyndene crying is not a welcome image.

A little bit of empathy goes a long way when someone needs comfort. "I know it must be hard. I haven't…lost anyone in a very long time. But I haven't forgotten what it feels like."

"Yeah. I forgot. Your parents. I guess I'm too young to remember, but I know my parents and my sister mentioned it at some point. Losing a brother is beyond words. Losing a parent, not to mention both at the same time, must be such a burden to bear. The Shadows have taken from all of us at some point or another, I guess."

The deepest parts of me fold in on themselves, invading my senses and filling me with a dull sense of anguish at the memory, but I squelch down the unexpected sensation of melancholy before it registers on my face.

She continues, "Do you…do you believe any of what that lunatic was saying? I mean, it does explain a lot. A whole lot." A heavy sigh escapes her swollen lips, and I begin to wonder just how much of her usual demeanor is a facade.

Her posture shifts suddenly as she flippantly remarks, "But he's obviously talking out of his mind. I should have known that idiot wouldn't know anything. And here I thought you might actually be onto something. Half my night is gone now thanks to you. Why did we even go down there? What a waste of time."

And there it was.

I'm stunned into speechlessness. Or not. *Who asked you to follow us down there, dear?*

"Who invited you anyways? And while we're at it, how exactly did you manage to follow us without so much as a sound to alert three normally resourceful pairs of ears? Don't act so smug. Forget it. Here I thought you might be a decent person under all that spite. But no. You're just like your mother and your sister. Always have to put others down to make yourselves feel better. No one invited you, so don't you dare act as if we let you down just because you didn't hear what you wanted to hear. What *do* you want, Cyndene? The only eyewitness tells you your brother was alive the last time he saw him. Maybe that doesn't amount to much, but in my book, it's something. And if you choose to ignore that possibility just because you want to close your eyes and ears just like everyone else, then go ahead. You just finished saying how blind everyone else is. But you know what? You're no different. In fact, you're worse. You want to know why? Because you had the potential for truth right in your hands, and you crushed it before it could even take root. Good night, Cyndene."

Without giving her a chance to respond, I whirl around to rush home before the stinging in my eyes erupts. Why did I let her into that room with us to begin with?

Trust is overrated.

CHAPTER 11

With everything that has happened today, I'm not sure another trip to the Hall would be the smoothest plan. Yet I know I must because I won't sleep until I do. Something just isn't sitting right in my thoughts with all of this. I want to believe Jocabin's words, but how can I? I refuse to act like Cyndene and completely brush it to the side simply because it doesn't flow with what I already know to be true. Perhaps everything I think I know is unraveling into chaos and confusion.

Whom should I believe?

Considering the risks for only a brief instant, I turn around and head back to the Hall. I'm only a dozen or so yards from home, where I could hide away from all of this and pretend it doesn't exist.

But I cannot do that.

The ramifications of this mess are too vast, too significant, to ignore. Even in the face of danger. I'm not even sure of what the danger is exactly, other than being caught by a Primary. But I do know that the cold prickling sensation I keep getting is a clear warning that this is bigger than me, bigger than the Primaries, bigger than all of us.

I'm halfway to the ladder leading up into the Hall before I even realize that I'm not outside. My mind is so absorbed in thought I must have lost track of my movements. But my body knew the way. I've done this so many times before but not since I was young. It feels strange being here alone, almost creepy. But this is something I have to do. I don't know why. I just know I'm being pulled further and further into the storm.

Turning left out of the entrance room in the Hall, I head in what I think is the right direction. Memory or instinct—or perhaps something else—guides me down the passages as I hold my breath, hoping that no one is down here to run into before I reach Jocabin's chamber. I'm not even sure he's still down here, but something tells me he wouldn't have told them about our earlier appearance. It also doesn't seem likely they would have moved him in so short a time for any other reason.

Somehow I find the door, and turning the knob slowly again, I open it just enough to peek into the small cavity. The only thing within view is the back of someone's robe.

A Primary.

Despite my panic, I make sure to close the door back ever so gently before I rush off into the torch-lighted maze. Not knowing which way to go, I stumble along in the half-darkness, turning down corridors I've never seen before and getting myself so incredibly lost that I am sure I will never find his room again. Not to mention the way home.

Eventually I come to a dead end and turn around to look at the options before me. There are doors on either side of me at the end of this passage. For some unknown reason, I choose the door on the right. Again, I carefully open it just a crack so as to peek in before I enter. What I see thrills me beyond belief.

Books.

Tons and tons of books. More books than I could read in a lifetime. And I can read a great deal of books.

But these books are mostly huge tomes, bigger than anything I've ever read. Scattered throughout the room on shelves, piled in corners, and sitting open on the long table in the middle of the room. Where did these books come from? Why are they here instead of in the Room of Records? Suddenly I begin to feel sick. Something, once again, is not right about all of this. All books go to the Record Keepers. That's what they do. They maintain our books.

Obviously, the Primaries don't want others reading these books. Maybe they have good reason, but the secretive nature of this room leaves so much unanswered. Perusing the open books on the table, I notice that many of these seem to be explanatory in nature, with drawings and diagrams of many things that look familiar to me. One is the steam-pipe system connected to the fire and another is one of the grinding machines in the wheat mill. I also spy a list of crops we plant, along with a diagram of the planting fields. Strange that all of this is stored here and not with the Record Keepers for everyone to see. I wonder if these were written by the previous Primaries.

Looking to the shelves, I notice that one section is higher on the wall than the others are. I have to lumber over several piles of books to reach the spot, but when I do, I'm dismayed to realize that I can't reach the shelf. I've never used books in this manner before, and I hate to start now, but seeing no other alternative I begin to stack several books at a time until I'm confident I can reach my goal.

Getting on top of the books without falling is another matter. I'm now not so sure this was a great idea. It takes four tries before I manage to refrain from falling. Leaning against the wall for support, I try to steady myself before I even look up. Once I'm sure that I can reach my arms up, I look to the books and scan the spines. There are approximately six or seven titles here, all extremely large. I suddenly realize that I may have trouble lifting them, especially from my precarious perch.

Something occurs to me in this moment. Unlike the books below on the table, most of these have titles on the spines. It was only out of habit that I even looked at them without thinking. Most books we have in the Room of Records have writing somehow carved onto the spine and outside of the book. The ones on the table were written by our people, bearing no mark on the outside cover. That ability was obviously lost to us when the Old World fell away. Pulling a few of them out just enough to look at the front covers, I see a few strange symbols as well as some odd words. I notice one of the books does not have writing on the spine, so I decide to grab it.

I lean down and drop it gently on the floor beside me, slowly climbing down from my makeshift ladder. Grabbing the book, I head to the table and place it on one of the only empty spots. Since there are no chairs in which to sit, I change my mind and sit on the dusty floor with my treasure. I open the heavy volume and let it choose a course for me to follow.

Nothing could have prepared me for this.

CHAPTER 12

Everything has changed around here. Nothing is sacred anymore, and no one remembers. We should never erase them from our memory. Without them, we wouldn't be here.

*****

The Primaries are wrong. They are destroying our people, and our culture, with their poorly made decisions and deluded ways of thinking. They think we should forget. Move on and just keep living like none of it ever happened. How dare they demand that we forget who we are?

It has been difficult to get some of the others to understand, to realize the importance of all that we are doing to insure the survival of our heritage. Many want to protest with us, but some are frightened. They do not want to upset the balance, and our way of living, by insisting we keep the past alive. We must continue to tell the stories and help our children remember. Why shouldn't they remember? It is our history.

They think we don't understand, that we lack a sense of community. The Pure understand the anger, the feeling of betrayal and abject disappointment. We have all been abandoned. That is a fate we all share, so there is no disagreement on that point. But why lay the blame at their feet by forgetting who they were? Why purge the past?

*****

Resources are becoming scarcer by the year. We have not heard back from the group who headed north several months ago. They were supposed to bring back any materials they could find, but no one has spotted them. We even sent a scouting team to the coast to check for any sign of their boat. No word has come back yet. I fear they are not returning, and I cannot blame them. The temptation of a whole new world of possibilities at their disposal.

Perhaps they can pursue our mission by creating their own colony and keeping our past alive through their children. There were both males and females among that group, all old enough or almost old enough but not yet mated. I can only hope they are finding comfort with one another and can experience love with such a limited array of options. This is my hope and my prayer.

CHAPTER 13

Words whirling around the room, blinding me to my surroundings and numbing my senses.

Thinking. Only thinking.

A whole new world?

More thinking. Can't think. Can't move.

It's obviously a story. I clumsily close the book to look at the cover in detail. The fact that it is completely devoid of writing only heightens my anxiety. I'm not sure why.

Coast? Their boat?

I turn to the very first page of the book and pause. *The Journal of the Pure* by Katronus and Those Who Remain Loyal.

Loyal. Loyal to what?

Or whom?

Why does this all feel so wrong? It's just a story.

Right?

Prayer? What does prayer mean?

All the unfamiliar words. Relics of the Old World. It has to be. Language that has been lost to time and tragedy. Urging myself to get up from the dingy dust-covered floor, I find my way to the door and exit into the hall. Jocabin was my original target. I need to speak with him. I'm halfway to his room before I realize I've brought the cumbersome tome with me. My mind is really off in a daze tonight it seems.

Approaching the room far more quietly than before, I peek in to see that he is, thankfully, alone this time. I proceed into the space unannounced, a motion that earns me a crooked smile from the slightly senseless man in the corner. The gesture is unnerving at best.

"Happy now, are we?" I'm fairly certain he's been medicated.

"Not fooled by them, are you? You got a good head on your shoulders for a young woman."

I'm not sure that I like his slightly condescending tone. I think I prefer the simpering version.

"Only a fool is fooled. And I'm no fool. I know the cruelty behind the masks more than anyone does. I've seen the scars, the ugly naked scars they hide. That's why I can smile and move on. With nothing to believe in, with no connection of love, no shared compassion … how can they be other than what they are?" Realizing I've deviated from the intended meaning behind the question, I stammer for a moment before ceasing completely to stare stupidly at my enraptured audience.

Again, he smiles.

Creepy.

"It seems you know more than I suspected. Sharp eye. Sharp ear you've got."

What does that even mean?

"What are you talking about, old man?" In fairness, Jocabin is nothing close to old, perhaps eighty or ninety, yet in this light—this *room*—the effects of this catastrophe weigh heavily on his face and body. He has thinned considerably in so short a time, especially in the face where the pale skin is piling in on itself in an effort to fight against gravity. His eyes, sunken and bloodshot, no longer offer the vacant stare from before but still lack the gleam that a man of his age should still possess. Whether he has been starved or refuses to eat, his treatment in this wretched place has not been kind. Either way, he must sustain himself or die.

"You think I'm crazy." It wasn't a question.

"Perhaps. A little, I admit. Much of what you said is completely impossible."

"Why?" Such a simple, straightforward question, and I cannot think of a single answer that fits my turmoil of emotions right now. Why is it that my heart can know the truth while my mind protests?

"Because it's not the truth."

"You mean *their* truth." And there it is. The one thought I've been submerging deep within my heart to the recesses that even my mind won't traverse. *Don't think don't think don't think.*

Suffocating it beneath a mountain of self-delusion, heaping massive amounts of filth layer by muddy layer to hide the ugliness. The belief that they would never—*ever*—lie to us.

That conviction drowning, drowning in a sea of tears that will not—*cannot*—fall. Buried in the ashes of my trust until no sign of life exists. The death of hope. It is only an idea, a dangerous idea.

A deadly idea.

Because if *they* are not truth, then what is? The Primaries hold our very lives in balance, keep our people going, moving, trudging on through survival.

Existence.

We are merely existing. Existence is not life. It is the absence of death. But death still comes to us all. And what do we have to show for it. What have we accomplished?

I think again to Jinsa's little boy. Milana's children. My own. *Someday.*

But there will be no someday if the Healing Tree is dying.

Images flashing in my mind and thoughts that feel foreign yet familiar. Thundering rhythms pulse and pound through my head. *I can't breathe.*

Shock reverberates through every inch of my body. I can feel an arm wrap around my waist and a rough hand clasped within my own trembling one. Some part of me feels numb. The thoughts and sensations I am experiencing don't feel as if they are my own. Yet here I am watching the pieces of the puzzles slide into position with a final product that I loathe to see. It all fits together, yet nothing makes sense. Someone is speaking to me, I think. Some version of me still composed of life and breath and beating heart.

Innocence.

The past that I left only moments ago, yet it feels a lifetime away. My ears are ringing and the sounds are muffled. The *words that are not my words* come into focus.

The fire. The wood for the fire comes from the Healing Tree.

INTERLUDE
~ B ~

No messages. No word. No guidance.

They are *alone*.

Without any direction, life can turn down so many different paths. The way becomes unclear, and time rolls on in an endless whirligig of difficult decisions and impossible choices.

She knows this, certainly. She recognizes the helplessness of their situation. Yet they cannot stop the churning emotions that landed them in the eye of the storm. The storm of their own creation.

What else are they supposed to do?

Is this all a big mistake?

CHAPTER 14

Those same arms wrap tighter around me and lower me slowly to the ground. I am unable to protest, to move or think beyond the sphere of shock that has enveloped me.

The fire is dying. It's dying because the tree is dying. And no matter what we do, nothing will stop it. I'm not sure how I know that, but the moment the thought enters my mind I know that this is the absolute truth of things. But why is the tree dying? That's the question we should be investigating. Everything depends upon the tree.

The Pure. I wonder now who or what they were. I realize I have no idea how old that journal is or what else there is to discover within its pages.

Does this business with the Shadows even matter now? Isn't the destruction of our livelihood of far greater harm than the death of one man? No, not death. Jocabin said he wasn't dead.

And I didn't believe him.

Glancing to the side with more effort than is warranted by the small gesture, I look up into the pale face of the man whose sanity might just exceed my own right now. Am I losing my mind as well, doomed to spend my eternity in a tiny cell with a man who smells like rotten feet?

Only one way to find out.

Forcing my mouth open and my brain to revive the circulation in my body, I start with the question foremost on my mind.

"What did the Shadows look like?"

He pauses, hesitates, looks around the room, at the floor, the walls. But not at me. Once again, he shifts his gaze over at me from the corners of his eyes, just for a fraction of a second.

"Told you I *heard* them. Wasn't close enough to see much. It was dark enough as it was, but in the trees…you don't know what it's like in the trees. You've never even been close, have you? Blacker than the sky on a moonless night. Black so thick you can smell it in the air. Taste it. Feel it. Like it's a living, breathing thing."

"But…you must have seen something."

They wouldn't have seen it coming.

"Barely saw anything, much less a shadow in a sea of black. Tall dark creatures, looking for the world like something out of a nightmare. I couldn't see features too well. They moved as if the very air around them was bendable. Seemed like the figures would appear and disappear at will. All murky and misty like I was losing my vision or something, but I knew I wasn't. I saw enough. I saw the eyes. The *eyes.*"

I shiver involuntarily at the word. I have no idea why. Maybe just the way he said it.

But they would have seen the eyes.

"What about them?"

"Nothing. Forget it. I'm not in the habit of frightening young girls."

"I'm not a young girl! Nor am I a child to be coddled and sent off to bed. I'm a grown woman, and I have a right to know what happened to them!"

"Them? Them who?"

With a sharp gasp, I slam my fist to my mouth, striking my teeth so hard I flinch in reaction to the sudden jolt of pain. Pain less sharp than the one in my chest, the one inching down into the pit of my stomach. I feel the tears welling up.

And this time, I don't hold back.

Surprisingly, Jocabin's shoulder is almost immediately at my chin. I'm not even sure how it got there, but nonetheless I take the proffered crutch and let everything come pouring out at once. The words are only garbled nonsense to anyone else, but I speak them aloud anyways to release the tension and emotions bottled up inside of me.

Still slightly damp and runny, my face cradles into the bony pillow as I sigh away the last of the flood. I pull back to look at my cellmate. Suddenly he seems far saner than any of us.

Delicately, he utters, "I'm sorry. I…wasn't thinking. It's always difficult to forget, isn't it? That poor girl. His sister. She's suffering hard. Whole family is, I'm sure. Time doesn't help much either I guess. You miss them, don't you? Well, of course you do. I just mean…it still hurts even now. You were young, but I guess that bond is hard to forget. We always say we move on from these things, but we never really do. Not when ones are taken before their time. But your parents, they were brave people. Those two young men owe their lives to your family."

"What good does that do for my parents? They had their lives taken away all because of the stupidity of a couple of children. If they had never gotten the water trellis open, mother and father would have reached them in time to stop them from getting out. Once the grate was open, they should have just let them go if they wanted to die so badly."

"Your parents stopped those boys from making a horrible mistake," he argues. "The boys weren't on some death wish; they just wanted to explore their curiosity, to see the outer world. We all had that craving at some point or another when we were young and too naive to understand the danger involved. They just decided to act on it."

The desire for freedom is something I can understand, but I cannot condone an act that took away a mother and father from us. My mother was such a gentle creature, always helping around the village in whatever capacity was needed. At least, that's what Gani always tells us, and I do remember people always stopping by our home to thank her for something or other. When my great-father was still alive, Gani would always tease him, telling him my mother got her compassion from him because he was too soft. My father, bless him, was always smiling or, in many cases, laughing at the most trivial things. He found joy in everything and rarely showed anger or frustration with anyone or anything. *I miss them so much it hurts.*

I decide to tell Jocabin the whole of the situation, including what we discovered at the Healing Tree. He must have already known about the issues we've been having lately with the fire, for he stopped me midway to exclaim his understanding of what I had only just a moment ago realized. The fire is dying because the tree is dying. But why is the tree dying?

Suddenly I feel so very tired. It must be halfway through the night by now, and I've been going full steam much of the day. But I came here to get answers.

"Jocabin," I start hesitantly. "What you said before about the—about Winslir. Why do you believe that he might still be alive?"

He looks at me, puzzled for a moment. "I never said I believed he was still alive. I only said he was alive when they took him and seemed to prefer him that way. I don't know if he is still alive now. He may be, but I doubt they would have kept him alive after they made him talk. No one would blame him for that. Who would be able to withstand whatever kind of torture beings like the Shadows could inflict?"

"And what exactly," I continue, "do you think they will get from speaking to him? I'm not saying I believe any of this about them speaking. But even if they could, what could he tell them?"

"Everything, Rinni. Everything. All of our secrets."

"What secrets?"

"Ask the Primaries. They have all the secrets, don't they?" He looks at my book knowingly. I had forgotten it was there.

"Do you … do you know what's in this book?"

"No. But I know the Primaries don't take kindly to having their things taken. I know you wouldn't have stolen it had it not contained something … *interesting.*"

His steely gaze is unnerving, and my mind drifts back to the words I had read.

A whole new world of possibilities, it had said.

Creating their own colony.

Keeping our past alive.

There are others.

There could be more of our people out there, somewhere, struggling for survival just as we are. Or maybe they have found a better life and can help us find the resources we need. Maybe they would know what is happening to the Healing Tree.

Maybe they would remember.

Remember what, I'm not sure. But they were supposed to keep our past alive. There must be something we have forgotten, something we no longer remember that could help answer all of our questions. They could help us.

And the Primaries knew. They have known about this possibility all along.

Why would they keep this from us? We don't have secrets. Not like this. We are supposed to support one another, and the Primaries have the responsibility to keep things in order to insure our survival.

They know about the fire. They know about the tree. They also know what Jocabin has told them about the Shadows. And they knew there was a way.

The rush of anger is exhilarating and terrifying. I've never felt like this before, not since my parents died. I feel betrayed.

No. We have all been betrayed.

And I'm going to stop it right now.

CHAPTER 15

Not sure of my exact heading, I stumble out the door and storm off in the direction of what I hope is the main area of the Hall. Something tells me, though, that I will run into a few Primaries before I reach my destination. They will be close, keeping an ear and eye on their visitor.

Prisoner.

I'm furious for him. I'm furious for me. I'm furious for everyone I know.

How *dare* they? How could they lie to us like this? To keep something this big from the rest of the village is monstrous. Never in my wildest dreams could I have imagined that something like this was being held in secret, literally right under our feet. No wonder they don't allow anyone down here.

I'm walking briskly down a long hallway that appears less dusty than the previous ones when I realize I don't have the journal.

Without the journal, I have no proof.

So I turn around, irritated, and head back toward the other side of the building, hoping all the way that I don't get lost again. Jocabin is asleep when I reenter, the medicines finally having their intended therapeutic effect. Pausing in the doorway, I look back to his sleeping form and then at the hefty book tucked precariously underneath my arm. It suddenly occurs to me that I might perhaps need more strength before I go barging in making accusations. I haven't slept for more than a couple of hours in over two days. My anger begins to fizzle, but only slightly.

"Tomorrow then," I resolutely say aloud to absolutely no one.

I need to know who the Pure are. I need to know what they were protecting.

When I get home, I curl lazily into my cozy blanket and fall into a dreamless sleep.

I wake up to sirens blaring throughout the stillness of the night. Not so still now. I hear men running around shouting orders at one another, and women screaming into the darkness. It's still pitch black out. I must have just dozed off. Perfect.

Looking over at Mori's bed, I realize he's not in it, so I assume he's run off to offer his help. When I reach the kitchen, I see Gani standing in the open doorway with her back to me. As I reach her, she turns to me with a look of horror. I question her with my eyes, but she only points outside. I look.

The Healing Tree is on fire.

Its branches are blazing with a burning brightness that would rival the sun on a cloudless day. The terrifying reality is too much to bear. *The tree is gone.*

And so is our only hope of survival.

I run, faster than I ever thought I could. What help I could offer is not in my thoughts, merely the idea that *this cannot be happening*. When I reach the outskirts of the clearing, the heat radiating off the tree pushes me back with the others. I look around at my people and spy Bhradon amongst them, but Mori is nowhere to be seen.

I grab the front of Bhradon's shirt, shielding my face from the blistering intensity. Looking up at him, I ask if he's seen Mori. He shakes his head.

"Where could he be?" I wonder aloud. Again, he shakes his head.

Suddenly the fire shoots up and out with a pulsating power, forcing us back even further. The tree begins to glow with a white-hot radiance that expands exponentially every few seconds. An explosion is imminent, and I desperately grab Bhradon in an attempt to pull him away from the danger. He refuses to budge, and I cannot move him while he resists. I look into his eyes, not understanding his intention but understanding what is about to happen. I cannot stop it, and I cannot leave him. So I brace for the impact as silent tears fall, only to dry up from the heat before they can reach my cheeks in the face of the deadly inferno.

Goodbye, Bhradon.

CHAPTER 16

A scream erupts unbidden from my throat. The sweat is pouring down my body. I look down to see that I am twisted up in the covers in such a way that I may never escape. Just as well. Apparently, trouble follows me everywhere, even in my sleep.

The exhaustion I felt last night isn't satiated much, not surprising considering the mental torture I just endured. Not so dreamless it would seem. However, there is no way I am getting back to sleep now. Images of the nameless man from my recurrent dream begin to pour into my now fully awake mind, and I'm suddenly wishing for those over the one I just endured.

I lie in bed for a few moments, thinking how odd it is that no one came running when I screamed. I look over and, once again, Mori is gone. This time I'm not concerned, but I do wonder where he went. Then I remember.

It's our turn to tend the fire. Correction: from the looks of the light pouring into the room, our turn started many hours ago. Why didn't he wake me up? I guess I should be grateful, but it looks really bad when someone doesn't show up for their duties. Maybe he told them I was sick. Which isn't too far from the truth. I'm sick to my stomach over this whole thing, and I need answers. But first, I need to find Mori.

Grabbing a pastry—or two—on my way out the door, I head for the firehouse with the conspicuous journal nestled under my unseasonable, but useful, overcoat. A few people stare at me funny as I pass by bundled in my odd garment, but they are not my problem. I'd prefer not to draw attention to myself before I have a chance to talk to Mori. Bhradon is most likely with an irrigation crew in one of the fields, but there is no telling where he might be, and I don't need to waste more time looking for him when I'm already ridiculously late.

By the time I reach the firehouse, I'm dripping with sweat and flushed from the brisk walk. The heat inside the building only adds to my discomfort, so I quickly take off the offending article of clothing before saying a word to Mori. Before I can open my mouth, he glances at the book that is no longer concealed and meets my gaze with concern in his eyes.

"You didn't come home last night." His tone is impossible to decipher.

"What do you mean? I was in the bed when you left this morning, or else I wouldn't have woken up there I'd imagine."

"What I mean is," he begins, "that you didn't come home last *night*. You showed up hours after I got home. Hours, Rinni. After a while, I walked all the way to Cyndene's place and back with no sign of you. Before you say anything, I'm not stupid. I know where you went, obviously. I just can't believe you did it alone.

The sun was almost on the horizon when you got home. I don't know what you did," he nods pointedly at the book in my hands, "but I'm guessing I'm not going to like it."

I sigh as I set myself down on the ground at his feet. He takes my cue and joins me on the dirt-covered floor. Placing the book on his lap, I open to the title page and point to the words written there that have been haunting my waking steps ever since I discovered them.

"*Journal of the Pure*. Okay, Rinni, so what does that mean?"

"It means you should be patient and brace yourself for this. Notice what else it says? 'Those Who Remain Loyal.' That has to mean something. But perhaps you should read this first." Opening the book to the same page I had read before, I allow him time to read and absorb the words there. It occurs to me that I need to read more of the journal before I can get a good sense of what it means. For right now, however, I just need someone else's eyes on this so that I'm not the weird girl with the crazy story.

I watch Mori's eyes widen as he gets nearer to the end of the entry. Finally, he looks up, but instead of looking at me, he gazes into the fire for a moment. I'm just about to shake him, thinking that he's zoned out, when he utters, "I don't know what to say right now. This...it has to be just fantasy, right? Did you get this from the Record Keepers?" But the way he says this I know he doesn't really believe that.

"It was in a room in one of the passages below the Hall. Sort of near Jocabin's room, but closer to the area leading upstairs. It was up on a high shelf, and there were many other books. Several of them looked really important, but this one caught my eye for some reason." Pause. Not sure how to continue, I let my hand drop from where I'd been pointing to the page without thinking. "They were keeping this from us, Mori."

"There has to be a good reason. Some reason why we shouldn't know about this. Maybe all the people who left died, and they didn't want other people to try to follow them. Maybe they're just protecting us from leaving...." His face turns pale.

Oh.

I could smack myself right now for sheer stupidity. It was *right there*, and I didn't even see it. Even when I sat there earlier sobbing on about it, I didn't realize the import of what I was saying.

It couldn't possibly... *could it?*

CHAPTER 17

No one ever told us. No one probably ever would.

Except now, we're purposefully searching. Gani would never tell us. We've never asked, never wanted to, but somehow I know she won't tell us. Neither will Bhradon for that matter. I'd be putting him in a terrible position to even ask him. So I won't.

It's evening again, just after our shift, and Mori and I are heading to the one place in the entire village that I never wanted to visit again. The one group of people who wouldn't hesitate to tell us the truth, if just to spite me. The one person I really don't want to see right now.

Cyndene.

I want to let Mori take charge, to let him knock and explain why we're here. But this is Mori we're talking about. Resolutely—with just a twinge of begrudging hesitation—I push him aside to step up to the door and announce our presence. Before I can even speak, Cyndene is directly in front of my face looking for all the world as if she is so very happy to see me.

Oh, joy.

"Hello again, Cyndene." I let the words roll off my tongue in what I hope is a pleasant manner, though in my head I'm mentally strangling her. Just a little. "We…that is, Mori and I, were… well, we were hoping to come in and speak with your mother and father."

The corners of her mouth tilt downward in an alarmingly rapid descent. She declares, "Whatever you found out, you'd better share with me. He's *my* brother." At this point, she's shouting, and her father comes outside to see what's going on. I nod to him as a sign of respect. I have to admit that he's never actually treated me like the women in this family have. Not that he's ever been kind, but I've never really spoken to him that much.

"Corinne, good evening. What brings you here?" His voice is calm and smooth, but his tone belies an anxiety hidden beneath the surface.

I decide to be as straightforward as possible. "This isn't actually about your son." I swallow down my nervousness to still the trembling in my hands. "At least not directly."

Cyndene looks far beyond annoyed. She spits out, "Then what is this about, and why are you disturbing us in our time of grief?"

"I am so very sorry to come here, but we need to speak with you about our parents."

Her father must see the shared grief written on my face, as he motions me into their home without another word. I wait for Mori to follow and allow them to lead us into the kitchen, where Cyndene's mother is busy cooking supper for the family.

She looks up at our approach, visibly startled by the presence of strangers. I jump in to explain, hoping to quell any ill feelings on her part before they begin.

"Very sorry to disturb your family, but my brother and I had some very important questions to ask you. And…we are very sorry for your loss, but this isn't directly related to your son's disappearance. It's possible there may be a connection, however. May we speak with you a moment?"

Immediately I realize my mistake, and as I continue to roll words off my tongue, my mind is thinking furiously for a way to backtrack against my own stupidity. Maybe they didn't notice?

"Disappearance? What do you mean…*disappearance?*"

My big mouth. Guess I should have brought Bhradon after all.

"She means the disappearance of his body," Mori steps in. "We are looking into something regarding the Shadows." Score one for my brother.

"Something as in…?"

I take a deep breath before plunging headfirst into the icy water I see swimming in her eyes. "We'd like to know the names of the two boys who…who were saved by my parents the night they died."

Dead silence sweeps the room on a chilly wind that gives me a sudden uncontrollable tremor. No one speaks. No one moves. I'm worried that I may be literally frozen in time, doomed to stare for all eternity at the horrified faces of my biggest adversaries. A cough interrupts the stillness, and I realize that Mori has moved to sit directly in front of Cyndene's mother.

"We aren't looking to start something negative here. We just want to know more about what happened that night, and those boys are the only witnesses." His face is almost ashen, and I see tears begin to form in the corners of his eyes. "Please," he adds almost in a whisper.

The look exchanged between the two adults is hard to decipher, but her father looks to me and says, "Those two young men have had to deal with the guilt of that night for many, many years. I hope you can understand that."

"Yes," I lie because I have no other words to say. "We just want to speak with them, to find out more about what happened and why."

He nods. "Both of them live in the south near the Healing Houses," he responds. "One is unmated and lives with his mother and father. The other lives close to his birth home with his mate. They have one child, I believe. You've probably seen him around town a good bit." He hesitates before adding, "The other tends to stay nearer to home more often than not. Please do not tell anyone where you got this information."

"Of course," I return. "We mean them no harm whatsoever."

"Thank you," Mori chimes in.

Minutes later, armed with names and directions, I follow him back out the door as we head off into the night in search of answers to questions that, until now, we never thought to ask.

The Healing Houses are in the south part of the village, but it's getting fairly late, so I imagine that most of the Healers are home with their families by now. We still need to speak with them about the tree, but things are getting so tangled together I'm losing track of our focus.

Winslir's death. *Disappearance,* my mind insists.

The recent issues with the fire. *With the Healing Tree,* my mind screams.

The Primaries keeping the journal a secret. *The others leaving our village,* my mind ponders.

It seems I am of two minds on everything. Then again, all of this seems to want to come together for some reason. I don't know how I know this, but I do. Even the Shadows play a part in this game, somehow. And I'm determined to solve the puzzle before it's too late.

When we reach the bridge, I spin around to look at Mori. "Whatever happens," I say, "whatever they tell us, we have to be objective about this. I miss them, and I know you do, too, but this isn't about us. Or them."

"Right," is all he replies back.

I had considered getting Bhradon to go with us, but no matter how professional this visit pretends to be, nothing will over-shadow the fact that this is very personal for Mori and me. Not that I wouldn't want to involve Bhradon in something important to me, but the truth is that it wouldn't be fair to Mori. They were his parents too, and I want to respect his privacy and his feelings in this.

We arrive at the house we were directed to, the home of the boy—*man*—whose name we were told is Nehemor. His mate, or what I presume is his mate, answers the door with a curt nod to both of us.

"Can I help you?" asks a very soft, high-pitched voice. She looks very young, not much older than us, but somehow she reminds me of my Gani. The soothing effect almost puts me into a trance as I struggle not to lose my nerve.

I cough. "My name is Corinne." Inwardly, I cringe, but it seems appropriate. "This is Mori. I mean Morick. My brother. We were wondering if it would be a bad time to speak with your husband. Is he home?" I look around inside at the small amount of space I can actually view, but no movement meets my cursory glance.

"Yes. He is home. Why do you want to speak with him? If this has something to do with Allysar, I'd prefer it if you just left." Allysar. That name. The other young man who tried to escape that night.

I try not to let my face register any recognition of the name. The last thing we need is to be thrown out before we even get to the bottom of anything.

"Madam, we just wanted to speak with him about a family matter." Best to leave things as simple as possible and tell as much of the truth as I can.

She just stares at me for a moment then turns her gaze to Mori. "This way," she states as she ushers us into the small dwelling. Cyndene's father didn't specify the age of the child, but I assume it must be asleep. Looking around for Nehemor, I notice that the entire abode is not much bigger than the size of our kitchen.

A short, stocky male with hair black as night and features to match—even darker than our own—enters the main room from a small enclave to the right. Glancing at his wife questioningly, he then looks in our direction for the first time. I watch as the blood drains almost instantaneously from his face the moment he sees us. His body remains frozen in mid-step.

Oh, yeah. He knows exactly who we are.

CHAPTER 18

What does one say in these situations?

Hello. My name is Corinne.

Remember that night you tried to escape town and my parents died trying to save you from the scary monsters you should have known could be out there? You do?

Good. Well, I'm here to make you relive that horrific night in excruciating detail.

No pressure. No guilt. Got it. "Hello. My name is Cor—"

"Yes. I know. I know who you are, and I guess I probably know why you're here. Bound to happen eventually I guess." The look on his face shows sincere pain and a touch of sympathy that makes me uncomfortable for some reason.

Mori steps forward with his middle three fingers touching his forehead, slowly unbending his elbow to lower his hand to chest level with his palm facing upward: a sign of respect and greeting.

From the change in Nehemor's stance, I gather that he was certainly not expecting this response. Nevertheless, he returns the gesture before turning back to me as we exchange the greeting in kind as well.

The awkward silence that follows is interrupted by the loud squalling of a very unhappy-sounding infant.

"I better go tend to the baby," the woman tells the room in general, leaving us with a concerned glance backward. Her mate returns the look with a half-hearted smile and nods toward her destination just a few steps away in a tiny room.

"We'll be in here talking when you can join us," he replies. He directs Mori and me to the only set of chairs in the room, other than the cooking stool in the corner by the fire. We sit across from the man who could change our entire lives with one conversation, and neither of us knows where to begin.

Nehemor jumps in after a brief moment of contemplation to comment, "Every time I see either of you in town, I convince myself that you've found out who I am and are heading over to speak to me. For twenty-six years I've worked myself up about it each time I saw you, but still I have no idea what to say to you. No words could even…" he hesitates, shaking his head sadly. "No apology would be appropriate, but I feel I have to say something. I have to try. I just don't know where to begin. The excuse of boyhood fantasies only worked for our parents' sake when they desperately needed something to grasp onto. I think it almost destroyed them. To know what we had done and to know that we'd bear that burden for the rest of our lives. But none of it compares to the burden you've had to bear ever since that night." He adds lamely, "I'm so sorry."

At that, he begins to sob loudly, and the woman hastily returns to the room to check on him, throwing her arms around his shoulders from behind and laying her head on top of his. The gesture does seem to comfort him somewhat, but there is desperation in the air that cannot be relinquished over a few mere words. This man has suffered, perhaps more than we have. Ironic but heartbreaking nonetheless.

"Saying it's alright doesn't make it so," I comment with a surge of hope in my heart that forces me to push onward through the murky waters of gloom and sorrow. "But I think it helps to share the grief, not to bottle it up inside and let it destroy you. Thing is, we came here looking for answers, not apologies. Words won't bring our parents back, but maybe…" I look to Mori with trepidation over the mountain we're about to climb, with no idea how the other side may look.

"Maybe we can make the future better," Mori states, "if we know the truth. The truth about that night."

Nehemor suddenly stands up with nothing short of fear showing on his countenance. He exclaims, "We told them. We told them what happened, and now I've made my apology and expressed my everlasting regret. That's all there is to know."

Mori sidles over to him, much taller than the older man but lacking the air of intimidation that comes with confidence, and retorts, "Seems like we'd be entitled to ask a question or two, don't you think? I mean, what's the harm in recounting the details, right?"

After a moment that seems to go on for hours, Nehemor relents and slouches back in his chair reluctantly. "What do you want to know?"

This is my cue. "We want to know why you tried to leave the village."

"Told you. We were young. Stupid. Not much younger than the two of you."

I aim all of my self-assurance directly at his pupils as I answer back. "That's a lie. And you know it." *Please please please.*

"Excuse me?"

"You left for a reason. You found something. Saw something. Something that made you question our past. Something big."

I see the sweat immediately pop up on his forehead just to slide down to his jaw in a noncommittal pattern that speaks volumes. My gamble looks to be paying off.

He eyes me warily without actually looking me in the eye. "This isn't…this is not part of who I am anymore. Allysar keeps going on and on, but I…I have a family and a life and I'm just so tired of being a part of any of this. I'm sorry I ever listened to him. If I hadn't, maybe your parents would still be here, and everything would be just as it's been. They said it was better that way. To stay how it's been…."

And there it is. The little piece of the puzzle that's been hiding under the table all along in plain sight. Slowly, Mori and I look at one another with a mixture of delight and panic. This glance does not go unnoticed by Nehemor, who is busy trying to find a way to backtrack out of his previous statement.

"You don't understand!" he cries. "It would ruin us! The entire village would suffer if any of this gets out."

"How? Tell me that. How would we suffer by knowing the truth? The truth of our past. How can that be bad? Don't we deserve the chance to find out?" I'm panting from the anger at this point. Not anger at him, but anger at the Primaries who so obviously made him keep everything he knew to himself all these years. But we still don't know what he knows or how he knows it.

"What did you find, you and Allysar? Was it a book?"

A look of apprehension is replaced with one of confusion. "No, not a book exactly. It was a group of documents. Some papers left sitting in a room."

The guilty look on his face speaks for itself. I continue, "A room in the further reaches of the hall, perhaps? A forbidden area?"

His refusal to answer is enough. I decide not to play games with any of this. "Did you and Allysar find a way in through the underground tunnel next door?"

There is something sad in knowing that Bhradon and I weren't the first ones to find the secret passage, but thinking on it now, it only makes sense that each generation would have its own set of childhood explorers. Children are excellent at discovering things they shouldn't.

A sharp intake of breath across the room alerts me to the fact that this woman obviously has no idea what really happened that night to the boy who would become her mate. A rise in temperature, a haze in the air: the possibility that this is all just a dream floats by, and I try to grab onto the idea, reaching out to grasp the comfort it offers, but the deep voice drifting through the mists of my mind brings me back. Back to uneasiness, back to the disquiet left in the room. The pain and the hurt pushing down, down, still further down until I feel I might choke on the bitter taste of my own sorrow and my own personal regrets.

Refusing to indulge in a random fit of self-pity during this poignant moment, and unwilling to acknowledge anything that would result in any sort of empathy from our hosts, I focus on that voice and erase any hint of emotion from my face. I need to know. Oh, help me, but I need to know.

I realize he has been speaking throughout most of my transcendence into self-absorption. He must have accepted our knowledge of the tunnels and passageways, for at the moment he is describing some in particular. None of it sounds specifically familiar, but I spent most of my time there as a child, either running or hiding.

Wait a minute.

So did he.

"Weren't you very young the last time you went down there? How can you remember so much detail?"

I scrutinize his eyes, his face, his body movements as he responds. "I don't know. I haven't been down there since…that night." Truthful, *yet not truthful.* Something. There is something.

"What aren't you telling us?"

"I told you. I haven't been down there in a long time."

"But someone else has." The stark revelation hits me at the same moment I involuntarily speak the words my subconscious mind had been shouting at me the whole time. How could I know that? Yet I know I'm not wrong.

And I know who that someone is.

Allysar.

CHAPTER 19

Mori turns to look at me quizzically. I shrug my shoulders and look back to Nehemor, expectantly awaiting affirmation of my unintended disclosure.

"How… I don't…," he starts. And finally, "Well." At least he has the decency not to deny it. He knows what I'm thinking, and I know what he's thinking.

"No, we haven't been following him. Let's just say we may have more in common than you probably expected. But he found something else, didn't he?" No answer. Avoiding even looking at me now. "Didn't he?"

"There was… something he said he found. Never brought it to me. Never showed any proof. Said he was leaving it there so they wouldn't suspect, but all he'd come back with is more nonsense. His condition just keeps getting worse. I knew after that night that I'd let him manipulate me with his incessant talking, his overly dramatic speeches about 'the truth' and 'the outside world.' But I was young then. I made my mistake, and I'll have to live with it for the rest of my life. Allysar…he can't let go. Just can't let it go. He never saw the wrongness in what we did. Now I'm not saying he didn't feel horrible about your parents. But he always felt that his rants were the most important thing. Bigger than all of us."

"What do you mean?" asks Mori.

"He said that the truth would save us all. That it was for the good of all of us, and that one person's life wasn't as significant as the whole village. I could understand that if we were at risk. But we're not. Otherwise, his stupid theories would have come true by now. He thinks…he thinks all kinds of things that rang true to a gullible adolescent. But I'm not that person anymore. Trouble is, he *is*."

"You mean his mind is off?"

"Yes. Well, no. Not exactly. He's sane as anything, but he still keeps going on about this stuff and spends most of his time working on it or thinking about it. Or bugging me with it. I try to go and visit. At least, I used to. It gets harder and harder every time. My family needs me, and he is bringing me down with him. His parents don't seem to mind looking after him, but he's a grown man, and that isn't right. Not right at all. Every now and then, he talks about trying to leave again, but he never does. He just keeps going on and on about that book—"

Book.

Journal.

I'd left it back behind the firehouse, well hidden under the firewood bin, under mounds of blankets we use on chilly nights for our shifts. A rare occasion.

Head cocked slightly to the side, I gaze at him, perplexed. "I thought you said it *wasn't* a book."

Sheepishly, he responds, "No, I said what we found back then wasn't a book. I've never seen a book. This is something more recent. We had some papers back then, loose papers with family trees drawn on them. Some of them just ended suddenly, and in our ignorance, we assumed it meant that people—some people—had left before mating or having children. We never stopped to consider that it was simply a matter of poor archiving on the part of previous Primaries. They admitted to that probability after that night, after they found out what we had. Told us it was a terrible situation, but that they were trying to resolve it. If we had spread our wild imaginings to others in the village, imagine the backlash and the chaos. No one could be calmed down enough to listen to reason and be told the truth after that."

"The truth." The words singe the tip of my tongue even as I utter them.

"We messed up. Such an understatement, but we messed up on a huge scale. It could have been worse, I know, but for you…"

"For us, we've moved past this," Mori adds. "Mostly."

But not if we can't even get to the bottom of it all. Not if the truth eludes us at every turn. Allysar found a book. Recently. And he never showed it to Nehemor, his only true perceived ally. If he never showed it, he never had it. That doesn't mean he never saw it though. Or maybe he found a different book. Something more.

"Why do you believe their story about the records?"

"Why shouldn't I? I mean, why would the Primaries lie to us?"

Why, indeed.

"Yeah, well, what if they were? What if you were right?"

"I don't…understand what you're saying. Why would you

think that? Have you been talking to Allysar? Has he poisoned your minds as well?" There's that look of pity again that makes my insides shift around in strange ways.

"No! I mean, we've never met him before. We came to you first, but we were going to—"

"Do not under any circumstances speak with him!" he explodes in a fit of sudden rage. "He is completely obsessed with all of this, and all you'll do is feed his paranoia. Please. Please don't. I've spent years and years trying to stem his excitement and talk sense into his deluded mind. But he won't listen, and you going in there talking like that would be the worst possible idea."

"What if I told you I have the book he's referring to, or else one very similar?"

Silence. Infant whimpering. Heart pounding. Heavy breathing. "What?"

"I … have … the … book. Or *a* book at least. It's a journal actually. Describing some particularly damaging evidence against the integrity of the Primaries. Past *and* present it would seem."

"But he … where did you get it?"

"Same place he found it I imagine. Only I took it with me."

He looks shocked, terrified. "No! No, you have to put it back. Now! Before they realize it's gone. They'll blame Allysar, and he'll be punished."

Punished?

"Punished how? What could they do? Publicly reprimand him? Won't exactly work if their goal is secrecy, now will it?"

"No. You don't understand. We swore we'd never—they made us promise. Made us promise we'd never go back. They'll blame him for sure."

Why all the secrecy? Why would it matter so much if we knew the truth?

Growing weary of this tired dance, I cut him off. "That book is a journal. A journal that seems to say there are—or at least were at some time—others like us out there. The person, or people, who wrote it believed that those who went away found new places to live. That was a long time ago, but who says their descendants aren't out there still? Maybe they have resources we don't. Maybe they have an answer as to why the tree is dying, some knowledge of the past that those who stayed behind seemed to be fighting to hold onto, despite efforts from the Primaries of those days to move away from the past. Our past could be the key to everything. Some truth or knowledge that would explain what's going on and why things are falling apart."

"Did you say the tree is dying? The Healing Tree?"

"I don't know of any other trees in the village, do you?" Realizing I've let slip a piece of information that we'd hoped to keep quiet for the moment, I allow myself to face reality.

Maybe there is no solution.

Maybe we are going to die.

CHAPTER 20

Leaving the home of Nehemor is like stepping into a bright day full of sunshine. I know he means well, especially considering how long he's been helping to look after Allysar, but he just doesn't understand what's at stake. Actually, I don't think that's entirely true. I think he chooses to ignore the implications because he was threatened by the most powerful entities in the village.

How can the Primaries think to force us into blind submission when the fate of our entire population—at least the part that we know for certain exists—rests on finding an answer? What purpose does it serve to look the other way? If they've known there were other things at stake for all these generations, was that information passed along from one group of Primaries to the next? The idea strikes me as odd, but I have no other answer.

Allysar's parents are genial enough people, if a bit anxious over even the mention of their son's name. They graciously offer to bring us fresh root tea as we head into the furthest room in the back to speak to the sole man who, sane or no, shares not only our facts but our fears as well.

He doesn't stand when we enter the room, as is proper custom. In fact, he doesn't even exactly look up, yet somehow he knows.

He *knows*.

"Well, I thought perhaps you'd come. Found the journal, have you?"

Silence.

Astounded, Mori finally exclaims, "How could you possibly know that? We just left his home!"

But I know better. This isn't some clandestine encounter. We are dealing with a professional sneak. A sneak long before Bhradon and I ever got into the business.

"How long have you been following us?" I ask him with a knowing hint of a smile, just enough to show him that I'm stepping up to play this game of wits.

"As you like. Well, seems it's been a while now, hasn't it? But I only began to take a serious interest recently. The silliness of children is of no concern to me. The nocturnal habits of a poorly organized group of adults—and I use the term loosely—has, on the other hand, piqued my interest as of late."

Mori's bewilderment amuses me to a degree. "How would you know about our *nocturnal* habits?" he questions, not expecting the self-assured response that follows.

The man laughs. "Stealth is certainly not your strong point from what I've seen." Mori looks like he's about to lose it, so I step further into the room to diffuse the situation. Leaning against the table he's sitting behind as he peruses what looks like a very brittle piece of parchment, I decide I like him. In a bizarrely fascinated sort of way.

Finally, he decides to look up at me, merely raising his eyebrows without actually lifting his head, and places the paper on the table face down. Pushing himself back in his chair, he crosses his arms over his chest and stares at me pointedly, as if he's waiting for me to speak first. *This could take all night,* I sigh resignedly.

But something makes him decide to say, "Your decision was brave, but stupid nonetheless. They'll be onto you quicker than you can imagine. At least you're not stupid enough to bring it here." He looks around me to glance at Mori. "Your brother should learn to speak more quietly when sneaking around in the middle of the night. If he wants to avoid being caught, that is."

I raise my hand up without looking back to Mori in case he had any thoughts of rushing forward. Not that he usually listens to me, but I hope he can see our situation here is precarious.

I'm growing very weary from lack of sleep, and my head is pounding. "Our expedition last night is beside the point. Nehemor seemed to think they'd come after you assuming you'd taken the journal. How could they possibly know it was us?"

He looks at me as if I've grown an extra head. "The prisoner, of course."

"The pris—you mean Jocabin? He's not going to tell on us. He's scared and alone. He just wants to forget about all of this."

"He will tell them," he says matter-of-factly. "He will tell them because he will have no choice. Because his loyalty lies with the ones in charge just like all these other deluded fools." He leans forward again. "No matter what he told you, his fear will outweigh his common sense. He will tell them."

Shock registers slowly, spreading to my limbs with an oddly intoxicating sensation. My legs can't support my weight any longer. I lean against the table for support, and I see a flash of concern melt across Allysar's face for a moment before quickly disappearing. Still, he jumps up out of his chair to allow me access to a seat, the only seat in the room. He doesn't exactly rush to help me over to it, but the gesture is still appreciated and unexpected. Mori hurries over to guide me to the chair, but looking at his face, I see that Allysar's assertion has hit him hard as well.

What if we're wrong? What if this is all a huge misunderstanding, and now we face punishment for acting like a bunch of paranoid children?

…a whole new world of possibilities at their disposal. Perhaps they can pursue our mission by creating their own colony and keeping our past alive through their children….

No, there is too much at stake here to ignore it. Allysar may be a tad weird, but he's smart. Too smart to be simply living some deluded fantasy from his childhood. He's not crazy. And neither are we.

"Nehemor also said the two of you found a document that night. Some sort of historical record or family tree that seemed to show the sudden disappearance of whole branches along some family lines."

"Yes, we did. Or I did. He was just tagging along as usual. But he saw the same thing I did. The Primaries tried to make up some excuse, but no one in their right mind would ever believe a bunch of nonsense about poor record keeping. All of our records are virtually *spotless*. The ones that are still there at least. It's the missing documents that concern me. There is virtually nothing in our archives from the time of that journal and before. Except for the family trees. And those with the missing pieces are the *only* ones not in the Room of Records."

I need Bhradon. I need to know what to do. I have no clue what we should do.

We head out, excusing ourselves with the honest pretext of a complete sense of exhaustion. If he's been following us, then he knows the truth of that statement.

A restless and fitful sleep glides uneasily into the gloomy predawn atmosphere. At first light, Mori and I head straight over to Bhradon's home to discuss the details of last night, leaving out some of the more emotional bits. After a very solemn breakfast, the three of us march over to the firehouse to retrieve the book.

Only it's not *there*.

"It's not here," I observe stupidly. *Why is it not here?*

"Are you sure—" Bhradon begins before I spin around to stare at him with anger and frustration oozing from my eyes.

"Of course I'm sure! You think I'd forget where I stashed *the one thing I can't afford to lose*? Besides, Mori saw me put it here. He helped me cover it up."

"She's right," Mori comes to my defense. "We both put it here. I know we did. But no one ever touches this area." He looks just as perplexed as I do, pulling on his hair by the roots with both hands and turning around in circles as if there might be *another* reticule we had heretofore never discovered in all our shifts as Tenders, yet somehow found, used, and conveniently forgot in one day. But I empathize with the sentiment.

"That's not what I was trying to ask, Rinni. Someone had to have found it then. That's the only explanation. *As I was saying*, are you sure no one knew where you hid it?"

I flush with the realization that I shouldn't have lost my temper with him. "No, we didn't tell anyone where we hid it. Nehemor and Allysar knew I'd found it, but not where we—" My mouth is halted mid-sentence as the word 'hid' dies on my lips.

I can't believe it: Allysar.

Sneaky, sneaky.

CHAPTER 21

Furious, I storm in the direction of his hut without so much as a backward glance to verify they were following me. After a few seconds, I hear Bhradon shouting, "What good will this do, Rinni? He'll just deny it."

But I know better. He won't deny it. In fact, I think he'll enjoy basking in the glow of his success.

The one thing I don't understand is *why* he did it. If he planned to use it, he would have done so already. If he's not going to use it, then why take it?

The pleasantries Allysar's parents offer only intensify my frustration. Eventually, I just walk around them, trying to sound calm as I explain that I really need to speak with him. I guess they don't get many visitors.

He is asleep on the extremely small bed with his back to the door when I burst into the room. Before I can speak, he comments, "If you're looking for the book, it's not here." And just like that, my step falters halfway to the bed.

"What do you mean it's not here? Where is it?"

"I put it back where it belongs. You're welcome."

"I'm sorry, but why should I thank you for stealing my book?"

"It's not your book. And you stole it first."

I'm so confused. "But why would you give it back to them? I thought we were on the same team here, Allysar!"

He rolls over to face me, and I feel one of my comrades behind me step closer. "Let's get one thing straight. We are not *a team*. I work alone. I found that journal long before you, and I had the sense not to take it with me. I meant it when I said they'd come for you. As soon as Jocabin tells them about you, they'll go straight to that room to check his story. And what would happen then, do you think? Your great-mother would be pleased, I'm sure, to have her home swarmed by a pack of angry Primaries." Amused, he adds, "Looks like you had the same idea, huh? You are an extremely pushy young woman. Do you know that? Almost makes me wish it had been Primaries knocking down my door."

Bhradon steps up beside me, ignoring the tension emanating from my body. "If no one confronts them, how do you expect anything to change?"

"Oh, I didn't say not to confront them. I merely suggested that the element of surprise is lost thanks to your girl here, and, therefore, you need to gain it back."

"And how do you propose we do that?" Mori asks from behind us.

"With this." He reaches under his bed and pulls out some yellowed pieces of loose parchment, similar to the one I had seen him looking at the night before. No, not similar. Exactly the same.

Some of the words on the top page catch my eye, and I almost faint with joy. And horror.

The Journal of the Pure.

CHAPTER 22

A lifetime passes as I realize the import of what I'm seeing.

Pages from the book. *From the book.*

The initial sound is unassuming, a soft, if shaky, breeze gradually rising in severity until it reaches storm capacity. Sound. Voice. Apparently mine. "You … *why* would you … I can't … how *could* you? That book is … it's a piece of our history. You've *destroyed* it!" Now I've gone shrill in the midst of my panic.

"Are you saying that our past is more important than our future? A future that will most assuredly crumble right through our hands. A future that is slowly but surely coming together just as it falls apart. As they—*we*—sit idly by and do nothing. *Nothing.* And you want to discuss meaningless issues over a *book?* People's lives are at stake. *We* are at stake."

I'm stunned into silence, but Mori doesn't hesitate to ask, "But what's the point of keeping the pages if we aren't going to confront them? If we're using it, we might as well have kept the whole book."

Allysar breaks out in a grin that is as unexpected as it is disturbing. Then casually replies, "Like I said, the element of surprise is with me now. Those old bones aren't climbing to get that book down. They'll see it's on the shelf and assume it's intact. Why wouldn't it be? I mean, who would rip out pages from an old book? That's just crazy." His smile widens, and his meaning begins to dawn on me.

He plans to have them make fools of themselves. They'll see the pages and immediately run to the book to open it, thereby incriminating themselves in the process and lending full credence to our story. I'm not so sure we had to destroy the book to reach that effect, but I don't say this last part aloud.

"So what's the plan?"

"The plan, my dear, is for you to leave me in peace so I can get some rest before I continue on."

Now I'm getting agitated again. Why does he have to be so frustratingly ambiguous? "I meant the plan for the pages you took."

"Yes. *I* took. Therefore, you didn't. I told you: I work alone." Unbelievable.

Wait. Why should I be concerned? He's going to handle the difficult bit. All we have to do is show up to provide moral support. Not that I'm extremely happy about supporting this lunatic. Still, he does share our end goal no matter how it's reached.

"Alright. But we aren't walking away from this. We want to back you up if needed. Just to be there when it happens so you aren't alone."

"Oh, I won't be alone. I imagine almost everyone will be available as witnesses."

Bhradon's deeper voice bounces across the room in echoes that add an eerie quality to the discussion. "What do you mean *everyone?*"

"I think you know what I mean," Allysar continues. "What use is it to tell the Primaries what we've found? They already know what they're hiding. It's all the rest that need to know the truth."

"This is about you, isn't it?" My brother's voice is wavering only slightly. "You're just trying to vindicate yourself by proving you were right. That somehow my parents' deaths didn't matter because you were right all along. And that's all that matters. To you." I guess I'm not surprised by the tear I see rolling down his cheek, but I respectfully keep my eyes averted and trained on our dear host.

"Young man, many things I may be: stubborn, strange, obsessed, even paranoid. But even I know that this is a huge discovery, and perhaps savior, for our posterity. Well, yours perhaps. If I have to consider the good of the village over the grief around the death of two people, if I have to rip apart *books* to preserve *people,* I will. I will do what I must do to save our people as a whole, but I'm no fool. Everyone still blames me for that night, and maybe it was my fault, but my intentions, however poor my lack of forethought, were honest and sincere."

Strange words from a self-inflicted recluse who has never—as far as I can tell—been interested in starting a family. So all this talk about *posterity* has me scratching my head. His parents will probably be gone before he is, and he has no mate, no children. The only person, besides us, who even bothers to visit him is his childhood friend.

Nehemor.

Of course. What new father doesn't brag about the wonder

and amazement of caring for a life they helped to create? I'm betting that, if he hasn't seen the baby, he's at least heard Nehemor talk about it. And here I thought he had no heart.

Bending down beside the bed, I stare into his eyes knowingly, hoping to impart some of my newfound compassion onto his rough nature. From the way he's looking at me, I'm certain I've only succeeded in making him uncomfortable. Well, that's something at least.

"I believe you," I finally manage. Ignoring the looks the other two men in the room are giving me, I push on and say, "I'm guessing you're planning on announcing this at the next Gathering." The only other reason we ever use the Festival Grounds besides harvest time. Gatherings occur maybe two or three times a year, but they are combined celebrations of recent events from the last few months, including births and mating partners. Bhradon always gives me a wistful look, just before Gathering days, but only when he thinks I'm not paying attention.

But I am. And my stubbornness ebbs a little each time, knowing that none of this is fair to him. His longing to have our relationship endorsed and officially sanctioned by the community breaks a little piece of my heart each time. He may understand, but he doesn't. Not really. His patience is beyond words, and I am thankful every day that I have him in my life.

Allysar interrupts my melancholic daydreaming for a dose of reality, albeit a reality I was already considering. Nodding in affirmation, presumably at my declaration that now seems ages ago in hindsight, he states, "Indeed. I have it on good authority that we will be gathering next week. I intend to put them in a very tight spot amongst the masses."

Next week. The Grounds Keepers will be kept very busy over the coming days. But can we manage to keep this secret for so long? How can we sit by and wait until then? From the looks on my companions' faces, we are all thinking along similar lines.

Bhradon speaks up first. "Allysar, I'm not sure that waiting is the best plan with this. Weren't you the one speaking of not sitting idly by? Well, how can we do just that for an entire week?"

Allysar's face turns dark. "You think you know how this game is played? You think you can jump right on in and tell me how to handle things when I've been biding my time for almost half of my life? There's a difference between doing nothing and doing something right. Running in there right now would be the very epitome of wrong. No witnesses, no audience, no accountability. I've been waiting for the right moment, once I had all the documents and information I needed, to spring this on the Primaries. Giving them nowhere to hide." A subtle but disturbing grin spreads across his face.

Some part of me is wondering exactly what we've stumbled into. And if we should dig our way back out or not. I'm thinking we keep digging until we come out the other side. But that's just me. Not to be left out of the main event, I find myself blurting, "Whether you like it or not, we're in on this as well, so you might want to accept that as a fact or else you're in for a very real surprise. I'm not all for the waiting aspect of this, but we have to do this. One way or another, we have to confront them and find out the truth."

Without the slightest hint of negativity, without even the tiniest of battles, he shrugs. "Very well. But leave the talking to me." A little too easy if you ask me.

Looking over, I notice Bhradon and Mori silently

communicating with one another. I guess perhaps it's time to leave so that we can discuss everything. I say goodbye, and the boys follow suit without a word, exiting through the main door right behind me without a glance to Allysar's parents who are sitting in the main room.

We travel a little ways in silence before Mori explodes, "What was that about?"

Compelled by his outburst of anger, I stop mid-stride and spin to face him, feeling the emotions of the last few days boiling up inside of me in what I can only describe as a force of determination. And then I realize what's been bugging me.

The tree.

"We're overlooking the real problem here."

Bhradon interjects before I can continue. "And what's the real problem then, Rinni? Seems like there's no shortage of real problems these days." I can tell he's still exasperated by Allysar's demeanor.

Sighing, I explain, "The Healing Tree is our number one priority, right? I mean *our* as in the whole village. If it's dying, waiting a week could be disastrous."

"And what about the papers? Allysar has them, and I'm sure he'd expect us to try to take them, so the element of surprise is definitely not on our side. And besides, he's right about the festival. That's the only time all of the Primaries will be out together, and we need this out in the open with other witnesses as well. Seems we have no choice."

But there's always a choice. "So we get all the Primaries out together in town during the day when lots of people are around." Simple enough.

Two blank stares.

Silence.

Blink blink stare—blink blink stare—

"We just have to give them a reason to come out."

Mori stares at the ground a moment, and then suddenly looks up at my face with a dawning realization written on his countenance. A moment passes between us, and I know he can see exactly what I'm thinking. The future is laid before us. All we have to do is walk the path and jump off the cliff when we reach the fork in the road.

A fork we're going to create.

Coming out of a slight daze, Bhradon shakes his head and replies, "There are only three reasons the Primaries all come out at once. Gatherings, the Harvest Festival, and—"

The birth of a nameless inconceivability plays out in front of my eyes as I watch him physically—almost imperceptibly—move away from Mori and me. His unconscious way of putting a wall between himself and the uncomfortable, downright scary, notion of what I now know we have to do. What we're going to do. Because we have no choice.

So we just have to figure out who gets to pull the siren.

CHAPTER 23

It turns out that pulling the siren is the easy part.

The difficult bit is facing hundreds, soon to be thousands, of terrified stares as everyone races to the gate with a nameless fear chasing at their heels and whirling in their heads. The slightest edge of guilt begins to creep into my own head, filling me with dread and a desire to hide under the nearest things I can find.

But this is bigger than me. Bigger than each of them individually. As a whole, we are all affected, and we all deserve to know why we've been lied to and what the truth really is. And in exchange, some measure of trust is about to be levied from these innocent beings.

Trust. I'm beginning to loathe the word entirely, perhaps even doubt its existence.

For now, we must remain strong and united in dealing with the crowd developing in front of us. The three of us are searching out for signs of the Primaries. Without them, this whole endeavor is pointless.

Slowly, oddly, they come out with the still developing crowd as time stands still for the three of us watching it all unfold. Four pushing in at the back. Two over to the left running from somewhere in the village. Six heading straight down the path leading here from the Hall. Several single Primaries rushing in from all directions. Where are the rest?

A few more edge in as time begins to move forward again. Many are now standing in front of us, waving their arms around and asking questions. Someone has to swing the axe here.

Might as well be me.

Clearing my throat, I begin in a softer voice than I intend. "Primaries, we are calling a meeting of the town. We will begin once everyone is present. Including *all* the Primaries."

One steps forward from the rest. "I don't know the meaning of this, and I can assure you that this sort of behavior is not tolerated and certainly is not expected from grown men and women." There have been occasions in the past where a naughty child has somehow managed to pull the siren. Punishment is swift and severe, if only to demonstrate to children the dangers involved in our livelihood and how seriously we take any issue with the siren. Like now, for instance.

Mori repeats my previous statement with more force than I was able to muster.

Another Primary speaks up with, "Some will be asleep in their homes, especially if they were just on duty in the Hall last night. You cannot expect them to wake up and join this ridiculous nonsense. What is the meaning of this?"

"If they are asleep, you will go wake them up. I sincerely doubt they could be sleeping through the alarms." Mori is certainly right about that.

And, sure enough, belatedly, many more people show up, including more of our esteemed leaders. After a few moments, in which we stoically ignore those Primaries that are present, it appears that all thirty-three have arrived and are making their way to the front of the congregation. Some are shaking their fists. Others are merely glaring at us with what I can only assume is barely contained hostility.

Now that we are ready to begin, I find that I have lost the words I wanted to convey. Staring out into the thousands of faces waiting anxiously for what they know has to be bad news, I feel a sense of longing for the life I had just days ago. Innocent and ignorant of all this sadness, all this anger. All the lies.

And I find my voice again.

"We apologize to everyone for having to bring you out here today and for taking you from your homes and duties. However, we have a message we must deliver to all of you. We ask you to be our witnesses and to allow us to show you what we have discovered." I hesitate, not out of fear, but out of distaste for bringing all these people out of their own blissful ignorance and into the grim reality that we face. Taking a deep breath, I continue in a much louder voice in an attempt to reach as many ears as I can. Many on the outskirts and in the back will not hear my words directly, though the message will be carried around by word of mouth.

"I apologize for having to bring you this terrible news, but it is necessary. Yet there may be a bright light in all of it if you allow us to tell you everything we now know." Whispers, murmurs sweep through the crowd. But mostly there is silence. Expectation. "We—that is, the three of us standing here before you—have discovered a part of our history that has been kept from us for what I can only guess is generations upon generations. The truth has been hidden by those whom we trust above all others. These men and women," I say, pointing to the Primaries, "have had a piece of our past passed down to them from their predecessors, for no other reason than to keep it from the rest of us. The lies we have been told are like dust covering the true object beneath."

Ever since he knew we were going to pull the siren, Bhradon has been severely quiet and thoughtful. It was obvious he wasn't going to be the one to pull it, so Mori and I did it together, our twin minds sharing the burden and the understanding of what it meant. But I have been nervous this whole time, wondering if this is all too much for him. If he plans to back out.

But he has found his voice, it seems, for now he steps forward and, in one swift but decidedly purposeful motion, grabs my hand in a tight embrace. Looking up into his face, I smile and nod in encouragement. His voice rings deep and loud as he shouts out to the crowd, "The Primaries have known, and have been hiding from us, some very important information. As of late, several strange things have been occurring, prompting us to investigate. What we have found is shocking and disturbing, and it must be shared. For starters, everyone seems to be ignoring the fact that we never saw the body of Winslir when he died the other day. The Primaries have been keeping his patrol partner, Jocabin, locked away in secret, probing him for information. We spoke with him, and what he told us is almost unbelievable. Yet we believe him. Does no one question the absence of Winslir's body?" More murmurings among the people, louder and more assertive, yet no one actually speaks up. "What if we told you the Shadows—"

I have no choice but to cut him off. Surely he realizes we can't tell them that the Shadows can speak? Do we even believe that to be true? Either way, we have no proof other than the ravings of a man whose sanity is currently in question. We must stick to the facts. The evidence at hand.

The evidence we no longer have.

But then I remember Allysar's plan. It could still work now just as well as it would have at the Gathering. Only, who's going to follow them down into the bowels of the Hall? We can't expect all of these people to follow us, much less fit, into the sub-level passages under the Hall. New plan: we come clean and tell them everything.

This is not going to end well, I know.

Still, I calmly interject his sentence with, "What if we told you the Shadows were not always a threat?" Now that gets their attention. The murmurings cease almost immediately. Bhradon and Mori both look at me quizzically, but wait expectantly with the rest of the audience to hear me out. "What if we told you that some of our people left the village a long time ago to search for resources, only to form new towns in other places? This was a long time ago, and we have no way of knowing exactly where they went or if anyone is still there." My voice is wavering, and I can feel myself growing dizzy with the intensity of *all these eyes* staring at me.

A slight touch, a squeeze against my palm, and I remember. Where he is, therein lies my strength. When I look up into his warm eyes, I forget the icy ones in front of us, and I remember. Encouraged by his presence and his strength, I gather my nerve and continue. "But these scouting trips were apparently a routine part of their lives. Our ancestors' lives I mean. So either they knew how to defend themselves against the Shadows, or the Shadows did not exist then. Either way, they left. Some never returned, and it was assumed that they decided to start their own colony. Somewhere north of here I think, but many of the words were unfamiliar to me. All I know is that these people who left, along with many others who remained, were unhappy with the way some things were being handled by the Primaries. There are still many questions we need to ask, and that is why we are here. To get the answers we seek. We deserve to know the truth. We, as in all of us. So we ask you," I state, looking directly at the thirty-three grim-faced elders at the front of the crowd, "to please be truthful and honest with us. Tell us what our true history is and why it has been hidden from us for so long."

They look back and forth at one another, a silent but nervous jittering that shifts and evolves into a whirlwind of agitation. Stirring. Murmuring. Until one speaks up. "We were aware that trips were made in previous generations to search for supplies when provisions were low. It became necessary to travel further and further away as the surrounding area became depleted. Obviously, the group that did not return was killed by Shadows. That is the most likely conclusion given all that we know. The reason we do not give out this information is to avoid tragic events such as what happened to your parents. If people start to believe there is anything beyond what we know out there, others will get the idea in their heads to attempt an escape."

Escape.

"What a strange word to use when speaking of leaving the village. Is that what it was, Primary? An escape attempt? Not two young men leaving of their own free will? But they had to sneak out, didn't they? They had no choice because everyone is forced to stay here inside these gates whether they want to or not." My usual calm demeanor is starting to melt away in the heat of this ridiculous debate. Of course they're going to feign innocence until the moment we can prove them guilty.

An angry outburst arises from another Primary. "And look where that got them! Look what happened to your parents as a result? Don't you think we have these rules in place for a reason? The safety of these people is our number one priority."

"No, it isn't. Your duty is to the success of our livelihood as a whole, to keep the peace and uphold the sanctity of our historical documents. Safety is in the hands of every individual and their own free will. Parents have the responsibility to watch over their children. Our border patrols maintain and secure our harvests to ensure we have enough food to eat. My brother and I," waving my hand in his direction, "help tend the fire so that our mills run and people have a way to refuel their home fires for cooking. You have the job of maintaining order, not locking us away! In the meantime, the fire is behaving oddly, seemingly a direct result of what we found at the Healing Tree. How do you justify temporary safety as a priority over the longevity of our *entire population?*"

That last part seems to have gotten the audience back into the conversation. Immediately everyone is shouting, asking about the fire, the tree, the Shadows. All at once, and with an ensuing cacophony of the earsplitting variety.

A lifetime passes before the volume lowers enough for someone to address my accusations. Prime Julos steps forward, laying a hand on my shoulder as if to demean my credibility by a mere gesture. His tone with me the other day is not forgotten. *Child, indeed.*

"While I can understand the concern you might have over not

being told about the trips to the outside in the past, it is of deep concern to me that you would go so far in your accusations. You claim we are holding Jocabin against his will and that somehow Winslir's body not being here proves...what? Why would you say these things? Just because Jocabin has not returned home does not mean we are keeping him."

I see the game he is playing. Very well. "We know you are, and we know that he is not allowed to leave. We know that you are forcing him to answer questions about the Shadows and about Winslir. We know that your treatment of him leaves something to be desired. And we know about the book." This last part leaves my mouth before I have a chance to snatch it back. Not that it matters much now. We have already jumped into that hole head first.

Thirty-three pairs of eyes flash in unison. Then, "What book?"

"You know what book. *The Journal of the Pure.* You might have the book back, but we have the pages we need to prove that you've been hiding things from us. And not just the records of the trips to the outside, but something else. Many people at that time were very upset with the Primaries for some reason."

"How would you even know about any of the goings on within the Hall?" This question comes from Prime Julos. *How fitting.*

"Because we know how to access the hidden tunnels underneath." Pausing for effect, I continue. "From a nearby entrance to the passages. We found Jocabin there, and we found the book. Well, I actually found the book, though it seems I'm not the only one. And I'm sure your great-daughter would be happy to tell you all about our adventures down there, including our conversation with the man you claim isn't locked away down there. Admittedly, the door itself wasn't locked, but, nevertheless, he cannot leave. A fact he is very aware of as he sits in his confinement." Wholly rushed without taking a breath or moment to think. Seems to be my style.

All through my speech, he remains stoic. Until I mention *her*. Then his eyes grow wide, and his face drains of color. Huffing and puffing, he stands there in mute horror as I wait for the decisive moment to arrive. What will she say? Time to choose sides. I don't think she believed her own denial any more than I did.

Noticing a small movement in the far corner of my right eye, I turn my head and see what could possibly be Cyndene pushing through the crowd to reach the front. Being such a tiny girl, she could easily be missed if you weren't watching closely. But I saw her unmistakable sparkling head, luminescent locks dancing as she struggled through, locks of hair a shade or so lighter than the usual deep brown of our people, sunlight rippling across the outer layers. Gani swears the women in that family all secretly wash their hair with tea. I have no idea what the purpose of that would be, other than to be different.

Cyndene sidles up to us, looking anywhere but directly at her great-father. Finally, she says, "He said that my brother was taken. Alive." I've never heard her voice so small.

Julos looks as if he wants to grab both of us up by our ears. I'm actually surprised he hasn't. He answers her with a shake of his head, saying, "I can't believe you would turn against us like this, child. How could you? Your brother's death was tragic, and I know you feel it harder than most. He was very close to you. But let's not make it worse by dwelling on it." Noticeably absent is any statement denying her accusations.

Cyndene notices this as well. "And what if he's still out there? What if we could help him? We're no safer here than we'd be out there if the Shadows keep destroying families and taking lives."

"There is no safer place than within these walls. There is no reason to believe anyone or anything exists out there now except for the Shadows. Your brother is gone. We have to accept that and move on."

I do not share Cyndene's hope in her brother's continued existence. He *may* have been alive when he was captured, but he is most likely dead by now. Whether or not the Shadows have command of language is something yet to be proven. I want to see the connection, but it alludes me. Either way, I'd sound crazy even mentioning that. Not exactly the impression we're going for here.

Out of nowhere, Mori pipes up, "And where do we move to, Primary? When the things we rely on are failing us, where do we turn? If the tree dies, if the fire turns to ash, how long do you expect the people to last?"

I see a number of the Primaries open their mouths to answer, and one by one, they turn to the crowd as the waves of onlookers move back to form an opening down the middle of the throng. Walking in our direction from the back, I see the last person I expected to see coming up the path, a wad of papers in his uplifted hand. Sigh.

Always full of surprises.

CHAPTER 24

Allysar walks up just as calm as anything, smiling charmingly at the crowd as he passes them.

Charmingly?

When he reaches us, his smile fades as he turns to look at the assembled Primaries who, by the looks of things, were expecting his presence about as much as they were expecting small yellow baskets filled with pinky toes to rain down from the sky. *Why is he here?*

"What are you doing here?" I pose the question to the back of his head.

"You forced my hand. This was not the plan, but seeing as you've already started the fray, my options in the matter have lessened considerably." Still facing the Primaries, he again lifts the papers in his hand. "I have here proof of what these people are saying. Personal accounts and historical documentation from a journal that has been hidden from us for generations. A journal that tells of a past we no longer have access to: a past beyond our understanding."

The shock on their faces ignites into an all-out uproar. Almost a third of the Primaries go running in the direction of the Hall. I guess they realized where those pages came from. The rest seem unsure of what to say or do, but the barely contained anger is duly noted. Allysar follows the others, so we follow him.

Reaching the inner pathways below the Hall from this direction is far less interesting than our secret entrance, but I don't fail to recognize the landmarks in case we need this information in the future. We continue following in a line until we reach the room with the book. The amusing bit is watching two old men try to steady one another long enough to grab the book from the high shelf. Pushing forward, I thrust my leg on top of the book pile and reach for the book while the men are still scrambling over one another, grabbing it and opening it in almost the same motion as I drop back down to the dirty floor. I find the place in question almost immediately, and suddenly I forget why I was even looking in it. For there, right where the torn pages should be… are the pages. *What is this?*

"What's going on, Allysar?" I spin on him, holding the open book in front of me to illustrate where my confusion lies. Everyone in the room looks at the page I'm pointing to, then at the pages in Allysar's hand, then back at the book.

"Clearly, those are the pages in question. Did you really think I would destroy an ancient document?" The smugness streaking across his countenance has a slimy sheen of sweat and self-satisfaction.

Bhradon practically leaps on him from behind, shouting,

"You...why did you tell us those pages came from the book? Why would you lie about that? What is going on?"

Shrugging himself out of Bhradon's grip, Allysar responds, "I told you that so you wouldn't be able to mess up my plan, and so you wouldn't go back to retrieve the book, which I know you would have done." He looks pointedly at me. "When you took the book to begin with, I had been surreptitiously following you on your little exploits. I followed you back to the firehouse and waited for you to dispose of it in the reticule out back. I then retrieved it and returned it. I made these copies over the course of my own perusals of the book so that I wouldn't *have* to take it."

"But why go through all this just to show them false papers? Why not just show them the book?"

"Because here we are, and there they are. Caught without any hope of backing out. We have questions. They have answers."

And I know which ones I want to ask first.

"Let's make this simple. I want to know what you know about this journal and who the 'Pure' were. Who or what were they loyal to? Why did the Primaries of their time want to hide the past and forget about it? Did something bad happen? And why haven't you told us any of this if you knew we were in danger?"

Julos looks at me with the saddest face I've ever witnessed. "We don't know who the Pure were or what they were trying to protect. If something bad happened, none of that knowledge has been passed down to us." He sighs the sigh of a man who has lost all will to struggle. "We keep these secrets simply because the danger has always been in revealing them. At least since the Shadows arrived."

"Arrived? You mean they came here from somewhere else?"

"What I mean is that they are here now, but they weren't

always around. Where they were, I don't know. But they are our biggest threat now. Nothing is worth that."

"Nothing?" cries Mori. "What about the fact that the Healing Tree is dying? Don't pretend you don't know about that. And the fire as well. The wood isn't burning because something is wrong with the tree. It's dying. Therefore, we are dying. Would you just let the entire village die out to keep everyone 'safe'? How is that even remotely akin to safety?"

"You are exaggerating, child. There is no reason to believe that the tree is dying. It is suffering from some sort of ailment, and we have the Healers working on that. But to send people out in search of help would be sending them to their deaths. If the Shadows can take our people even barely outside the gates, then what chance does anyone stand at reaching any sort of help at all?"

Take.

"You just said 'take,' Primary. I heard you. So you admit that Winslir was taken alive?" I manage to keep calm as I utter the words, knowing the impact the answer may have.

Two of the Primaries give sidelong glances to one another as Julos stumbles around with his words, trying to maintain his composure while mentally wrestling with his own thoughts. One of them, a female I've barely spoken to in the past, addresses me directly.

"We are not sure what happened to the young man on patrol. Perhaps he was still alive when they took him, but it is doubtful at best that he is anything but otherwise now. The fact that his body was taken, rather than desecrated, is a mystery and concerns us deeply. That is precisely why we do not want to encourage anyone to risk their life out there in the wilderness. Especially when those records are so old that, even if the claims of some leaving and starting another colony are true, the chances of anyone being out there seems slim when you take the Shadows into consideration. At that time, the Shadows did not exist, so they would have had no knowledge to bring with them on how to defend themselves, nor any means of surviving. The absence of fire alone would seem to prove that."

"What makes you think they wouldn't have knowledge of fire? Surely that's been a necessity since the beginning of...whatever our past is."

"That's true. But the knowledge and the means are entirely different matters. Once the Shadows appeared on the scene—and we can only assume they would gravitate toward other life forms since they seem to thrive on the destruction of our people—any villages without the means to keep a fire going such as we do would eventually die out. Either from cold, if their climate differed from ours somehow, or the inability to sustain themselves with properly cooked foods. Without fire, many things we eat would not be available."

"What if they built around a tree, such as our ancestors did here? If they have a constantly replenishing supply of firewood, they are just as likely to exist as we are."

The Primary starts to speak, and then halts the motion before a single sound escapes. She looks to the others, seemingly in search of an answer to a question she has not asked.

A man behind me clears his throat. As I turn to him, he begins, "Child, it is not possible. Our tree sustains us. Without it, our people will die. You are right in that. But think about it. It is the tree that keeps us alive; therefore, anyone who leaves its safety would surely die. Perhaps not right away, but they would perish.

From the records and the journals, we know that our lifespan is prolonged by the tree. Or some sort of proximity to it. Leaving would be a death sentence. We will find another way."

All the details swirl inside my head until they place themselves in the correct order, in the correct chain. Logical sequences lock together, bonding themselves into an impenetrable wall of resolve. The laughable part is I knew this was my destiny all along.

Our past is out there. There is no denying that fact. Maybe they're gone now, but there were some of us who were out there at some point. Some who believed in whatever these Pure believed in, and fought to keep the past alive through whatever means necessary, sacrificing their safety and any ties to family and friends in order to preserve some vital piece of the puzzle for posterity.

And I'm going to find them.

INTERLUDE
~ C ~

Her cries pierce the stillness of the evening air even as he touches her face in rapt concern and pity. She tries to form a sentence, any words to express something, *anything*, but the racking pain continues without pause or relief and he *hears* it and he *feels* it and he *can't* get the gnawing *guilt* out of his *head*, out of his *heart,* because, oh, he *knows* it: this is *all his fault.*

Sweat covers every inch of her body. How many times over the last several hours had she screamed in agony, calling out, begging for it to stop? But her hopes had not been fulfilled. The child within her is desperately trying to make its entrance into the world, but try as she might, she cannot seem to end this unbearable anguish and suffering for the both of them.

He looks at her again with the naked torment of fear in his eyes.

Is this punishment for what they had done?

CHAPTER 25

As it turns out, deciding was the easy part.

I'm not sure if getting to say goodbye to Gani would have been better or worse. But we definitely can't tell anyone. We, as in Bhradon and I, with a very determined Mori intent on staying by my side no matter the cost. And as close as we are, his thoughts seem to invade my own. Both the danger and the importance weigh heavily on all of us.

Mori and I are special. Rare, I guess I should say. That's what they always tell us. The Primaries used to say that twins are so uncommon that our birth was celebrated in grand style at the Gathering that season.

But we're more than just uncommon. As we got older, it became very evident that we were extremely alike, both physically and mentally. Even emotionally. Laughing, crying, yelling: it was always in unison or near enough to make the neighbors uncomfortable. When one got angry, we both got angry. When one was sad, the other was sad. We've even dreamed the same dream on a few occasions, though not always at the same time.

And we look so much alike, far beyond the dark skin and features we share with everyone among our people, far beyond what twins of differing genders should share. Uncanny. Inexplicable. Yet perfectly natural to us now. I don't look like a male, and he doesn't look like a female. Yet our appearances are so similar that, according to Gani, it sparked many a debate among the Primaries at one point. Apparently, there are books in the Room of Records mentioning some aspects of these matters, and someone took it upon themselves to study up on it when we were younger. Like there was something wrong with us. The idea of "polar twins," as they called it, was apparently an enigmatic phenomenon even to our esoteric ancestors. Gani says it just means we complete two pieces of the same puzzle.

Gani.

My heart is bursting at the very thought of leaving her alone, with no explanation and no goodbye.

When Mori and I return home, she is sitting in her normal spot in the kitchen. But nothing about her is normal. She seems to have aged a great deal in a matter of hours, and I can sense a sadness in her eyes that overcasts everything of her usual demeanor.

She clears her throat before speaking. "You know they loved you very much. And they'd be so proud of what you've become."

Mori looks at me with a glimmer of nervousness. "Are you talking about mother and father?"

"Yes, dear. They're looking down on the two of you and smiling right now."

Stepping up, I interject. "Do you really believe that, Gani? I mean, are they looking down on us? How could you know that? None of us do." I trail off into thought, but she continues.

"Truly, child, I don't know. But I believe it nonetheless. Call it what you will. I just can't imagine that death is the end."

Mori says, "What does it matter if they can't be here with us? Where are they if they aren't here?"

"I don't know that either. What I do know is that your mother and father would have been so proud of you today. You stood up for our people, despite the consequences. That is exactly what your parents did. They paid the consequences, but they tried to help."

Astonished, I burst out, "So you aren't mad at us?"

At this, she smiles a smile full of melancholy and the wisdom she keeps locked away inside her head. The wisdom she doles out in increments, just enough to make a point. "No, Corinne, I'm not mad. I'm unhappy that things are the way they are. But that doesn't mean I'm unhappy that you did what you did. You did the right thing, albeit perhaps in the wrong way. But your intentions were pure."

Pure.

"Gani, do you know anything about the Pure or any of this? I can't wrap my head around it, but I know there's something there."

"Of course there is. People don't go around keeping secrets that don't contain something of substance. Think about it, child. The world is unknown to us, and we've never questioned that. Yet maybe our lives depend on doing just that. Maybe today will open minds and get people thinking." Sighing, her shoulders sagging under a heavy weight, Gani adds, "Who am I kidding?

These people lack the capacity to think for themselves. They walk around in a daze and trust everything they're told. Nothing will change."

The single tear rolling down my cheek belies my calm exterior. Standing, she opens her arms, and I fall into her warm embrace, shuddering with the burden of knowledge. The burden of responsibility. She's right. No one will do anything about this. Except for us. We have to go.

Pulling back to hold me at arm's length, Gani gazes into my tear-filled eyes with such intensity that I can feel her searching for something. I'm not sure what. But eventually, she nods several times and smiles, this time with less melancholy and more joy. At least I've somehow made her happy again. That's the closest thing to a goodbye that I can give her.

With a solemn look, she says, "Never forget that life is rarely easy, and decisions rarely simple. The more we strive for what we believe is best, the more we sink into the mire of indecision. Questioning our beliefs and searching for the truth almost always leads to destruction. The right decision isn't always the best decision."

"That makes no sense, Gani."

"Think about it, child. So often, we see others make mistakes out of good intentions. Striving for what's best is not the same thing as doing what's right."

"So which one is better?"

"I'll leave that up to you to decide." With that, she kisses my forehead and reaches out to hug Mori as well.

"Thank you, Gani. I'll keep that in mind." Her words continue to echo in my head.

After we eat our midday meal, Mori and I head out to find

Bhradon. We need a plan, not to mention provisions. And a way out of the village.

Allysar told me that he and Nehemor had escaped via the southern water trellis, a contraption built in the days before our known memory to allow the free flow of water through the town walls. The water enters from the northern water trellis, moves downstream through the center of the village, and continues on its way unimpeded past the southern trellis. The only time they are ever moved or opened is to allow debris that has collected around the opening to be extracted so that the water can flow through. The very idea is nauseating and beyond what my mind is capable of bearing at the moment. So I am choosing to keep moving, thinking about nothing other than the book and where it is leading us. Thinking about our future rather than our present.

So far, I'm failing miserably.

It takes two days to sneak out all the necessary materials: food, clothing, a few bits of firewood to last us until we can gather more. On that note, I have to make sure that Bhradon remembered to get an axe. We store all we know we can carry in an empty shed behind the Healing Houses. Now we wait until the moon has shied herself away from the world.

A tapping. Everything in blackness, my vision adjusts to see a familiar face at my bedroom window. Again, I feel a bit ridiculous at the color that rises to my cheeks and the giggle that threatens to erupt and give us all away. Why do I feel like a young girl whenever the thought of him entering my bedroom comes to mind? It's all rather silly, and I know it has to do with the fact that Gani is in a nearby room, sleeping the sleep of someone oblivious to the proceedings. Blissfully oblivious, I hope. That sobers me, and the impending laugh dies on my lips.

Mori takes over at my momentary hesitation, intent on climbing over me to let Bhradon into the room. After he almost breaks my anklebone, I shove him off in as gentle a manner as I can so as not to disturb Gani. I step back to allow room for our midnight visitor to enter, mentally noting that he briefly pauses atop my bed on his descent, only to immediately scramble down to the floor. Smiling in spite of myself, I pull him into a warm embrace, which has the added benefit of making Mori uncomfortable as well. So be it. He'll have to get used to this if he's going to insist on going with us. We would, of course, be more discreet when it comes to anything further.

Without a word, so as not to make any more noise than necessary, we gather our currently empty packs, along with any last minute items we feel we may need. Bhradon helps Mori roll the bedrolls up for us to tie to our packs. Whatever we take, we must carry. Those are the rules. Following Bhradon, with Mori slinking along right behind me, I creep through the house and into the moonless night.

Sneaking around the silent houses on the short trip from our house to the water trellis south of us is, quite literally, child's play to us now. Bhradon knows the patrols and routes better than just about anyone, so the timing on this venture is supposed to be simple and easy as long as we stick to the plan. Our packs are made of strong material with a watertight seal of hardened sap from the Healing Tree. We carefully load everything into them, careful not to forget anything. Bhradon wraps the axe and larger items inside of clothing pieces for the duration of this initial phase. No need to cut our legs off trying to swim out.

My skin barely registers the tepid water as we silently swim against the inner wall of the village, making for the center of the main waterway. This far south, the waterways diverge into far-spread appendages heading down to the southern fields, where they dissect the area into crop sections and provide irrigation. I'm not a strong swimmer, so I quickly lag behind the others, at once feeling the stark loneliness of the dark, the unceasing current that threatens to carry me through the wall itself into the wild unknown.

When I reach the trellis, Bhradon is already huffing and puffing in his attempt to get it open. Mori, being much smaller, is trying his best to help but only seems to be getting in the way. My heart stutters out a wild staccato pattern as thoughts of drowning enter my already bewildered brain. The current is bashing us repeatedly against the wall, so powerfully that the idea of death by force doesn't seem all that unlikely.

A creaking sound interrupts my thoughts. I allow myself a glance in their direction and notice the grate lifted up. Now comes the hard part. We have to swim down and *under* the wall all the way through to the outer edge. Without being swept away downstream.

Thinking I hear something, I turn around to face the bank, but Mori grabs my arm and ushers me right above the opening. Bhradon is nowhere to be seen, so I have to assume he made it out on the other side and is waiting to help me get to the bank in safety. I have to assume this, or I won't be able to go through with it. I can't hold my breath very long, and the current is relentless in its steady yet forceful rhythm. This isn't going to work. I'm going to die.

A soft voice whispers, "Deep breath, Rinni," and barely gives me enough time to comply before shoving me down under the water. An unending plane of darkness envelops me, and I start to panic, only finding my sanity at the last moment. The grate should be right over my head, so I swim forward, reaching out with my hands to keep from losing the last vestiges of anything resembling a sense of direction.

Immediately the water surrounding me surges forward, dragging me along in a frenzy of motion and speed that propels me in a lateral direction until I feel a hand on my forearm yanking me back up into the comparative stillness of the night. Before I can scream, Bhradon's face comes into view, and I remember. We are outside.

We are outside.

The thought paralyzes me for a brief moment, but he is too busy dragging both of us toward the bank. Based on what we knew, we had planned on the current fighting against our attempts to reach land, but our hope was that, by the time the line we would make could converge with the bank, we'd be far enough south of the patrols as to have no need to worry about them.

Helping Bhradon by swimming as hard as I can is the only aid I have to offer at this point. Turning around for a glimpse of Mori, I'm terrified by the empty space behind me. Perhaps he decided against coming after all. As much as I want to believe that, I know it's not true. So where is he?

Seconds pass.

A tug on my arm.

I almost yank free, but thankfully, we are within reach of land. Bhradon jerks me out in front of him, and I grab hold of whatever I can. He still manages to get out ahead of me and reaches down to help me pull myself up. Once I'm standing, I begin motioning and whispering loudly. My brother is still nowhere in sight.

And then it happens. A large round object pops up above the level of the water, and for one nightmarish fraction of time, it appears to be Mori's pack, floating along with no sense of urgency. But then I realize the object is moving against the current to some degree, slowly weaving a course in our direction. I sigh with relief.

Until I realize it's not him.

CHAPTER 26

The moment he reaches us and drags himself up, I pounce, pummeling his girth full-force to the ground in my rage.

"Where … is … my … *brother?* What did you do to him, Allysar?"

His face is contorted from what little I can tell in the darkness. "Get off! I can't … breathe!" He manages to pick himself back up into a sitting position once I feel inclined to step back long enough to give him air.

He raises his hand to me. "Relax, sister. He's coming." He adds, "He was right behind me."

"He was right behind *me!*"

"Yes, well, he felt obliged to let me go first. That is, once I told him what I had. You couldn't possibly think to do this without me, now could you?"

At that, a sputtering, bedraggled, but fully alive Mori comes into view. Bhradon and I help him up, and I can't help but stop myself from throwing my arms around him just to be sure he's really there.

"I thought…I thought…" I begin but am unable to finish the thought without threat of tears.

"I'm sorry. I didn't think about it like that. But our friend here was following us, and, believe me, I was tempted to take off without him, but you'll understand when you see what he's brought with him to help us." I watch the concern on his face melt into shock as he stares off into the darkness behind me. He lifts his finger to point into the water, and I turn in trepidation of what I might find there.

Another large round object is floating along, coughing quite loudly and somewhat missing the point of swimming against the current. Bhradon runs downstream, traveling along the bank in conjunction with the object, presumably in an attempt to grab it. Reaching out a good deal farther than he should have been capable of, he wraps his hand around something and pulls it free of the water, dropping it to the ground just beside the current that nearly carried it off. I almost—*almost*—wish it had.

Cyndene.

"What are you doing here?" I ask in what amounts to a barely contained scream.

She looks as though she's about to respond in kind, but she sighs and stares at the ground instead. Raising her eyes back up at us, she replies, "Look—you were right. The other day, I mean. I'm not saying I agree with everything you and the crazy old man were saying, but I can't believe my great-father could be a part of something so…I mean, how could do they do this to us? Lie to us. Lie to me." She squares her shoulders and continues. "I believe this place may exist. I don't know if anyone is still there, but I bet there's something there that could help us. If nothing else, we'll be the first ones to ever leave the colony. Except them, of course." She smiles, actually smiles. As if this was some afternoon lark through the village center.

There is nothing we can do at this point without having to give up our plans to slink off into the night and avoid any notice. Suddenly I feel very naked in our current position, far enough from the further edge of the fields to avoid direct contact with the patrol, but close enough to be seen if the moon were to make a grand appearance. Either way, we need to keep moving, with or without our "friend."

Then I remember where we are, and I turn to see the immense vastness of the trees leading off into nowhere, or perhaps everywhere. The outlines are too dark to distinguish much in the way of details, but the sheer number is something I have never before seen in the whole of my existence. The Healing Tree is the extent of my personal experience with these incredible entities.

And then I remember the Shadows. I imagine we all had the same thought, for we move as a group, swiftly but silently, in the direction that will take us around the village and past the main gates. From there, we head off in a northerly direction, following the path of the water upstream.

In the footsteps of our ancestors.

CHAPTER 27

Rain.

Not a storm but a downpour, droplets edging down my already blurred vision, obscuring the line between nature's sorrow and my own tears. I wonder if the spirits of nature are troubled by our abrupt departure. Will they whisper a farewell to Gani for me tomorrow with the caress of a sudden afternoon breeze?

Gani would like that. She used to tell us about the books we never see anymore, the ones the Record Keepers won't let us read. Books about nature, about mighty—and often strange—men and women of old. Books about long passages of time where everything was recorded in painstaking detail. Stories of beings who created the world, some cruel and some kind, but always, always there was some element of nature involved. *We are all a part of nature,* she would say. That you can look at the simplest

of things in nature and see the hand of a deity. That word—
deity—was forbidden. But Gani was never one to follow the rules
blindly, especially when she didn't agree with them. Funny how
much like her I am, yet neither of us has ever been willing to
admit it. For different reasons.

Whenever she would tell us these stories, either Mori or I
would invariably ask her why some books were forbidden, unable
to contemplate the intricacies and complex entanglements of
human behavior at that age. *The Primaries.* That was always the
answer. And talking about such things in public would have
brought nothing but trouble for our family. Looking back, I wish
I had taken the time to learn more.

Looking ahead, I notice how far I've fallen back from the rest
of the group: a dangerous move to say the least. My feet, slowed
down by the water-logged mire that encompasses the entire area,
attempt to catch up to the others who seem to be stopping up
ahead in a clearing surrounded on three sides by trees. At least I
think they're trees. Thick night permeates the air and my vision,
so that I can only sense the looming presence amidst the absence
of it. We've skirted in and out of small thickets since leaving the
village a few hours ago, but for the most part we are following
the path of the water north in the hopes that our ancestors would
have done the same.

Allysar's death grip on the map is relentless: he insists on a
retainer against waking up one morning to find himself tied to
a shrub and stripped of all but the barest of necessities. Mori has
told him several times to stop being ridiculous.

Apparently, the shrewd little man can read my thoughts.

That map he brought is the only reason I'm even tolerating his
presence right now. *We are not a team. I work alone,* he had said.

Well, we'll see. For now, that sacred scrap of paper is all we have in the way of anything other than pure luck right now.

Cyndene, on the other hand, has been unusually quiet since we left. Though I can't say that I've been overly talkative myself. Thoughts of home snatch me back inside my head over and over to relive the painful emotions as if to punish me for their own existence.

The choice of encampment leaves me with an odd sense of foreboding. Not dread, not exactly. Just a feeling. And not for the first time, either. I felt it every time we neared the pockets of trees, the dense underbrush a flimsy barrier between me and my imagination. Like something just out of reach yet breathing down my neck—my spine—as it whispers foulness into my ear....

It's that kind of bizarre thought that makes me doubt my sanity at times. And then...

This. Bhradon's arms are a welcome diversion from my mental journey into an episode of insanity. My conviction wanes as he holds me tight against him in the dissipating rain, the last vestiges of cold seeping from me with a lingering farewell sigh. But tonight is not a night for us. This is our first camp, and everything is miserably wet. Tonight's fire will be a pitiful, or perhaps nonexistent, sight.

Bhradon goes to help Allysar in his attempts to keep our small reserve of firewood dry long enough to get a fire started. Mori is trying to spread the tarps across nearby protruding branches so as to keep us as dry as possible. I see Cyndene watching him, eyeing the proceedings with an air of detached curiosity. I wonder if she's ever had to do anything other than make the deliveries from the mills to the bakery and storage houses. They never made her carry the heavy stuff. I know because the younger, and in some cases older, boys would go out of their way to look like complete idiots just to compete for a smile from her. The rare ones she did give away showed nothing but contempt and bitterness in their depths.

The rain is lessening, but the effects are still here, the air rife with dank moisture in the aftermath. Sleep will not come easy, even with nature's lullaby pitter-pattering in the background.

I wake up to sirens blaring throughout the stillness of the night.

The night is a solid wall of pitch, but somehow looking over I can just barely discern the outlines of empty bedrolls. Where have they gone? And why did they leave me here alone?

As I shove my bedroll away from me, I begin to shiver with the cold, with the realization that I'm alone. With fear.

I run.

The trees, the wind, whispering in my ear. The sentiments vulgar and full of hatred, shockingly violent. A hoarse, throaty gurgle reaches the apex of my senses, and I realize it is laughter. The whispering dies out as I come to a dead stop.

The sudden flash from a nearby tree is lighting up the night sky, burning brilliantly as a scorching blaze swallows it whole and paints the night with a glow of red, then orange. A ball of flame so intense it's impossible to look directly at it.

The Healing Tree is on fire.

But why is it here?

Not happening not happening not happening—

I look around and spot the others on the far side of the tree. At least, I think I see everyone. There are four figures faintly lit by the light of the flames. Then I realize only two are human-shaped, and with a sickening feeling I know what the other two are. As I call out to them in warning, the *feeling* that Mori isn't there is a living entity inside my head. I know his form, and I know when he's nearby. I can't sense his presence at all. Where is he?

Suddenly the fire shoots up and out with a pulsating power, forcing me back away from the group assembled on the other side. I begin to make a wide arc along the outskirts of the clearing where the tree is located in the hopes that I can reach them and find Mori. The tree begins to glow with a familiar white-hot radiance, swelling in size at an alarming rate. I won't reach them in time, I can't escape, and somehow I know that it wouldn't matter. So I stand my ground and await the impact. This time there are no tears.

Goodbye, Bhradon.

CHAPTER 28

Through the trees. Through the trees. Through the trees. Oh, the trees, trees, trees.

I've never seen so many trees in my life. Not up close, at least. Back home, the Healing Tree is the only one in the village, our only source of all that it provides. Gani and some of the other elders would speak of days long past when our people cut down trees around the village to use as firewood, but the Shadows made it impossible and downright dangerous to continue to do so after it became necessary to travel farther and farther away from the gates. Besides, those trees were only good as firewood. They didn't provide any of the other benefits of our tree.

For so long, that was enough. And now, here we are in the midst of enough trees to keep us going for a very long time. Truthfully, I know that will not help us. The Healing Tree, the life force of our people, is dying.

And so are we.

Mori insists on stopping at every sunset to set up camp when all I want to do is keep moving. I feel a pull, a subconscious tugging that keeps dragging me on, not wanting me to stop. But we have to sleep. We must rest in order to keep pushing forward.

A deathly silence follows us, surrounds us, closes in on us. Silence that is deafening in its intensity, a booming nothingness that reverberates in my ears until I feel as if my head will burst from the acoustic void. We've never experienced a true stillness before, this flattening peacefulness that reeks of passive fierceness. No auditory sensations. Not a whisper on the air. No sound. Such calm would not be so shocking were it not for the constant motion and humming throughout the village every day. Now there is nothing. Absolute nothingness.

The trees really are beautiful. Some of them, at least. I guess because I've never been in a forest before, everything seems unreal and unnatural, almost like I'm floating through a dream. Stopping to admire one particularly fascinating specimen, I feel a sudden aching in the pit of my stomach. That pulling sensation is becoming stronger the farther we travel into this never-ending sea of green.

Today is going to be rough.

I got very little sleep last night, so intently focused on not falling back into my nightmare that I thought of little else. And Bhradon is trying. I can see that. Trying to comfort me. But today there is no comfort to be had. I'm not sure if Mori's absence from my dream is a good thing or a bad thing, considering the outcome. Nevertheless, it disturbs me as nothing else ever has.

We end up walking for most of the day in the hopes of reaching a safe spot to camp before nightfall. But as the last rays of pink and gold ebb away, so does our hope of finding a decent clearing. We will just have to make camp in the forest tonight. Although we've been following the water upstream for most of the journey, our current path has taken us further away than we'd expected. The soothing sound of flowing water was a welcome presence that I'm sorely missing today.

After the fire has had a chance to settle down, and our exhausted bodies have had their fill of the night's meal, all of us are sitting around in an ill-disguised attempt to seek solace in the company of one another. I guess anything is preferable to whatever might be out there, and the likes of Allysar and Cyndene are no exception tonight.

The stories being told tonight are mundane at best, my eyelids beginning to close of their own accord without the luxury of a bedroll against my back. When I begin to fall headfirst in the direction of the still-smoldering fire, my subconscious mind slaps me across the brain in warning, but it's too late. My eyes pop open, sensing Bhradon as he leaps up to grab me, but something to my left grabs me around the waist from behind before I have a chance reach for him.

We land in a heap, and I hit my forehead on a rather large stone jutting halfway out of the cool ground.

"Ouch!" I hiss, rubbing my head rapidly with my palm as I turn to face...Cyndene.

Huh.

Without a clear indication as to what she's expecting me to say, I mumble a word of gratitude as she picks herself up off the ground. I think she's about to offer me her hand to help me up, but I realize she's pointing at my head.

"Is it that bad?" I laugh uncomfortably.

"Depends on what you mean by 'bad' and how attached you are to your hair." I'm expecting smugness, but her tone implies pity, which strikes me as far worse considering the source.

The acrid stench of singed hair. Ah, yes. There it is.

Perfect.

"Probably doesn't matter, I guess. Though I wish I had a way to cut it off." I notice Bhradon eying the axe tied to his pack just a few feet away, so I shoot him a look that I hope screams *not even remotely funny.*

Gathering myself up since no one seems to be coming to help, I sit back down between Cyndene and Bhradon. One by one, fatigue hits each of us, forcing us into our bedrolls as the night rolls by in inky shadows of nothingness.

Sometime later, I'm awakened by a light tap on my upper arm. Again, I'm achingly aware of the silence: a loud, pulsating thing that surrounds and suffocates us. It takes a moment to rouse myself from the vestiges of that same familiar dream, thankfully filled with the nameless man instead of burning trees and burning flesh. Bhradon's dark eyes reflect the moonlight cascading through the interwoven branches overhead, but it's the look he's giving me that gets my attention. Snuggling into my bedroll as best as he can considering the cramped space, he rolls over to face me, his lips already against mine before I can fully turn around. For a moment, I forget where we are and relax into the familiar feeling.

Then the thought of the others just yards away brings me to my senses. Pushing him gently back, I say, "We shouldn't do this here."

He looks over at the sleeping forms and whispers into my ear, "Okay, let's go for a walk."

My face must have mirrored my fear because he gives me one of his simple smiles, takes my hand and kisses it softly, and starts to inch his way out of the bedroll as he takes me with him. His look says "I'll protect you," but I'm still not comfortable given our current location in the middle of the forest.

Something strikes me out of the corner of my eye. Looking over, I see nothing, hear nothing, but still the feeling is there. I can't shake the thought that something is off. Then I realize the fire is now completely out. The fire made with wood we brought from home. From the Healing Tree.

Bhradon sees it too and gives me an odd look. I shrug, but I'm still getting a strange sense of wrongness….

There it is again. This time I see something. Nothing I can pinpoint, but something nonetheless. Panicking, I tug on his arm, beseeching to know if he saw it as well. Despite the inability to see more than a few feet in front of me, the look on his face is perfectly clear.

He did.

The air is full of noise in the utter silence. The wind whispering, yet there is no wind. Faint, so very faint, yet so very loud I feel as if my ears might rupture from the pressure.

A sudden fierce chill skirts across my skin, moving from a crawl to swiftly envelop my entire body in a fevered embrace that I cannot fight my way out of, a sheen of sweat already forming before I can speak.

Eyes.

Red, glowing *eyes*. Hovering, suspended in mid-air as if separated from any part of the natural world. But I know better.

And I know we don't stand a chance.

CHAPTER 29

Run run run run run run run run run run run run run—

My mind screams, begs, pleads. In the space of time between the flash of an eyelid and the breath that has lodged itself halfway to my lungs, impotent in providing any necessary air, the others are awakened with what seems to be an invisible hand floating across the camp. All at once, they are on their feet, some grabbing packs, others taking off in a blind panic. But we are all on the run now.

Run run run run run—

I can barely make out the shapes of the others in the moonless night, but I feel Bhradon's presence nearby as we run for our lives. I want to find Mori, to scream out his name, to assure myself that he is one of the dark forms in front of me. But I know that this would be a deadly mistake. For all of us.

Before long, a gurgling sound reaches my ears, and a wave of relief washes over me for no apparent reason. Maybe, just maybe, the Shadow can't follow us into the water. Almost as quickly, the thought vanishes. My parents were killed as they attempted to rescue two young boys from the Shadows.

They were all in the water.

We continue a path along what I can only discern as the water's edge by sound alone. Nothing is coming to me: no plan, no thought, no action. The gurgling sound is suddenly replaced by a thunderous crashing cacophony that envelops the night air, making it hard to think of anything else. I try to look ahead, but the darkness is absolute. An oblivion of black on black. The figures that I think are Mori and the others begin to slow down ever so slightly, and I realize that I am doing the same. We can't keep up this pace forever. The Shadow will reach us eventually. Or Shadows. There is no way to know how many are actually out there right now. Who knows what levels of endurance they possess?

The deafening roar surrounds us, pounding out an indiscernible rhythm of continuous beats. The thrumming sound is hypnotizing, lulling me into a dreamy state as my legs persist in moving of their own accord in an attempt at self-preservation. My stubborn mental senses want to fight this feeling, but it seems as if we've been running forever.

Then I hear it.

A piercing scream erupts somewhere in front of me, and I force myself to keep moving forward despite the raging battle in my head. My senses are shouting at me to turn around or jump into the water. But I don't know whose voice I heard. Images of Mori being torn to pieces by a Shadow force my legs to go faster.

Bhradon is right beside me as we come closer to the scene.

I still can't figure out the identity of the shapes, but they are slowing down for some reason.

Two.

There are two shapes. Someone is missing.

Before I can examine the details any further, a dark form leaps from nowhere, black as night, virtually invisible, a Shadow in the shadows.

It grabs the nearest person, and we stare in horror for a few mute seconds. Then we run.

Only a few strides ahead, I realize the source of the scream from a moment ago.

The ground slips away from underneath my feet, and an identical scream escapes from my throat as I feel myself falling into nothing.

CHAPTER 30

Mist hits me full force, a spray of water washes over me, pushing me violently downward. Plunging feet first into water that wraps itself over my head, filling my lungs and forcing out the last remaining tendrils of oxygen, I feel myself sinking further and further into the abyss.

Until I'm grabbed from above, yanked out of the water with a sudden motion, and dragged onto the bank. Though I'm fairly certain this is all in my head.

Please, please, please no.

But the pressure is real. Pressure everywhere, pushing brutally against my chest with an unsteady rhythm that feels out of sync with my heart.

My heart.

Rinni, please no, please, please, please. Come on!

Sounds, far away yet so close, echo in some crevice of my

consciousness. Rapid expunging, torrents of liquid gushing up into what I might have once called my throat. A purging relief leaving a trail of burning heat in its wake.

Massive quantities of air suck down into my chest, unbidden but not unwelcome, though the pain and the burning are so intense I want to scream.

"Oh, please, thank you! Oh, Rinni! Thank you, thank you, thank you." Realizing that my newfound exploration into life might be squelched by the suffocating embrace I'm involuntarily wrapped up in, I push Bhradon far enough away to make my predicament clear. My throat is raw, stinging, and I don't trust my ability to verbally communicate at the moment. Not to mention the intense roaring sound that persists in my ears.

Red, swollen circles circumscribe his eyes like the walls of a fortress. Like home. And I can see that Mori is close beside me, partially responsible regarding his own involvement in my would-be asphyxiation. A group smothering is a minor mishap in the grand scheme of things.

Bhradon's hands don't leave me, but he backs away enough to allow me the necessary air for recovery. Mori scoots around my right side, laying his head on my shoulder like he used to do when we were children.

A jolt slams me back, the force of it almost landing me in the water once again, but both Bhradon and Mori reach out just in time, each grabbing an arm to pull me forward onto dry land.

What was that?

"Did you … feel that?" The look of shock on Mori's face does nothing to alleviate my swirling emotions.

Slowly, sound manages to escape my throat with a raspy,

choking cough. A hoarse "yes" is all I manage to get out, so I nod my affirmation in case he didn't hear me.

Sensing Bhradon's confusion and curiosity, I look pointedly at my brother in the hopes that he can explain the unexplainable.

"That was odd. More than odd, I know. It was…like lightning, or what you'd imagine lightning feels like, I guess." He shrugs, unable to articulate the strange experience that we just shared.

"Well, whatever it was, we've got to get a move on. Now." Bhradon's tone of authority snaps me back into the present situation.

Now my mind is reeling with the acute jolt of clarity, and reality sinks back into place. "Who was it?" My voice is a throaty whisper in the darkness, the pregnant words hanging in the air, floating among the tendrils of mist and spray, defying gravity with their weighty implication.

Both of them look at me, and then turn to glance into the trees behind Bhradon. A figure stands there; I can see that now. A female form by all appearances, crouched low to the ground, with long hair skimming the grass and fallen leaves.

So Allysar is gone.

No one seems to know what to say, what to do, how to move forward. But we must move on before the Shadows figure out what happened and where we are.

I'm still unsure as to what exactly *did* happen. All I remember is running and running. Falling and drowning. Breathing and living.

"What happened? I mean, where are we? What was that?"

Cyndene raises her head from her knees and looks at me. She stands up and walks toward us, but I can see that she is avoiding the edge of the water by a wide berth.

"It's a waterfall. Like in the stories, you know. Mother has a picture book she likes to look at when it rains, and she showed it to me many times." She sighs and glances up in the direction we fell from. I follow her gaze and gasp audibly. I've never seen something so terrifyingly beautiful in all my life. Even in the near darkness, the majestic beauty of the rushing water crashing down to continue on its way is breathtaking in its violence. Perhaps it wouldn't seem so scary had it not just tried to drown me.

Mori breaks into my thoughts by declaring, "We've already lost time backtracking downstream, but there's no use worrying about that now. We were all running blindly, I know. They are still out there somewhere, and we need fire badly." He's right.

Immediately, we take off our packs to survey the damage. Our packs are fairly watertight considering they are coated with a layer of sap from the Healing Tree, but we took a pretty hefty plunging. As Bhradon pulls out some firewood to start a fire, a sudden horrible thought comes to me.

The map.

"The map!" I manage to croak. Shaking, trembling with chills not wholly attributable to my impromptu bath, I continue in intermittent blocks of words as my throat slowly begins to heal. "Not to be cruel—really upset about Allysar—scared—map in his pack—now we're lost."

Mori stares at me for a moment with an odd look. Finally, he says, "Rinni, I have the map. I was looking at it this evening after we ate, so I just put it in my pack since Allysar was already asleep. But I think as long as we stay by the water, we'll be okay."

I nod slowly at him, and we share a moment of silence for our lost friend. The friend we never wanted, the friend who stood apart. The friend who wanted nothing more than to give his best friend's children a future.

After the fire is started, instead of making torches and moving on, we decide to take turns watching the fire and keeping an eye out for Shadows. Maybe they think we are dead, or maybe they are on their way now. The fire should keep them away, as long it continues to burn bright. No one can sleep, but no one wants to leave just yet.

We are up before the sun rises, eager to leave behind this awful memory, but resistant to continuing on like nothing has happened.

But something *has* happened. We are now painfully aware of our vulnerability, horrified at the thoughts and images that pervade our minds as we try to block them out.

Peace be with you, my friend.

Walking becomes automatic, just another part of us like an arm or a leg. The trees seem to be a permanent fixture in our lives right now. Days pass as the nothingness continues on its way past us, bringing not a sound or a breath of wind to ease the painful silence. Silence that is made all the more heavy because we cannot speak without thinking about him or talking about him. Mori has become our guide, utilizing the map as best he can, but truthfully, I think we are merely doing as he previously stated. But I guess following the water makes sense.

After making camp one evening, Bhradon suggests that we keep watch in pairs, each covering half of the surrounding forest. It makes sense, but Cyndene and I insist on taking the first watch. The boys are exhausted from chopping firewood and setting up camp, refusing to let the two of us help. They don't argue at this suggestion, and before long I can hear my brother's light snoring and the heavy breaths of my love. How I wish I were lying there with him.

An hour or so into our shift, I hear a hoarse cry echo in the darkness. Without a thought, I race in the direction the sound seemed to come from, my mind filled with images of Shadows and darkness. Luckily, I manage to keep ahold of my torch as I scramble through the black of night.

When I reach an open clearing, I see Cyndene crouched down on the ground, her back to me and her shoulders hunched over. I can hear distinct sobbing, and my fear turns into concern. Her grief is still fresh. I have not forgotten that. Cautiously approaching her shaking form, I lean down to put my arm around her, the only comfort I can offer. Then I see it. She is stooped over a dark shape, her hands draped across the still figure. Bringing my torch closer, I fear what I will see. The firelight illuminates upon a bedraggled body with large gaping wounds across the torso, the mark of evil that we know too well. Shaking my head, I try to push reality from my mind, yet I know that this is perhaps, more than anything, what she truly came to find.

Her brother.

CHAPTER 31

Cyndene raises her face to mine, looking like a lost child. Her mouth begins to form words, but no sound emerges.

"I'm so sorry" is all I can think to say.

"No, this is"—silently sobbing, she shakes her head—"this is just the end of what we already knew. I guess some part of me still wanted to believe he might be alive, but deep down I knew that possibility was just wishful thinking. I just want to give him a proper burial if I can."

"Yes, of course. I can go get Bhradon and Mori to help."

She nods and gives a slight smile. "Thank you."

As I head in the direction of camp, I realize we may need to get creative with the tools to find ways of digging. Bhradon will be able to handle that part better than I will.

I'm running as fast as I can manage, with the campsite in view, when I hear it.

A blood curling scream erupts in the night air, chilling me to the bone and freezing me in my tracks. That was not the same cry as before. And that was not the wailing of a distressed and grief-ridden sister.

That was the scream of someone in fear for their life.

Two heartbeats pass before I manage to turn around. I yell back to the boys over my shoulder, hoping they can hear me and wishing I had more than just a torch for protection.

When I reach the clearing, Winslir's body lies exactly as it did when I had left, only there's no one here, but another cry soon pierces through the forest, and I take off in that direction. Within moments, I come across a horrific scene.

Cyndene is trapped in the grip of a Shadow, its sharp claws digging into her small frame as it lifts her into the air with a jarring movement. A gaping mouth reveals teeth like fangs, sharp enough to rip through human flesh with ease. The rest of its form is a hazy fog, black on black, pure darkness. But I can discern the presence of a human-like shape, albeit far taller and with completely different features. But legs and arms and torso in some form nonetheless.

None of this registers until after I react. I'm already charging the beast with all of my fear shying away to make room for something else. Something I've never felt before.

And I attack.

I whirl my fire-lit torch as I run, lashing out with the end toward the creature. Immediately, it drops Cyndene, and without warning, tries to run around to my right-hand side. I twirl in that direction, simultaneously launching my makeshift weapon at the snarling creature.

Fire erupts all around the Shadow's leg where the torch

manages to embed itself, the flames licking higher and higher as it shrieks its fury to the sky. Not stopping to watch the festivities, and grabbing the shaking mass of Cyndene lying in a questionable state of consciousness on the forest floor, I drag both of us in a direction that might vaguely lead toward camp. Before we get very far, two shadows emerge from up ahead. Too small to be the enemy, the figures quickly come into view and confirm their identity. Mori grabs Cyndene from my trembling grasp as Bhradon grabs onto me in a life-threatening embrace. Just as I'm about to pass out from lack of air, he releases me, and I point into the trees behind us.

"I killed it, I think. Lit it on fire. But Bhradon," I whisper as I grab his retreating form, "there's something else." He stops, glaring at me impatiently. "Winslir. He's dead. She found his body. He needs a proper burial."

Nodding tersely, he runs back to camp to grab some tools. I'm not sure what all we can use for digging, but we have to try. Cyndene is sobbing uncontrollably at this point, but Mori has her locked in his arms. Mori. My brother. Holding a girl, emotional wreck that she is.

I wish Gani were here to see it.

Refusing to let my tears get the better of me, I wait for Bhradon to return. When he approaches our group, I tell Mori to keep Cyndene comfortable while we go attend to her brother's body.

"No!" she screams. I'm taken aback by her outburst, but she continues, slightly calmer. "I mean, I want to help. I *need* to help. I'm the only family here right now." Smiling at her with what I hope is a friendly expression, I help her to her feet and we head back to the fateful spot as a group, leery of what we may now find.

It's gone.

The Shadow isn't there. No remnants, no pile of ashes, nothing save the charred end of what used to be my torch. I didn't kill it after all. So we take turns keeping watch and digging a shallow grave, the best we can offer Cyndene considering the circumstances. But the gesture seems to appease her somewhat, and as we place the last bit of dirt back on top of his final resting place, she grabs the scorched bit of stick left by the creature in what was apparently a mad dash for escape. Which seems extremely odd to me. The Shadow running from us being the odd part, not her picking up the spent torch. But she places it atop the mound, smiling and nodding as she looks back at our work.

"Well, that is the best we can do, I suppose." Turning around to look at us, she adds, "Thank you. All of you. Especially you, Rinni. You saved my life back there, and I will never forget that."

Huh. I guess I did. But the act had been purely instinct on my part. I don't know what drove me to attack, or how I managed to embed the torch into the thick hide of that evil creature.

"I'm just glad we're all safe now. But we'll have to be extra careful on watch now. No splitting up. It'll lessen the ground we cover on our shift, but I guess we just stay closer to camp."

The night is slowing waning, but Cyndene and I attempt to get some rest while the boys take over the watch. Very little, if any, sleep will come this night.

The next day, we head out later than usual, only stopping twice during the daylight to calm our fatigued bodies and blistering feet. The sun is slipping, slipping further down its path to obscurity, the fading light still illuminating the world as twilight approaches us. Up ahead, the scenery changes. Bhradon notices it first, calling out to us as he runs ahead in a mad frenzy. Crumbled ruins of buildings are in the distance. Is this what we have been searching for? Are there others here?

Sadly, no.

The remains are empty, devoid of any life. But there is no denying that this was once a city. How could these buildings have crumbled away so swiftly? Perhaps they were wrong on the timing for those that left the village. Still, this all seems very odd.

We decide to explore around this treasure trove of decay. Who knows what could be lying within one of the buildings? Another journal, a map, supplies, anything that might be useful. Bhradon never seems to let me out of his sight these days, so we pair up to search, leaving Mori with Cyndene. The look he shoots us is clear: *help me*!

Ever wary of the Shadows, we cast furtive glances in every direction while we search among the ruined city. Heading down the left-hand side of the town, Bhradon and I look around desperately for a sign, a clue, anything that would lead us in the right direction. Something to explain the existence of this deserted settlement. Underneath our feet, fading pieces of stone disintegrate into dust with every step we take. I wonder briefly as to their purpose, why someone would feel the need to place stone in what appears to be the middle of the walking path.

My musing is interrupted by the sound of frantic shouting. Looking over at Bhradon, I freeze in my tracks as we both decipher the mix of cries and shrieks shouted in unison from the other two.

Up ahead, the hazy form of an inky-black shadow materializes.

CHAPTER 32

Horror beyond comprehension envelops my entire body, making it impossible to move.

Vaguely, I recognize the sensation of Bhradon pulling violently on my hand and dragging me off toward the buildings on the left. Only too late do I realize he is heading straight for the Shadow. With a crazed bewilderment surging through me, I viciously yank away from him to scramble back in the direction from which we came. Frantically, I search for the nearest intact building, something to provide shelter and safety, only to be once again pulled back into the eye of the storm.

He may be speaking to me. The words don't register at first. My mind only recognizes the instinctual need to run away from the monster.

"Rinni! Stop! Just stop fighting me! There's no way to protect ourselves here. We have to find a secure place to hide!" Looking around swiftly, I realize that he is right. All of these buildings are completely exposed, with no way to keep out our assailant.

Our *enemy*.

The enemy is moving slowly, or perhaps it only seems that way. The haze around the creature obscures the reality of its movements and speed, not to mention its shape. Its size is extremely—horrifically—apparent: at least twice my own height and much wider than a normal man. Beyond that, I cannot discern anything other than my own terror.

A nightmare incarnate.

In a frenzy, we dash ahead, searching for a safe haven. One building we pass by looks fairly solid. We run around the perimeter until we find the outer doors, slamming them behind us in our haste. Bhradon locates what appears to be a disheveled bookcase nearby, and we quickly barricade the entrance. He grabs my hand again to retreat further into the chamber we've entered, and my brain finally allows me the freedom to think rationally.

Only then do I realize: Mori and Cyndene are still out there.

"Wait," I shout as he begins pulling me again. "We have to find my brother! They're still out there!" My voice is choked with sobs as I realize that Mori could already be dead.

Or worse.

The rational part of my brain looses the game as my hysterical half runs to the door in an attempt to retreat back outside in search of the others. Bhradon yanks me around by the shoulders and shakes me hard enough to snap my head back in an awkward, uncomfortable way. In fact, it hurts. But I gather my senses.

"We can't, Rinni. We can't go back out there. We'll all be caught if we do that. Believe that they found a safe place to hide. Mori is smart and resourceful, so I'm sure they're fine. The best plan right now is to hide and wait it out. Hopefully it will leave soon if it can't get in."

He's right. As usual. I will believe that Mori is safe.

Because I have no other choice.

Now that I have my wits about me, I notice the interior of the building we currently inhabit. Row upon row of what I assume is seating, with pillars that reach high above our heads. A raised platform stands at the far end of the room, decorated in rich colors that stand in juxtaposition to the grim, ashen atmosphere surrounding us. A small, infinitesimal shaft of light stubbornly pokes its head through a colored glass pane near the top of the wall to our right. But none of this can compare to the view above our heads. Starting near the top of the pillars, weaving its way across the entirety of the ceiling until it blends with the columns on the opposite wall, is a sight that my eyes cannot conceive as reality. For nothing in my own little world of existence can propose a name to properly define or explain this substance.

Glittering perfection.

It is the shimmering sparkle of dreams. The light at the edge of vision that cannot be caught. Yet still it is there, shining with a dazzling array of metallic prisms that mirror the effect of sunlight on a clear day.

A luminous element unlike, yet so much like, the gleam of a roaring fire. Yet it is distinct and separate in its own shiny world. A color never before imagined.

Beautiful radiance.

Striking in its ability to glow, stunning in its burning brilliance. Bhradon stares at it as well, his mouth hanging open in mute adoration, a mirror of my own. He looks over at me after a moment with a look of child-like wonder. How handsome he is when he smiles. How long has it been since I've seen that smile? These past several weeks have taken a part of him from me that I will possibly never get back. Yet I feel the same changes within myself.

Almost blinding, the ceiling is a phenomenon we will have to find a way to share with Mori and Cyndene. When we find them again. We need to move along, away from the door that is surprisingly, yet eerily, silent.

Sensing my fear, Bhradon reaches out to embrace me in his arms before we head down the main path through the center of the rows of seating. Behind the platform at the front of the room is the strangest object I've ever seen.

A carven man hanging from two blocks of wood laid perpendicular to one another, half-clothed and half-dead by all appearances.

What a depressingly odd scene to depict.

Pausing to grab Bhradon's arm, I point at the strange artifact. He, too, looks perplexed by the oddity, but diligently continues to drag me down the row, turning left at the platform with the bizarre backdrop. A door ahead of us leads into other rooms full of strange relics and, astonishingly, a vast number of books that seem only partially damaged by time.

As a lover of books, back home I would constantly curl up under the Healing Tree or in my room with a tome from the Room of Records. Mostly, it was just a mixture of things that had been salvaged or saved over the years, well before any of us were born. But the Record Keepers tried their best to maintain and preserve the books we had. Some were about imaginary places with mechanized transports that sped from place to place. Others were about romantic adventures between characters in a vast number of invented worlds. Either way, I enjoyed them all, simply because they were different. Different from my home. Different from my world. Different from my life.

Eagerly I begin to explore the shelves of books, most of which have tumbled into the floor or rotted away completely. Many of the books are damaged beyond repair, but quite a few are legible and mostly intact. One in particular catches my eye almost immediately. The cover is strikingly familiar.

Two long rectangular blocks crisscrossed in a perpendicular fashion.

Intriguing.

There is something oddly familiar about that symbol. Not familiar in a nostalgic, comforting way like mother and soft blankets, like lullabies and bedtime stories.

No. More like a queasy feeling in the pit of my stomach.

I've seen it before. Somewhere. Before the wooden man we just passed. I now remember a vague glimpse, an eyeblink vapor on the outskirts of my panic-stricken vision as we passed underneath the tall outcropping in our mad dash to safety. There. I see it now. On the top of the building. This building. A massive version of that same crisscrossed pattern.

But.

But that's not it. That's not the culprit, the offending subconscious memory giving me this strange *knotted* sensation. Something else. Something before. A memory from home.

How I wish I could remember what it was.

Here, now, we have our haven, if only for a while. All the time in the world.

Glancing over the first several pages, I allow myself to immerse within the words, to soak them in with a false sense of tranquility. I cannot help it, cannot avoid entering the world it creates, submersing mind and body into what appears to be what we call a mythos back home. A story of hope, of heartbreak. A fantastical, beautifully tragic tale, layer upon layer of confusing images. Frustration of mind, yet it enthralls my senses. I don't know why. There is far too little time to read even the remains of this tome, but what I do read speaks to some part of me that I cannot comprehend. I can't explain my fascination with its scorched-out skeletal fragments, the regrettably absent pieces only alive within some compartment of my imagination. The message is confusing, but bit-by-bit I begin to understand that it is meant to provide some form of comfort. Comfort for someone, but not for me.

There is no comfort when death is so near to your door.

Literally.

The Shadow that lingers outside of our refuge does not venture further. Why, I don't know. Does it lack the ability, or does it choose to wait patiently for our inevitable departure? We have little in the way of provisions. Perhaps it somehow senses this.

As I silently read, occasionally sharing particularly interesting parts with him, Bhradon is blocking off the room as best he can while inspecting every corner for food or water. Of course, there is none. This building was abandoned long ago. So long ago it seems to make no sense. Nevertheless, we continue scavenging in vain, he in the ancient rubble, and I in my newly acquired—and oddly prized—possession.

Both are fruitless pursuits of security in a world turned upside down and so far from home. Our intent perusals are halted as a sudden banging reverberates within the outer room.

Icy fingers put a death grip on what used to my living, beating heart.

I guess the enemy's patience just ran out.

CHAPTER 33

Nowhere to run. We are trapped.

Trapped in the sanctuary of our own creation.

Bhradon grabs my arm once again, only this time he lifts me over his shoulder like a sack of grain. Too terrified to register any momentary indignant ire or fleeting thrill at his sudden lack of appropriate social mores, I hold on for dear life as he runs directly at the solid wooden door that we entered through when we found the room.

The only barrier between us and it.

"Bhradon?" I squeak out the word that is both a name, a statement, and a question, barely audible above the pounding of my heart. I venture again. "What are you *doing?*" Without a word, he continues on his path to the door, his heavily labored breathing intensely louder than my voice sounds to my own ears. "Why are you leaving? It's out there, not in here! Bhradon!" Suddenly I feel a clammy hand clamped across my mouth as he swings my body around in front of him.

He holds one finger to his lips and gives me that look that screams *trust me*. Standing behind me with his hand still over my mouth, he brings his lips close to my ears, and I shiver involuntarily.

"We have to get out of this room. If it got in there, it can get in here. We'd be trapped with no way out." His voice lower even than a whisper, he slowly pulls his hand away from my face. I nod slowly to express my understanding. He is right, of course.

Silently, we edge closer to the door. He ever so carefully turns the knob until he can gently force it open just enough for our bodies to slip through. What had recently been the waning vestiges of twilight now leaves us with only the barest sense of vision, the darkness—in this moment—either our greatest friend or our ultimate foe. Again taking the lead, he pulls me against the wall just outside the door and pushes us both down to a crawling position. I look around desperately, certain that death awaits us the second we take a step. Bhradon appears to be doing the same thing, only his assessment seems to grant him added confidence about our current predicament. Actually *predicament* is not exactly the right word. More like *cataclysm of doom*.

And we're off, ducking under the seating benches and rolling to gain momentum. I'm just following along, trusting that he has a solid plan in mind. *Surely he has a plan, right?*

"What's the plan?" The question is asked with my lips rather than spoken aloud. He shrugs and points to the front door.

That's the plan? I could have come up with that one.

Nevertheless, we are rolling and crawling along at hasty intervals, within a few yards of the front door, when the banging sound strikes again, originating from the other side of the room and resounding in an echo across the whole of the building. This time it is much, much louder.

And right underneath the strange symbol behind the platform.

Only now do we realize how long and how much effort it will take to remove the barricade from the door. Panicking seems the right thing to do in this moment. A dark shape emerges from the floor at the back of the dais, rendering an escape back in that direction impossible. We have to move, and quickly, so instinctively we both rush to hide behind the nearest bench and begin to crawl around the side in the hope that the Shadow will head to one of the two side doors. The fact that this is a probable course of action negates our earlier skepticism as to their intellectual capacity. Frightening to say the least.

Expecting the creature to begin its search immediately, I'm baffled when it sinks back down to the floor and emits a strange guttural sound into the darkness around us. Slowly the Shadow rises back up from the ground...with another Shadow in its wake.

Like a dream that speeds up and slows down at random intervals, the two figures seem to be directly upon us one second and moving as if in a state of sleepwalking the next. The effect is mind-numbingly chilling, like some bizarre dance.

A dance that will end in bloodshed, and I cannot stop watching.

Threads of dim light bounce off the nameless glittering essence above us, but down below it might as well be midnight. Darkness around us and darkness upon us.

As we slip down the length of the room, sliding against one another in our haste to put as much distance as possible between

us and them, a faint whispering reaches my ears. I can't understand the words, but I'm certain I don't want to know. Terror
grips my core, winding its way through every outlying extension
of my body, until even my toes refuse to move. I feel a distant
sensation, Bhradon pushing me, urging me on, but I just can't.
The whispering has grown louder, but now my mind is too frozen
to even attempt at deciphering what's being said. I can feel them
nearing us, and I know there is no escape.

We round the front corner and realize we were mistaken. The
Shadows were never intent on reaching either door.

They were waiting for us to come to them.

CHAPTER 34

I scream the scream of the dead, the already dead, the dying. The scream I've heard too many times: back in the village, lying in bed, awakened by the sound of someone who was too careless, too close to the forest. Too late.

The claw that seized my arm now clamps over my mouth, and some part of my mind wonders if they don't like the sound of screaming. Maybe they've heard it one too many times as well.

"Oh goodness, Rinni! Oh, thank goodness!" Limbs grab at me, pulling me into a death grip. But I know that voice.

"Mori!" I scream with more passion than I had when I thought I was dying. His embrace is comfort. It is home, and it is a missing part of me.

Finally, we separate enough to talk. "We thought you might have escaped the city. That maybe you heard us and took off."

Bhradon's voice is a booming echo against the high ceilings.

"There wasn't time. We ran in here and barricaded ourselves in. That is, until we heard what we thought was the Shadow getting into the building. Turns out it was actually two of them." Looking at me, he adds lamely, "We thought Shadows were coming up from the floor. We thought it was over."

Cyndene pipes up with oddly cheery laughter, "We heard scurrying and thought it might be the creature. Must have been you. I think we were both too terrified to move." She bursts into nervous giggles, and I cannot help but join in the aftermath of what could have been a massacre.

Suddenly, we are all in a state of hysterical laughter, the anxiety and apprehension of these past weeks—particularly today—relinquishing their hold on our exhausted frames. As we wind down, edging back into seriousness, the unanswered question springs into my mind with instant clarity. *How did they get inside the building?*

"How did you get in here?" I ask with confusion and shock battling across my face.

Cyndene looks over at Mori, and they *share a look*. A look I can't decipher, which is strange considering the twin connection. She explains, "After we shouted a warning to you two, we ran. Ended up in a Room of Records on the other side of town. We spent a little while perusing the shelves, but ultimately, it was your brother who found it."

We all turn our glances to Mori, who is blushing under all the attention, either from us or from Cyndene. "I found a door leading into a tunnel that fed into this whole system of passageways that would make the Hall look simple and small by comparison. But there were maps, believe it or not. They were spread out all around, on tables, on the walls. So I followed the one that seemed to head to the side of town where you had been. Where you are, I guess. She's right. We thought you had made it out of town."

This is all so much to take in, but right now I am merely thankful that no one has been harmed. But the enemy is still out there.

Somewhere.

I can't resist showing off our finds to the other two. They are just as astounded as we were by the shiny material above us. Grabbing the book I had been reading, plus a couple of others, I follow everyone to the secret door where Mori and Cyndene emerged from nowhere.

I point out the bizarre depiction of the wooden man to Mori. He doesn't remember anything either, but the thought is still bugging me. We enter the underground tunnels, and I get a strange feeling of nostalgia for home, the feeling of being underneath the Hall so overwhelming that it hurts.

Until we begin to move on.

The passages are so complex and confusing that I wonder how they made it anywhere, even with the maps on the walls. Once we exit out into the Room of Records, I'm astounded by the sheer number of tomes it carries. This room has to be thirty or forty times the size of ours back home. I notice many that seem so completely foreign to what we have in the village, and that part of me wants to touch them, to open them, *so badly*, but I know that we have to keep moving.

We have no idea where the Shadow is, and the black of night presses in on us. Bhradon and Mori start a small fire and light torches for us, unsure as to whether or not the fire is still a deterrent against the creeping enemy of unknown whereabouts.

Charging along through the darkness, I grab a few random books on our way back to the tunnels, where we plan to hide out for the night in the hopes that the Shadows won't even know they exist.

A little more weight in my pack can't hurt.

INTERLUDE
~ D ~

She does not need to look in the mirror. But as she feels her strength ebb away and her body grow more and more fragile with each passing year, the inevitable is a hard thing to accept.

She is aging, slowly, ever so slowly, but it is there.

This is not *right*! This is not how it is supposed to happen. What happened to the plan, the promise? Why is all of this happening, thrust upon them like a sharp sliver of glass aimed right at the heart?

Her heart.

CHAPTER 35

In the morning, I wake up to the sound of nothing.

How wonderful the sound of nothing seems now. A breath of relief passes my lips, and I find myself smiling slightly. Periodically, I keep checking to see if the others are awake, but mostly I am absorbed in my newfound treasures from last night.

Some are similar in content to those I've read back home, and one is downright boring, but there are two that look promisingly exciting. Stories of old. Those are my favorite books. The ones that tell of adventures from long ago, and you can never tell which ones might have a grain of truth and which ones are outright tales.

The cover of the closest one is almost indecipherable, but turning to the first inside page, I can clearly read *Marlowe, The Tragical History of Doctor Faustus*. Flipping through the pages, it reminds me of others I've read, in form if not in content. These types of stories are almost always entertaining, often funny when I can understand them, but also very sad in many cases. Wondering to myself which way this one will lead me, and not desiring to put myself into a foul mood so early in the morning, I instead cast a cursory glance inside the other chosen book. *Le Morte D'Arthur by Sir Thomas Malory.* These people lived so long ago, yet they seem so near when I read through the pages and share in the experience of their stories. Often I find myself envious of their ability to weave narratives into life. It must have been easier when the world was much larger than it is now. When the planet was bursting with people, with life.

Stuffing the smaller tomes into my pack along with the large one with the strange symbol on the cover, I rouse myself to get things started for the day.

After our morning meal, we head out, stealthily despite the gloriously brilliant morning sun. I remember the beautiful ceiling and how it sparkled like sunlight. Another smile spreads across my face. There is beauty in the world, after all.

The panoramic views from the area are breathtaking. Utterly heart stopping in their intense arcs of green and blue, tree and sky, water rippling along with a clear purpose. The world around us is thriving, with no help, no Keeper to tend the greenery. No one to make it into something. It just exists, and that purity affects me down to my core. Nature prevailing against the odds.

After another few weeks, it all starts to blend together. Between Bhradon trying to stay so close that he runs into me every time I stop or slow down and Cyndene whining if we don't stop every few hours, the journey is reaching an all-time low. We haven't spotted a single sign pointing to life. No villages, only a few more empty ruins, and still we continue.

With a never-ending source of water, you'd think we'd be much better off. But with the water comes the falls. They aren't very big, not nearly as big as the one from that horrible night, but the simple act of navigating around them has become more tedious by the day. Obviously, we could steer farther away from the water, but our hopes of finding others diminish if we lose track of the water source.

Or so I thought.

Despite my rationale and heated protests, Mori insists that we leave the comfort of the water's edge and head slightly more east since the map suggests our ancestors went that way. Why they would have left the water is beyond me. Perhaps there is another water source in that direction. Perhaps the path of the flow has changed. Either way, we agreed to abide by the map, especially considering Allysar gave his life for us to have it.

A count of days—*weeks? How many? Two? Three?*—as we travel farther and farther east, through hilly terrain, walking, always walking. The sun has all but vanished behind the canopy of trees that surrounds us, haunts us. I am thoroughly convinced we're going in circles. The forest is dark enough even in the day, but at night it holds a power that consumes every blissful thought you might hope to hold onto.

And the trees.

Wonderful, glorious, nauseating plethora of trees. We're like old friends now.

Friends I'd like to push down a hill.

I'm joking. You can't push trees down a hill. I tried.

Stumbling along blindly in the haze of boredom and monotony that stalks our every step these days, we suddenly spy in the distance a remote shaft of light scarcely trickling through the never-ending wonderland of trees. With barely a glance to my rear to confirm a silent agreement among the rest of the group, I take off at full speed in my rush to greet the sunshine. Oh, sun, what a stranger you have been!

And come to a dead stop the moment my unaccustomed eyes adjust to the blinding intensity.

There he is.

The man from my dreams.

CHAPTER 36

Right in front of me.

With arms wide open, beseeching me to come forward. Just like in my dream. Only he's *huge*. Like a giant in the sky huge: the largest thing I've ever witnessed in my entire life. He's facing the wrong way, but I can tell it's him. And again, there's that brick wall slamming into me from behind. *Why does he keep doing that?*

"Bhradon, why—*why*—do you keep trying to run me over? In case you hadn't noticed, I'm a bit smaller than you are." Pausing for effect, I slowly continue, "Oh, and by the way, meet the man from my dreams." My arm outstretched in a dramatic pose, I turn to my friends with a forced smile on my face. On the inside, I'm losing my mind.

How can this be? How is it possible that I could dream of something I have never seen before in my life? My eyes bulging with recognition and confusion. And perhaps a mild case of insanity.

Far up on the massive hilltop in the distance, he stands like a frozen beacon meant just for me and me alone. That thought might seem thrilling, but it scares me beyond belief. None of this makes any sense whatsoever.

My friends are staring at me with matching looks of incredulity. Mori is the first to speak after the build-up of the awkward silence following my pronouncement. "Rinni, that's … incredible. And impossible. I think."

"Well, I'm telling you that is definitely the man I've been seeing. In my sleep. I know it sounds crazy. I know it makes no sense, Mori, but it's the truth. I'm sure that's him. Obviously, the only thing we can do is continue forward, up that monstrosity of a hill, and find out what's going on. Or prove I'm nuts. Either way, that … that *whatever it is* just seems to be where I'm supposed to go."

"Plus it's higher ground. We'll have a much better view of our surroundings from up there." Bhradon's logic seems to sway the rest of the group. But I can't ignore the pained and bewildered look he gives me before pushing past toward our objective.

We've been up and down some rocky terrain here this last week or so, the only variance we've encountered among the hills and underbrush. The feeling of being surrounded by an ominous presence has lulled, so hopes are a little higher now that we are seeing some alteration to the landscape.

And this.

This whole situation with the frozen man. It means something. I just don't know what. And the fact that he even exists terrifies me.

We make our way across more rock-strewn ground, trying to determine the easiest path to the hill in the distance. It takes several hours with all the inevitable stops for *her* sake. Mori insists we take a break every time she so much as utters a sigh. At least he is less intimidated by her now. But I think it is more than that, a proposition I do not care to dwell upon.

Up close, the texture of the object is all-too-familiar: stone. Most buildings back home are made of stone, much like the ruins we have come across. Our ancestors built them long before anyone living was around, or, at least, that's the story the Primaries always told us. Since our people no longer venture out for resources, we have to make do with what we already have, reusing what we can and repairing when sap or something similar will suffice.

The stone man stands patiently, waiting for our arrival, seemingly almost alive were it not for the crumbling exterior of rock. He has been here for a very long time. The enormous slab of rock he stands on is bigger than our wheat mill back home, and I wonder how it got here. The closer we get up the hill, the more his back is to us, but I am absolutely positive this is it. I can see that his clothes are similar to what the Primaries wear, a long straight flowing of cloth instead of tunics and pants like the rest of us. His hair is just past his shoulders, and his arms are straight out to the sides as he gazes out into the distance. And I can see that his hands are partially open, his palms facing an imagined audience.

When we reach the summit, I walk immediately around the left side to get a better glimpse of the face. A telltale texture resembling a short beard enforces my earlier conviction. This is definitely him. There is a mesmerizing air about his features, a warmth of security even as we stand exposed upon the high ground. His gesture seems as if he wants to welcome and embrace his onlookers.

Tearing myself away from the sight and the feeling it is creating, I look over to the others, hoping they are having the same experience as I am. But all three of them have stopped halfway to my position, entranced with something.

Something behind me.

My skin is alive with an awful tingling sensation when I force myself to turn around.

And stare into oblivion.

CHAPTER 37

Endless. Completely and utterly endless.

A deep blue void touched pink and orange in the now fading light. The horizon line dancing with the last rays of energy, their luminescence a breathtaking spectacle of never-ending light and shadow, brilliant color and blackest void. All swirled into one rich tapestry of pure wonderment.

"Is that...the ocean?" Cyndene cries in a voice rich with emotion.

Bhradon answers her, "Yeah. I think so."

"No wonder they didn't want us to know what it looked like."

There is no denying the amazing display of nature going on in front of us. I had figured out that the "coast" the journal spoke of was like the bank of the waterways, only for the sea. I never could have imagined the sea to be this beautiful. So inviting.

She's right. No wonder they didn't want us to see this.

Hypnotized as we are by the undulations of the water, the rough back and forth as it crashes onto the coast, Mori manages to take in our surroundings, looking around at the face of the stone man and back at me numerous times. He must think I'm crazy.

"That is him. I swear it," is all I say.

He nods after a moment, slowly at first but gaining momentum. We can understand each other this way. Whether I only think it's the man from my dream, or whether it actually is him, he still believes that I believe it.

He turns his back to me, staring off into the distance on the other side of the hill. The cry of shock he utters is unexpected, considering we've just experienced our entire quota of surprises for the day. I walk over to him, expecting another dazzling display of nature.

Ruins. A large, rather impressive, expanse of ruins is scattered all across the landscape in the distance, leading up to and encircling a small still body of water much closer to us than the sea with its crashing waves. I can't believe we didn't see it before, despite the fact that the enormous hill we now stand on blocks the view from the side we climbed. The landscape is incredibly surreal in the waning light, the buildings barely visible, light emerging from their midst nonetheless.

Light.

And now I see it. The light is coming from specific points within the ruins, and I'd swear they look like torches.

"Bhradon! Come here! Cyndene!" I yell despite our visible position.

When they reach our side of the hill, no one speaks for a moment. Then, all at once, we begin to ask one another questions that no one can answer.

"Is that what I think it is?"

"Are those torches?"

"That is fire, right? I mean, you do see the fire down there?"

"How do we get down there?"

"What should we do?"

"Do you think there are people?"

Our joy and excitement mix with fear and anticipation until we are practically delirious. Even though this is the sign we've been looking for, I guess I never truly felt we'd ever find it. Too many unknowns, too many guesses, too many dangers along the way. Amidst all the chaos, one voice rings loud and strong among us.

It doesn't belong to any of us.

CHAPTER 38

The young female stands just in front of two males who stare vacantly ahead, yet seem to be watching everything. Two others, one male and one female, have long spears aimed at us.

The striking part is not even their sudden presence. It's their *appearance*. Each of them must be more than one and a half again the height of Bhradon and almost twice as wide, with thick, sinewy limbs that defy human musculature. Considering his significant stature, that makes these…these *whatever they are* absolutely enormous compared to us.

They must be just as shocked by our small size. Staring at us with more than mild curiosity, the female in front speaks again. "Who are you? In which direction does your colony lie?"

Too stunned to speak, the four of us just stare up at the giant woman. Finally, Bhradon steps forward, touches his forehead with three fingers, and lowers his palm. Greeting them with this respectful gesture, he answers, "We are just travelers looking for resources. Our colony is in danger, and we thought we could find help here." Pointing in a vague southerly direction, he states, "We come from that direction. It's been a very long journey, and we've already lost one of our friends to the Shadows. Please help us."

At the mention of Shadows, her face softens. "You have suffered. I see that. Come. We will go straight to Orlianna. We'll get you some food and drink, and perhaps then we can learn more of each other."

This is all so confusing, and I'm not even sure what these beings are. But when the rest of the group follows without a word, I am forced to join them. I can see the apprehension in Bhradon's face when I catch up to him, but he reaches over to grasp my hand tightly. We make the journey in silence.

The ruins we had seen sprinkled with the firelight cover a large portion of the land, and up close, I can see the area that has been walled off and protected by fire sconces in the same way as we do at home. This can't be a coincidence, yet they look nothing like us. In features, perhaps yes, but there is no denying the strange difference in height. Every one of the five strangers looms over us, an unsettling predicament from which I see no escape. We have to find out. We have to find help.

Approaching the massive walls of the village, we head south and skirt around the edge, heading toward what I assume will be the entrance. When we pass by what appears to be a large ingress with a closed and barred gate—and a conspicuously absent guard patrol—Cyndene points and asks, "Isn't that the way in?"

The female, who appears to be the leader of this odd group, is the only one who responds. "That is the back gate. We no longer use it. For safety reasons." She doesn't need to explain further. There's only one thing that threatens the safety of a village.

We continue walking around the edge of the ruins, unable to see inside due to the size of the walls. I thought our walls back home were huge, but these make ours look like a child built them. They appear to reach toward the sky, a never-ending barrier between them and the outside world.

Once we reach another entrance, this one manned by two guards on top of the wall, our "guides" stop abruptly to offer a salute to the people above us. I notice there are three men and one woman, all holding strange objects, weapons of some sort I assume. The greeting is returned as the gates open, and we get our first glimpse inside the place that has danced in and out of our dreams for these past many weeks.

It's home.

Or something very near to it. Everything looks and feels familiar in some sort of way, from the thatched roofs to the torches. The village is spread out in a similar manner, at least from what I can tell. As if we hadn't left at all.

But the people.

The people aren't like home, aren't like us, aren't like anything I've ever seen, even in books. I don't understand who or what they are, but clearly they are not of our people. These are not the descendants of those who left us so long ago. So who are they?

We continue to walk in silence as our guides lead us to a house in the middle of what I assume to be their village center. One of the males turns to the side and opens the flap over the door, beckoning us to enter.

Having no reason to distrust these strangers, I'm somewhat shocked when my hands are pulled forcefully behind my back and tied together with some sort of rope or twine. The others are all protesting loudly until a woman steps forward from further within the hut. I can see her now, though she'd been there the whole time, sitting and watching from a crudely made, but rather large, chair at the edge of the room. She observes us with a strange look in her eyes, and from the accumulation of wrinkles there, I can see that she must be at least one hundred years of age. Her swift gait across the room would suggest not much older than that, but even her eyes exude a wisdom that only comes with age. Though far younger, she reminds me of Gani.

How I miss home right now.

When she speaks, her voice is low and slightly raspy, but still smooth enough to speak with eloquence and grace like no one I've ever heard before.

"Where did you find them?" she asks the female scout.

"On top of the Great Hill. They spent a good deal of time staring at the statue. We followed them up and watched for a while. I thought it best to bring them to you."

"I see," is all the elder woman responds with as she continues staring at us with… *incredulity*? Perhaps we do seem just as odd to them as they do to us. But I need to know what happened to the ones we journeyed to find.

"Please," I start. "We meant no harm in coming here. We are desperate, and our village is dying. We've been traveling for many weeks, searching for…" And suddenly I realize the difficulty in explaining our situation. We have no idea who or what these things are, or even if they are friendly. Considering the current state of affairs, I would guess that "no" is a viable answer to that question.

"Searching for?" The woman's query is no innocent curiosity judging from the sparkle in her eyes as she leans in closer.

Sighing, Bhradon adds, "We found information that led us to believe that some people from our village left a long time ago and came here to start a new colony. We came looking for their descendants. And for help. It appears we've found neither."

"Maybe you can help us by telling us what happened to them, if you know." Mori's voice breaks in with a dejected sense of loss.

I find myself responding back, "Obviously, this isn't the right place, Mori. We got it wrong. *I* got it wrong." There is no way to stop the deluge of tears that accompanies this confession. Everything had seemed so right. The map led us here. The stone man—*statue* as they called it—was supposed to be the key. Wasn't it?

Mori breaks into my self-pity by exclaiming, "No! The map led in this direction, and your dream...your dream, Rinni! How can this not be it?"

At the mention of my dream, every pair of eyes in the room looks straight me. The old woman comes closer, and in an even lower voice says, "Tell me about this dream."

Feeling somewhat uncomfortable, I explain what little I remember of the dreams. After a long pause, she asks me how long and how often I had been having them.

"Since more than a few weeks before we left, but only every so often." This all sounds ridiculous even to my own ears. Yet there it is. All I have to do is step outside the house and look up at the hill and the massive stone giant.

"Perhaps we may help each other out in some way," the woman begins. "My name is Orlianna, and I am the leader of these people. You say that your village is in need of resources and supplies. We are in need of help as well. Many within our village have passed beyond this life recently, more than we are used to and more than we can afford. Some from the Evil Ones. Some from old age. Some from sickness. But it is more than we are accustomed to losing at once." She nods as if deciding something, and her voice grows louder. "Stay with us. Only for a while. Help us where we have need. Lend us your hands and selves. Perhaps we can come to an agreement on supplies. And quicker, easier ways to get them—and you—to your home, I'm sure."

Looking at one another, four heads nod in unison. *At least they haven't given us to the Shadows. It seems that we have that enemy in common, at least.*

"Forgive our rudeness. The bindings were merely for my protection. Your appearance is certainly strange to us, but it may be that you can find your answers here."

At that, the ropes are cut by unseen hands. As we rub our sore wrists, the group leads us back out of the hut and into the moonlight. We are directed to a small building on the far side of the village and told to get some rest. Two of the males from the group stay nearby, guarding the door. It seems they still don't entirely trust us, but I can't blame them considering the circumstances.

With nothing to do but collapse from exhaustion and overexertion, we unpack and roll out our beds side by side, our bodies ready to sleep but our minds reeling.

Cyndene is the first to break the silence. "Do you think they'll know more about the Shadows or why they took my brother?"

Mori, in an attempt to comfort her, says, "I'm sure they must know something. They've had dealings with the Shadows, it seems. So maybe they can help, even if it's just the closure you need."

Wrong thing to say, dear brother.

As her quiet sobbing erupts into loud wailing, the two guards outside peek in with concern in their eyes, spears at the ready. When they notice the source of the sound, they immediately close the flap and resume their positions.

Males never seem to know how to react to a crying female.

While I attempt to comfort the girl, Bhradon has his thinking face on. I can see it clearly. He's assessing the situation, just as I am. Can we really trust these strangers? Can our people continue to survive while we stay here to help? Do we even have a choice?

No. Without help, we are doomed.

CHAPTER 39

At first light, we are *guided* back to Orlianna's home. This morning, she is accompanied by an even taller male about the same age. I assume he is her mate, and despite the voice in my head telling me not to pry, I ask if this is the case.

"Yes, Veynor is my mate, as well as leader of the Jadhenash."

"Jadhenash?" Cyndene cocks her head to one side with that snide look I've seen far too many times. Just like her mother.

"The Jadhenash are the name of our people. Jadhenash is also the name of our village."

Confused, I ask, "But didn't you say that *you* are their leader?"

"Yes, I am," she continues, nodding slowly as if contemplating her answer. "But he is also. We, together, lead these people. That is the way. Is it not also so for your own village?"

"No, we have a group of elders within the village who are chosen by their predecessors to be our judges and leaders. There's quite a lot of them, in fact. But they take turns and have specific tasks they perform. How do you accomplish everything between just the two of you?"

They glance at one another, looking perplexed by my question. "There is not that much for leaders to do. We must make sure everyone is fed; make sure the borders around the village remain safe from the Evil Ones; and keep peace and some sense of harmony among our people. We oversee those whose job it is to accomplish these tasks, but everything else is handled by the coteries."

"Coteries?"

"Groups of...like-minded or similarly skilled individuals who work together to perform the tasks needed around the village. For instance, Arithena"—she points to the female leader of last night's group—"is quite skilled with spear and long bow. Because of this, she has become a leader among the martial coterie. There are also those who serve as messengers, guardians, and bakers. Those who chop the wood and those who tend to the sick. Everyone has a purpose."

"We are the same in that respect. My brother Mori and I are Tenders for the fire. Bhradon is a Patrol Guard, similar I guess to your martial coterie, only back home it's more to have a pair of eyes watching out. We don't have weapons and don't generally fight back against the Shadows."

"Shadows. That is the name you give the Evil Ones, yes?" Veynor's sudden entrance into the conversation startles me.

Mori answers, "Yes. That's what our people have called them since...well, apparently since they first appeared. We were unaware until recently that there was a time since the Old World was destroyed when the Shadows did not exist. To know that sort of peace and not to fear…" he trails off. I know he's thinking of mother and father, and I wish to change the topic. Before I can speak, Veynor has another question.

"Why do you and your sister look so much alike?"

"We are twins. Do you not have twins here?"

"Yes, we do. But not like that. Not when one is male and one is female. It seems impossible, yet here you stand."

"The Primaries—our leaders—told us that the Old World had books describing something similar, called polar twins. But I don't think even the ancients knew exactly what it was. All they knew was it was rare, if it even existed. I have no idea how it works exactly."

Orlianna, who has been quietly listening this whole time, speaks aloud, almost as if to the room, "These leaders, your Primaries, they do many of these jobs themselves?"

"Yes. Their main duty is to keep peace, as you say, and to be our judges. But they oversee most of the other jobs around the village."

"That seems like an unnecessary amount of work for these Primaries, not to mention control. How do your people survive if they are not allowed to think and learn for themselves? Our community functions because the people are responsible for making it so. We are just here to keep an eye on them, and to make sure things do not fall apart."

I suddenly realize how much sense she is making. Smiling at our hostess, I nod my affirmation at her words. Bhradon is looking off into a corner of the room, into nothing, his thinking face back on again.

He's thinking the same thing I am. I'm sure the others are as well. Perhaps we can learn much from these people and help ours in ways we never even thought to question. My mind is taking all of this in, storing it for later when we can speak privately without our guards.

It takes a moment for me to register the fact that Veynor has been speaking through my thoughts. As he continues discussing more aspects of the village, Orlianna gently cuts him off as a figure blocks the light filtering into the room from the opening behind us.

"As my mate has been saying, there are many things for you to learn in order to help us, and we have members of various coteries who have agreed to show you and teach you our ways. But first, I believe a general tour around the premises would be the ideal start. This"—a slight smile playing at the corners of her lips—"is Taernus. He, like you, is not an original inhabitant of our colony. He comes to us from far north, where his village was destroyed by the Evil Ones before he escaped. Having been here for many years now, he has become a part of our family."

Trying to process this idea that there are, in fact, *other* colonies, I turn around to face the newcomer, and my heart forgets to beat.

For a moment.

And another.

He is beautiful. Bizarrely tall, yes. But a beautiful male nonetheless, more beautiful than any I've ever seen. Sheer perfection, radiating every possible promise from one being to another.

Everyone is looking at me. I must have been staring. I look to Cyndene, who only betrays herself with a knowing smile and a gleam of satisfaction in her eyes. I'm not sure if it's meant for him or for me. But he's introducing himself, and I should remember my manners.

"I have asked him to accompany you around the village and answer any questions you have," Orlianna continues.

Mori jumps in with, "It's kind of you to show us around, Taernus." Looking first at me, then at Bhradon, he adds, "We should get going then, I think."

Following Taernus out of the building, we head in the direction of the front gate. The sights and sounds of the village have come alive in a tingling vibration and hum of time. Endless time. It's as if we are back home, our friends and neighbors there to greet us and wave in earnest as we pass by.

But these are not our friends. They are not our neighbors. They are strangers, and we are entombed in a world of unfamiliarity, caught in a trap of our own making. Why are we here? What can we possibly hope to accomplish if we can't get back to our people? Trusting these…beings may be the best or worst decision of our lives. And our lives will forever change as a result. One way or another.

"I thought we should begin at the beginning, so to speak," Taernus states with a look of mild amusement on his face.

Bhradon nods at him, acquiescing with the rough gesture, but his body language suggests he is none too pleased with the situation. While I understand and empathize with his feelings, I see no point in going out of our way to make these strangers our enemies. Best to comply and put on a smile while we learn all we can. Maybe they will live up to their promises. Though, there is just something about Orlianna that strikes me as odd. The way she keeps looking at us is somewhat intimidating, almost as if she is looking straight into my head. The effect is unnerving.

I swallow my concern for the sake of what may be. Taernus takes us by the mills situated near the entrance. As we pass what appears to be a firehouse, my curiosity grows. I notice a look of partially concealed alarm on our guide's face as he winds our path into a wider arc away from the hut.

"Is this your common fire? The building looks so similar to our own." Eerily so.

Hesitatingly, he replies, "Yes, this is the firehouse. Each colony has brought with them the knowledge of such things. Each has their own ways, of course, but I believe we all share common foundations. Over the years, as the colonies spread out, they took with them what they could, along with those who knew how to build the necessary basics for a productive society."

"But we're not like you. Our ancestors were here at some point. They either died out or were overtaken." Bhradon's barely concealed wrath is threatening to spill over. *This is going to end badly.*

Taernus nods slowly, pondering the statement with serious intent. "Perhaps. Or perhaps it was something less sinister. One would hope that such violence would not come from any people, be they yours or mine. Though, as we all know, there are those who are less honorable than others."

I think of the Primaries and where their dishonesty and deceit have led us. Then again, I can't place complete blame at their feet. This all started long before them. Their predecessors are the ones to blame, but they aren't here to defend themselves. Why did they do it? And how could our current Primaries take the issue of our dying tree so lightly?

The Healing Tree. That's one major point we need to keep our eyes open for to see if they have something similar. If so, maybe they will know what's wrong and how to fix it.

We pass the bakery, and the smells are making my mouth

water. Mori looks around with desperation in his face. Considering we haven't had anything to eat since yesterday around midday, I know we must all be starving.

Putting on my most charming smile, I turn to our guide and ask, "Would it be too much trouble to stop for food? We can walk and eat, but we haven't eaten for almost an entire day." With a meek smile, I add, "I'm feeling fairly weak right now, especially with those wonderfully enticing aromas teasing me."

He smiles warmly. "Of course. You are guests. I apologize. Someone should have thought to bring you breakfast this morning. Have anything you like. We can stop here if needed. Take as much time as you like. My job today is to show you everything in the village. Pastries included." His smile widens, and I can't help but smile back at his infectious mood.

After devouring one pastry, we all grab another to take with us as we continue our walk. Taernus is unerringly graceful in his speech and the way he points to things with a slight flourish that makes everything seem grand and wonderful, despite the ordinary and familiar landmarks.

Until we reach the gardens.

A spectacular arrangement of the most beautiful flowers and plants I have ever seen, the gardens outshine anything our own Grounds Keepers have ever accomplished. It is a surreal playground awash in color and beauty, and I cannot hold in the gasp that forms in the back of my throat when I behold the splendor. Without thinking, I run ahead and stop at the gate. Peeking in, I take in every inch of the expanse. Nothing ordinary here.

"You like the gardens, I see. They are quite beautiful, far exceeding anything in my home colony." His eyes betray a wistful gleam, and I am saddened for his loss.

"I can't imagine what that must be like, to lose your friends, your family, your home. Everything. I ... I just ..." My heart cries out, and I feel it constricting within my chest, the image of losing Gani and Milana and all the others exploding in my mind.

"It is done. I do miss them, yes. But time has taught me that one can only continue moving, hoping to find some happiness in this world. I still look for that every single day. There are moments of sadness, moments when the despair seems to overwhelm me. But there are far more moments of happiness, moments when everything is full of light and life, and the world seems right again."

"That is a beautiful sentiment. I only wish I were that strong."

"You are stronger than you know."

"How would you know that? You've only just met me."

"I can see it in your eyes. You and your friends managed to make it here with enemies all around, just as I did. But you did not leave because you were forced to. You had a choice, and you chose to make that journey. That shows far more courage than I have ever known."

My voice fails me, the emotion welling up too great to express. As I stare into his sympathetic eyes, Bhradon's voice stirs the silence.

"Shouldn't we be moving along?"

I shoot him a look of irritation before saying, "Yes, well, I want to look in the garden."

"I think we should move along. We can check it out later when we have time. Let's get this tour over with." *What is his problem?*

"Bhradon, what is wrong with you? As he said, we have all day to look around, and I want to look at the flowers!" Storming off into the garden, with Cyndene mutely following behind, I glance back with a look that states my intentions clearly. I'm going in, with or without them.

I hear Mori speaking to Bhradon as I turn the corner. "Let's just have a quick look, and then we can head on. We might as well look around since we're here."

The colors are phenomenal, splashing rainbow hues against the backdrop of greenery that weaves its way around the edges and borders, along the ground within the spaces outside the walking path, and up the tree standing in the middle.

The *Tree*.

Large but not as big as our Healing Tree, it stands as a looming centerpiece among the exquisite blossoms within the garden. Its leaves are similar in size and shape, but nothing else graces the tangle of limbs and boughs besides a sprinkling of orange orbs. No kastana nuts. An ordinary-looking, but sizable tree.

"Does that tree hold any significance?"

Taernus looks at me with bemusement, and odd mix of confusion and interest. "Significance? Well, it's the center for the garden. It's a nice spot to come and sit when one has the time. The shade under the tree is quite refreshing. Would you like one?" He points up to one of the orange orbs, just out of reach.

"What are they?" Mori quietly asks. This place evokes a sense of calm solemnity.

"Aranjas. Fruit. Do you not have them in your village?"

Shaking our heads collectively, the four of us stare up at the strange round fruit. Cyndene bursts out with, "No, we don't have any trees in our village. I mean besides—" Her voice cuts off as she stares alarmingly at the rest of us.

"Besides the one we use for firewood," Mori chimes in quickly. Taernus gives him a funny look, but smiles and reaches up for one of the aranjas. Pulling a small knife from his pocket, he deftly slices into the fruit, shedding the colorful exterior to reveal a rather uninteresting inner core. The fruit strangely peels right away into sections with the slightest pressure from his thumb. He hands a piece to each of us. The temptation is rather strong despite our recent meal. The sweet, tangy aroma is enticing, but the white film around it is a bit off-putting.

He sees me staring at the aranja intently and looks at me with a quizzical gaze.

"It looks strange. Is this really edible?"

His laugh is loud and echoing in the still peace of the garden. "Why would I offer you something that wasn't edible? It grows on the tree. We eat them all the time. Go ahead. Taste it. You'll be surprised."

Tentatively, I bite into the fruit as I watch Mori stare at his piece. But the taste is sweet. Tangy yet smooth. Quite delicious, in fact. I smile in appreciation.

"Delightful. We should take some with us," Cyndene says.

Taernus's smile fades. "The aranjas must stay in the garden. You may come here to eat, but you must remain here." He shrugs. "Those are their rules. I guess they don't want people running off with a sack full of them."

His smile returns as he states, "If you still wish to have a look around the garden, I suggest we move along."

We stroll among the flowers for a short time, admiring the variety of colors and shapes all interspersed within the maze of blossoms. As we leave, I cast a passing glance at the tree over my shoulder. I have to remember to ask about the tree. But how do I ask without being obvious?

Continuing to head toward the northern end of the village, we pass by so many houses that I lose count. Many look to be empty or deserted, but still they outnumber our own. It's strange that the colony's walls are built around so many unused structures. Perhaps they were used by our ancestors. Maybe they built these walls before the Jadhenash came.

Mori and Cyndene are wrapped up in their own private conversation, pointing at the various features within the town as we pass, and Bhradon … well, Bhradon is busy looking sullen as he glowers at our tour guide. *What's gotten into him?*

Taernus is pleasant on our journey, pointing things out in a way that makes every mundane thing seem fascinating. For some reason, I am captivated by his voice. Soft, yet strong. Smooth with a touch of sweetness, musical in tone, a harmony among the noises of the village.

Before long, our tour is over, and I find myself feeling wistful despite the need to do our part here as quickly as possible in order to get back home. Taernus tells us that Orlianna and Veynor will delegate us to coteries appropriate to our skills. I assume Mori and I will be working with the fire or helping with deliveries. Before we became Tenders, my brother and I would sometimes help with deliveries and other Carrier duties.

"What do you do around here?" Bhradon's voice is sharp and irritated. Something is bothering him. I wish he would talk to me about whatever is going on. He's not usually so closed with me. This journey has taken its toll on all of us, I suppose.

We may never be the same again.

INTERLUDE
~ E ~

Her children are her heart, her home. And she is being forced to leave the home she helped create, not knowing where she is headed. From one home to another. Or perhaps not?

Perhaps nowhere.

He can see all of this every time he catches her eye. Not that he is blind to his own slowly unraveling limitations. The black shadow of death is in his eyes as well, plunging headfirst into his life stream to rip away his happiness. The passage of time is the cruelest force in the universe.

For is this not a happiness they created for themselves?

Why should they be forced to leave it?

CHAPTER 40

"How were you able to make it here without being killed by the…Evil Ones?" I'm still amazed by the fact that more people are out there, somewhere, beyond my mind's imagining.

"How were *you*?" Taernus quips back good-naturedly, strolling leisurely with me past rows and rows of stone houses with partially collapsing thatched roofs.

"That's different, I should think. I had companions. We protected one another. And shouldn't you be helping to thatch those roofs? Looking awfully neglected if you ask me." I try to mimic his light tone despite my constant worries.

"It is not my shift right now. Would you expect me to work all day *and* all night? Roghen, however, should be working on these. You are correct in that." He continually darts his gaze in every direction, presumably looking for the young man. "And to reply to your incessant questioning, my dear, I would say that I am just one person. Perhaps I was more difficult to spot, yes?" His odd logic doesn't really ring true, but it isn't my place to pry. These others are, in fact, similar in size to the Shadows. It's strange that they even fear them at all when they are larger in number. One on his own, however…

"Tell me about your village, Corinne." His request, while innocent, raises my guard back up as I try to step around any specifics. Internally, I cringe just a little at the use of my birth name, but for some reason it doesn't bother me so much when he uses it.

"We come from a village to the south of here. It is not dissimilar to this one, other than the leadership system." I try my best to explain about the Primaries, looking back to the others for help before remembering that we are alone. My words falter as I look back to no avail, but Taernus saves me by changing the topic slightly.

"Are all of your people like you?"

My confusion must have been apparent because he laughs and adds, "Are they all of your size? And as pleasant to speak with?"

I laugh along with him. "Yes, we are all hopelessly small I'm afraid." My tone grows serious as I ask, "Have you met anyone from other villages that were our size?"

"No, I'm afraid you are very special in that respect." The gleam in his eye is kind and gentle, so I ignore his teasing. It's hard enough to keep my head tilted back to look up at him when he speaks. If I had to guess, I'd say it is this continuous uncomfortable posture, and not the duties of a carrier, that is making my neck and back ache quite painfully. Now I remember what it feels like to be a child.

I catch him staring at me with that odd look again, similar to the one that Orlianna gives me, but less threatening. Almost as if he wants to tell me something, but can't quite find the words. He interrupts my thoughts when I realize he's stopped walking and is looking all around again.

"Where is that boy? He's supposed to be getting these done!" This is the first time I've seen him get angry, but his voice is not loud enough to carry far.

"Taernus, calm down. I was getting something to eat. Back to work as you can see." From nowhere, Roghen appears just where I'd been looking only a second before, walking casually as if he'd just strolled up to us. The lane is long and narrow with few side streets. Yet I'd swear he wasn't there a heartbeat ago. As he walks up, I'm reminded that he is a good deal shorter than Taernus, still young enough to be living with his parents, with frightfully long dark hair. He has a nice face, a kind face. He always waves and greets me when I pass him in the village, and always has a smile on his face.

"Something to eat? What, all day? Not one of the repairs in this section has been done. Now I'll be spending all night trying to make up for your laziness."

Roghen scowls at him, but turns to grab his supply bucket as he walks away. "I had to help Lanora with her section early this morning," he quietly replies over his shoulder.

"Lanora? Why?"

Roghen turns back to face us, the scowl still present on his face, marring the sweetness that usually rests there. "She was running late on account of her little one being sick, so she ran all the way out there." He stops, looking at the ground. "She fell and messed up her leg, Taernus. Bad."

Comprehension dawns on his face, but I'm still lost. "Did someone take her to the Healers?" I ask to diffuse the tension.

They both look at me, Roghen blinking away a sadness that I cannot understand. He tilts his head to the side and stares at me in despair.

"What good would that do, Rinni? She's got a broken leg and some really severe gashes on her arms from where the brambles caught her fall. They can clean up those wounds and tend to them. But they can't do anything about her leg."

"But…what about the aranjas? From the tree? Or the leaves? Don't you make medicine here?"

At that, Taernus's eyes grow wide for a moment. "Corinne, what are you talking about? The tree in the garden?"

Roghen breaks in with, "Aranjas? How is fruit going to help Lanora?"

I feel so confused right now. I had thought that the tree was like ours, that it had the ability to cure anything like the Healing Tree. The only thing our tree can't change is a death from old age. My breathing becomes erratic, and once again I'm fighting off a panic attack. I put my hands on my knees and try to stop the world from spinning around me.

All of a sudden, footsteps in the distance grow louder and louder. I hear his voice before my constricted vision allows me to see him.

Bhradon.

He's barely spoken to me these past couple of weeks. But there he is, his face inches from mine now, his hand on my back as he calmly whispers in my ear. I turn to drown myself in his embrace, desperate to calm the raging storm within my mind. My rock as always, but still not the same man I once knew all those many weeks ago, in a place we called home. *How did he get here so quick?*

"Why aren't you on duty?" My muffled voice adds a softness to counter the words.

"Sorry. I'll go," he snaps off before pulling away from me. *Cold.* It's seemed so cold lately without him nearby. Ignoring the chill that dances along my skin, I reach out instinctively for him, grasping his shirt as he walks off, heedless of my pleas for him to stop. I can't let him storm off like this. Something is wrong.

Despite the fact that he's only just walked away, it takes me a moment to catch up. I try to get his attention, grabbing his arm, calling his name, but he merely flings me off and keeps walking.

Standing, alone, in the middle of the empty lane, I can't ignore the feeling that's crawling through me from my toes to my head. There's nothing I can do but wait until he wants to talk to me. I head back to Taernus and Roghen, determined to get some answers instead of more questions.

When I turn the corner, Taernus is gone. I look up to see Roghen teetering on top of a ladder against the side of a rather dilapidated-looking building. Some of the houses in this area are inhabited, but many look as if no one has lived there for a long time. He stares down at me seriously for a moment, but then his face suddenly lights up with his usual smile.

"Rinni, you sure know how to make *all* the boys go running, don't you?" His mischievous smile belies the clear concern in his eyes, and I know he's still worried about Lanora.

"I believe you're the only one that qualifies as a boy, Roghen."

"Ah, well, perhaps Taernus is a bit old for you."

I laugh at the naivety apparent in his interpretation of ages. To the young, everyone seems old. "I wouldn't go that far. He can't be older than fifty, if that."

"Fifty!" Almost falling off the ladder in a sudden wave of

laughter, he steadies himself before adding, "Just wait till I tell him you said that. I wasn't even going *that* far!"

"What's wrong with fifty? I'm thirty-two. Bhradon's forty-two. That's not far off from fifty."

Immediately, I know I've said something wrong. Going completely still, his body is rigid near the top of the ladder. A moment passes before he climbs down, ever so slowly, never taking his eyes off my face.

When he's barely inches from me, so close, yet still I can hardly hear his whisper, "What did you just say?" He keeps staring at me in a very unsettling way, making my skin crawl more and more with each passing second.

"I…I just…I mean…why…what did I say?"

Eyes narrowing, he steps back slowly, pointing his finger at me with an incredulous motion. "Rinni," he starts, then stops. Then starts and stops again. Finally, "Rinni, how old are you?"

"I told you. I'm thirty-two."

"That's not possible. You look the same age as Lanora, and she was mating age not more than a few years back. She's just had her first child."

And I remember. *From the records and the journals, we know that our lifespan is prolonged by the tree.* These beings don't have the same duration on this world as we do. The tree in the garden is just a tree. They don't have the Healing Tree, and our ancestors wouldn't have either. Which is why they probably died out.

The tree in the garden is just a tree.

Forcing a smile, I say, "Yes, she would be about my age. We must measure time differently than you." Well, the first part was true. I don't like lying—not at all—but I don't think he'd understand even if I could afford to tell him the truth.

Perplexed for a moment, he eventually shrugs his shoulders. "I guess." But he continues to eye me warily as he gets back on his ladder. Since it seems that I have part of the day to myself, at first I decide to head back to our hut and read from my books. Then I have an idea.

"Do you have books here, Roghen?"

"Books?"

"Yes. Pieces of paper with writing on them that are bound together. For reading." Hesitantly, I add, "You do read, don't you?"

His smile returning, he chuckles again. "I know what books are, Rinni. I've just never known anyone to ask about them. We tend to keep mostly to our own stories around here. Pass them along and keep them alive that way."

"So you don't read? At all?"

"I mean, yes, we read. We all learn to read as children. But most of our stories come from our parents and great-parents. Yeah, we have some books, but they're fairly old and not used very often. The leaders keep a good portion of them. Studying the past and all. The rest are scattered around among the families. But I imagine most are over in the old chapel building southwest of here."

"What's that? Chapel?"

Giving me that wary look again, he stammers, "What's a chapel? Are you serious?" Again he starts up with the laughter. Apparently, I'm just here for his amusement today.

He stops laughing when he sees that I'm not.

"You really don't know what a chapel is? What do you … never mind. Did you not see it when Taernus took all of you out around the village? Southwest corner? Has a big cross on the outside?"

At my perplexed look, he explains, "Like this." And he crosses his arms in the air between us, one pointing up and down, the other pointing left and right.

The strange symbol. From the town. From the book. From something back home that I can't remember.

My look of shock must have alarmed him because he quickly puts a hand on my shoulder. I look into his eyes and realize I'm shaking.

"Rinni?"

"Yes? I mean, yes I know the symbol. I just didn't know its name. But we never saw this chapel. I haven't seen it the whole time we've been here."

"Well, it's up in the far corner, but you can't miss it if you head in that direction. We don't really know what they were for, but they tend to hold a lot of books."

"Thanks, Roghen." I turn to leave, but I'm not heading to this chapel. This is all too much at once right now. I need somewhere quiet.

Back in our hut, sitting at the table with my scant collection of books spread around me, I still find myself fascinated with the strange symbol. I didn't ask him what it meant. He probably doesn't know, as it's obviously a remnant of the Old World. Opening the book to continue my perusal, I begin to ponder the words before me. A flood. A disastrously enormous flood enveloping the entire planet. Could this be what happened to the Old World? So many possibilities, so many directions. Bhradon and I used to play a game when we were younger where we'd each try to come up with the most outlandish idea for what happened to those who lived before. How did some survive, and why wasn't their knowledge of the previous civilization passed down? We'll never know the answers, but now it seems that maybe these strangers hold the key to what's happening in our village.

Heavy footsteps approach the door of our hut. Recognizing Bhradon's boots before he enters, I'm out of my chair and by the door when he comes bustling in with a scowl still on his face. He tries to step around me, but I'm not playing this game anymore.

Squaring my shoulders, I say, "We're going to talk, and you're going to tell me what's going on."

Again, he moves to step around me, but I stand in his path. "No, Bhradon. No more. Either speak to me, or leave me." The words are out before I have a chance to register what I've said.

"Yeah, so you can run off with him. Yeah, great. Fine. That's just wonderful, Rinni. Thank you so much for the talk."

"Him? Him who?"

He narrows his eyes at me with a look I've never seen before. "You know exactly who. Your new friend. Taernus."

"Is that what all this is about? That's why you're upset? Because I'm friends with Taernus? Why is that suddenly a problem? I have plenty of male friends back home!"

"Not the kind that would try to steal you away from me!"

"Steal me away? As if I had no choice in the matter?" By now, I'm sure most of the neighbors can hear our heated exchange but too furious to care. *Does he think I'm that easily swayed?*

"Oh no, see that's just it, Rinni! You do! And you're choosing him!"

"This is ridiculous! How am I *choosing* him? Because we go for a walk when we're not working and you're on patrol? Do you have so little trust in me, Bhradon? After all these years?"

Trust. Who am I to speak of trust?

He stares at the floor and sighs audibly, the breath leaving his body and deflating it with one final blow. A sad and dejected man stands in front of me now, one that I've never seen before. And I feel the small sharp slivers of my heart rain down as it shatters with a single beat.

He drags his tired eyes back to mine and says, "Not anymore. Not after what I've seen."

What?

"What have you seen? I don't understand."

"I see the way you look at him. And I know what he's thinking. He gives me that look whenever—"

"Stop! Just stop, Bhradon! I can't believe you think that I would do that. That I could do that. And if all this is over some misguided sense of jealousy, then we need to step back a moment here. First, Taernus has never been anything other than a friend. Second, he's horrifically tall for me, don't you think? And third… well, third, we've gone through too much together to lose this now. This isn't like you. Not at all."

He reaches out, putting his arms around me, and I lose myself in that space for a moment. Or two.

"I just feel like I'm losing you, Rinni. And that scares me more than any of this. More than our problems back home. Every time disaster hits—being attacked by shadows, watching you almost drown, you fighting one off single-handedly, and now this—it feels as if you're slipping further and further away from me."

"Look at me." Cupping his face in my hand, I say, "Bhradon, I swear that I will never leave you. Ever. I will always be by your side. Even in the midst of disaster."

A slight smile tugs at the corners of his lips as the tension he's been holding in begins to fade away. I decide to share my findings from the book with him, and we spend the evening enveloped in old but comfortably familiar discussions. All thoughts about the past manage to slip away during the night as we try to focus on the present.

After a short group debate, we decide to get up early the next morning as none of us has work to do until the afternoon or evening. We need to determine what our plan is going to be before any more time goes by. Time is what we don't have these days. And any hope of finding more of our own people has vanished.

I'm up before anyone else, so I quietly eat my morning meal as I think about our situation. We've been here almost two weeks already, and the leaders don't seem too eager to hold up their end of the bargain. No time frame was ever specified, but our people don't have time to wait any longer.

Cyndene rolls off her mat and strolls over to the table, sitting down beside me without a word. The glassy look in her eyes tells me she's not quite awake yet, so I let her be. A short time later, the indeterminate shape that has amassed inside Bhradon's bedroll begins to stir. Eventually, I see the top of his head appear, and when he tilts it back I can see his still-closed eyes and sleepy mouth as he whispers "good morning."

Crawling out of that knotted up bundle is an amusing site, at least from our end. By the time he's free of bedding, his mood is somewhat dampened. I try to cheer him up with a cheery smile, but he just passes by me, grumbling under his breath.

"Bhradon! Stop fussing. Come join us for breakfast. Have a seat," I say, patting the empty seat to my right.

"I'm not fussing. I haven't slept well, and I have a headache right now."

"Oh! We've all been losing sleep," Cyndene pouts sleepily.

"If this is the way you girls are going to be on the return journey, Mori and I just might go it alone."

A sudden burst of frustration tickles the inside of my brain, forcing me to stand up quicker than I mean to, my chair knocking back against the wall. Clenching my teeth, I vaguely hear Cyndene's high-pitched squeal as I turn around to look Bhradon square in the eyes.

"I'm thoroughly sick of everyone being at each other's throats. We are all tired. We are all miserable. And I—"

Square in the eyes.

A gasp of shock echoes around the small room, and I glance over to see Mori's astonishment hiding amidst a pallor that seems deathly white in my hazy vision. Simultaneously, Bhradon jumps back a few feet, looking terrified, and I see myself gazing back and forth at the two, with Cyndene standing in the middle of the room, unmoving, a look of pure terror on her face.

Square in the eyes.

But it's Mori that eventually captures my attention, trying to vocalize the words that none of us can speak. The words that will confirm what my mind is screaming at in protest.

Square in the eyes.

"Rinni," his voice a desperate whisper in the near dark of the early morning. Again, "Rinni, you…you…"

He can't say it. But I know. It's not possible, but I know. I see it now, as I stare from my precarious perch, looking down over the world as it swallows every hope, every desperate thought. A glance downward confirms my living nightmare.

Square in the eyes.

A terrifying scream impales the stillness of daybreak, exploding into a shriek of revulsion and shock. The sound continues on ceaselessly. Then I realize.

It's me.

CHAPTER 41

In a blind dash, I burst out of the door into the sun's first half-hearted rays, ignoring anyone and everyone in my path. I stop just up the hill, unsure of my destination, just knowing that this is *not happening not happening not happening not happening—*

A firm grasp on my wrist spins me around, and I'm looking down at Mori.

Looking down at Mori.

The denizens out on the paths are staring and whispering, those nearby that had heard the screams are creeping out of their homes to stare at the bizarre spectacle that I have created. That I have become.

I stare back, my eyes seeing what was there, what *is* there, what I just couldn't see before. And now I know where to go.

Orlianna. She knows something.

Running, running faster than I ever have, my legs more than

extensions of my body now. They are solid mass, strong and lean. Almost as if I had been stretched overnight, my limbs molded and shaped into their new larger form.

Then I'm gone. Gone where? Dark space, floating, distant lights. And I return with a sudden jerk of my entire body, but with a start I realize I am not where I was.

How did I get here?

Having barely left the far side of the village, despite my speed and my new legs, I should have been a little less than halfway to my destination near the gates. I *had* been a little less than halfway. Now, in the space between breaths, I'm suddenly here. And I don't remember how. I don't remember the journey.

How did I get here?

Oddly, Orlianna and Veynor are standing just outside their hut, almost as if they knew I was coming. Slowing down my frenzied pace as I reach them, I can see they wear matching faces full of concern and bewilderment.

As I stop right in front of them, I voice my questions with a word: "Explain. Now." Okay, maybe two words.

They motion for me to enter the hut. Once inside, I turn quickly and repeat my command. They sit, and ask me to do the same. My patience is wearing thin, but it's doing better than my sanity. I've all but run out of that.

Orlianna sighs before beginning. "I wish I knew the best place to start. But I guess we should start at the beginning. Long ago, longer ago than we can imagine, there were two. Two people that loved one another so much that they acted on their shared feelings despite the devastation of the past. Their beginning is something we know little of, even less so the Old World from which they must have come.

"Once this world was full of life, full of people, and survival was not so difficult. They were not so cut off from one another, and the things we now see around us were intact and well maintained. There were even people living in these very buildings once. We know that much. These were built by those who existed in the Old World. But they are gone. We don't know why, no more than you do I imagine. There were creatures, animals of all sorts, that populated the entire planet. Now they are all gone. Our only experience with them is through books we have salvaged.

"But these two people existed sometime after all of that fell away. They created a family and started the beginnings of our society. They were well respected within their vastly growing community, and they watched as generation after generation bloomed right before their eyes. I don't know how long they lived, but it was far longer than any of us. Even you."

I interrupt. "What does this have to do with me?"

"You came here looking for answers. I'm not speaking of today. I mean when you first arrived. That's why you are here. I am giving you the knowledge that I have. Those two people are your ancestors. The knowledge that has been passed down calls them the First."

"You know about the First? Why didn't you tell me this before?"

"You did not mention them. You merely asked about your more recent ancestors. The ones who came here. And you were strangers to us. I wasn't sure who you were or where you came from. But I have since begun to realize the truth of your statements. You came from a village to the south. But you did not tell us the full truth of it. I understand that you did not trust us any more than we did you. I want you to understand that I am trying to put the pieces together and share them with you. You need to know the truth. The full truth."

Looking at her now, I begin to see what I refused to see before. That look she gives me, the way she stares at me with a strange expression on her face. I had known, but not known.

"You can see my thoughts."

She glances down at first, but pulls her head back up slowly. "It is something like that, but not like you think. Let me continue where I left off and we will get to that soon, I promise. The First and their children were different from their grandchildren and later generations. They lived much longer. But as time went on, they eventually died, and the life span of each generation slowly began to lessen.

"Their hurts and diseases were healed by a special tree. A tree they had built their village around. No one knows how or why it existed; it was the life source of these people. However, the tree, like the people, began to lose its power over time. This was a very slow process, but it continued without end. The flowers on the tree stopped blooming. The fruit stopped growing.

"Soon after the First passed away, the Primaries began to form. There was a need and a desire to replace the leadership they had lost with their elders. The loss of the First was devastating to them, but they wanted to keep their memory and their past alive. And that is what they did. For a time."

My thoughts begin to wander through all of this newfound information. "But why would they stop? Why would anyone desire to dissolve that connection?"

"Perhaps because of greed. Maybe there were those in power who wished to direct more upon themselves. Veynor and I have a similar leadership to that of the First. Our village is run in that traditional fashion. Over time, the Primaries warped their roles, and the community was drastically changed as a result. There may have been other reasons for the shift. I do not know the truth nor the minds of those who designed the idea. I only know what has been passed down from those who rebelled against it."

"Are you … are you saying that we are connected somehow? But we aren't the same beings! Our ancestors would have looked like us!"

"And what exactly is that, Corinne? Do you doubt your own eyes? You are no longer what you were! Can't you see the truth?"

Once again, against my will, I look down at my alien form, exactly the same but completely different. The same proportions, only larger in scale and somehow more solid. How can this be me? How is this even possible?

The others begin to arrive, dashing into the house and crashing into one another when they enter. Ironically, Cyndene is the first to walk over to me, with Mori shyly following at a distance. Bhradon holds back, glancing around with a palpable sense of insecurity.

Afraid.

Not of them. He's afraid of *me.*

Cyndene picks up my hand, squeezing it gently and saying, "I think we've finally found something that actually makes sense."

What?

"What are you talking about? What did you find?"

Shaking her head, she replies, "No, Rinni. This. You. It all makes sense, doesn't it? We came here in search of something, but we blinded our eyes when we found it. Who could blame us? It all seems crazy, but it makes total sense at the same time, doesn't it?"

"What makes sense?"

"This place. We found it. We found what we were looking for, only we didn't want to see it."

Bhradon storms over. "Are you suggesting that *they*"—pointing angrily in the direction of Orlianna and Veynor—"are kin to us? Are you out of your mind? Look at them!"

Slowly, I turn to him, my face and heart saddened by my shame in being so blind until now. "Bhradon, look at *me*." I stand up. Not quite as tall as them—*not yet*—but at least an equal to my once-towering mate, my limbs pure muscle, lean but dense and well formed. Mori strides over, taking my only available hand, and now, ironically, I feel like a child being led by its parents. Yet we have nowhere to go. The way we must tread is beyond my grasp, beyond my thoughts, a whirlwind of emotional chaos that is threatening to swallow me whole.

My breathing becomes shallow, and I sense that old familiar feeling. This time, I don't fight the panic attack, for I know it has been waiting for this moment. Letting it run its course is the only way to purge the turmoil and darkness within me, to open my heart and mind to all that is before me.

So I begin to fall, but, as always, he is there. Bhradon can sense them coming somehow, and he catches me despite my giant physique. Slowly lowering me to the chair, he holds me close as I wait out the inevitable.

A flash, an image, swirling, whirling, floating like a memory just out of reach. My mind is somewhere that is not *here*, somewhere just beyond my understanding. Luminous shapes fly by and dash out of my consciousness, forming into images and scenes just before disappearing. A dream. Like a dream, but not a dream.

Am I dreaming? Did I lose consciousness?

And just as suddenly as it began, it ends with an abrupt jolt that slams me back into reality. Bhradon must have felt me twitch. He leans back and looks at me, his face full of shock and concern.

"Are you alright?"

"Not entirely. I don't know what just happened. Did I pass out?"

Mori stands beside my chair. He leans down and says, "Rinni, you just completely blanked out. Your eyes were still open, but they were glazed over. You didn't even respond when I waved my hand in front of your face."

Bhradon adds, "Then you started shaking so violently, and I didn't know what to do. But only for a moment. Are you hurt? Are you in pain?"

"No, not in pain. It's just…I don't know what it was, but I thought I was dreaming. My vision went blank, and all I could see were these glowing shapes moving all around. Something though, something that I don't know how to explain. It was as if I was remembering a memory I never had, but I don't know what it was. It slipped away before I could grasp it fully. Just images, mostly. But it was different from dreaming. I know that doesn't make any sense."

My glance falls on the two people in the room that seem to have all the answers, but they are staring at one another intently, something akin to mounting alarm on both of their faces. Pulling her gaze to me with a slight nod of her head, Orlianna stands up and walks over to our huddled group.

Veynor's voice booms out to every corner of the room. "Has this happened to you before?"

My voice tries to unwittingly answer him despite my still

befuddled brain. "No. I mean, I—" and trailing off mid-sentence, it suddenly comes back to me as if I had somehow discarded it as nothing.

But it is far from nothing.

A harmony snaps into place in my mind, weaving its way through the whole of my essence, opening my eyes and revealing the truth.

I don't know why, but memories of home spring into my mind, and I find myself thinking back to all those years. Images flash through my head, a burst of knowledge overflowing until I cannot hold it in anymore.

Because I know. I *see*.

We are not who we thought we were.

INTERLUDE
~ F ~

Is there some part of him that now exists beyond this world? She will find out soon enough.

They offer her food, coax her, plead with her to sustain her own existence.

But why? What is the point?

She closes his eyes this last time, runs her hand from the crown of his head across the smoothness of his hair, down the nape of his neck, to the strong muscles of his upper arms. The arms that had held her, comforted her.

Arms that had built a civilization, a people. A family.

She sweeps that same hand across his chest, now devoid of the telltale movement of life. No fluttering of breath. No steady rhythm. *The heart that had loved her.*

Not one of them has known that pain. Not one of them has lost... *everything.*

Eventually they would.

All of them would.

CHAPTER 42

"Rinni?" Bhradon asks with trepidation, an unspoken question still lingering in the air. *No, everything is not alright. No, things will not be okay, at least not in the way we want them to be.*

No, we are not *us*. We are *them*.

My only thought is to make him see, make them all see. Somehow, Cyndene can see this, but I don't think she realizes the full extent of that knowledge.

"Bhradon," I begin, unsure of where to start. I look at Mori, still standing beside me, still looking as if the whole world is spinning around us. Maybe it is. "Bhradon, you know how you always know when my panic attacks are coming on, and you always seem to know what I'm thinking?"

He gazes at me in mute horror. "Rinni, please tell me you aren't suggesting that I can read your mind? Don't you think I'd know if I could?"

Finding myself nodding despite my disagreement with his statement, I try a different tactic. "You know how you sometimes say I seem to vanish and appear without you noticing me leaving?"

His sigh of frustration only adds to my impatience with this whole ordeal. "That's only happened a few times, and obviously I wasn't paying attention when it did happen."

Why can't he see?

"No, Bhradon. Today. I did it today, only I didn't know what I did until just now. It seemed like I was traveling through a dream, and then I was here. Until just now, I had forgotten, locked it away so I could pretend it didn't happen. But it did."

Cyndene pipes in, "So that's how you got here so far ahead of us! We were asking people where you went, but no one through town had seen you except the neighbors. Then we got here, and the ones poking around outside said you'd gotten here ages ago. I thought they were exaggerating. But you did! You really did! How did you do it?"

Mori has been staring at me ever since I started this seemingly insane conversation, not speaking a word, only staring. Suddenly, his voice rings out. "You were right, Rinni. About the statue, I mean. I didn't want to believe you, but when we got here, and I saw the look on your face, I had no choice but to believe you. And now, I know I have to believe you again. I'm not sure why, But I just know that I should. Besides, we almost share half a brain, remember?" His smile melts my irritation, my impatience, and all of my dread.

"You're right. We do. And thank you." I feel myself returning his infectious smile, and looking back to Bhradon, I say, "Orlianna has the same—whatever these are—as you. Look at me. The truth is splattered all over me. Literally. This is really happening."

Orlianna begins to speak again. "We call them gifts. But first, we must go back to where we were in order for you to understand. Or perhaps we begin at the beginning again since your friends need to hear this as well." She recounts the story as she had told me thus far, with interruptions and questions, and the same confusion and uncertainties that I held. That I still hold to some degree.

"Those who did not agree with what the Primaries were doing were disregarded by many in the community. They had spent all their lives, as did previous generations, looking up to the judgment of these leaders. They trusted them. But still there were a few who chose to keep and respect the memory of the First, to not forget them. Eventually, they had to speak of such things in secret as the pressure was rising against them. The Primaries began to enact laws forbidding any mention of the First, of the past, or even of the Creator. They did not want any of that part of themselves to continue on, for whatever reason. That is how our Creator became a distant memory for anyone who obeyed the rules. No one was to speak of their beginnings or teach about these things to their children."

Now my ears perk up. "Creator?"

"Yes. We are here because of the Creator. Our origins lie with him, but most of it is hazy in our memories at best. But you would have no knowledge of any of this. It was strictly prohibited to speak of anything related to how we got here, including the First."

"It is still prohibited, but we—Mori and I—were taught a very small part by our great-mother who raised us. She taught us in secret, and much of it was very vague, but she spoke of the books they kept hidden away from us. She would tell us stories about many different people, great heroes, and beings who created the world. And she always reminded us to respect nature because it was created for us."

"From the knowledge passed down from our ancestors, from those who lived in the final days of the First, we know that there was a Creator. But we do not know where and how the First came to be. For some reason, that part was never discussed. Perhaps the First did not know the answer or had a reason for keeping that knowledge. Either way, we keep what little information we have alive to the best of our abilities."

Mori steps forward, stopping right in front of Orlianna. "So you are descended from the ones who left our village? Your ancestors are our ancestors?"

"Yes. They left on a mission to retrieve resources for your village, but in the end, they decided not to return. They found this place and realized the potential for creating the society as the First had wanted. Since then, others left to start their own colonies. Out there in the wide world exists many of these groups who spread out to find new and better resources. They all promised to keep the memory of the First alive."

"But you are completely different from us! How can we be the same?" Bhradon's fury spills out into the room like a looming shadow.

"This is true. You are not the same as us. Not yet, at least." Veynor seems to be almost smiling, but I can see the tension in his face.

"What does that mean?"

"It means that Corinne has now become who she really is.

And you, I suspect, will not be far behind." Veynor turns to me. "I suspect there is a lot of power in you, young woman. You know what you can do, don't you?"

Nodding, I answer, "I can travel places with my mind."

Laughing, he replies, "Yes, well, it is something like that. It is called apparition. Not too many have that gift, and it is a confusing one from what I understand. The period of time when you are in darkness is a sort of passageway. I've been told it is quite beautiful and strange, but it is not of this world. You are actually traveling between dimensions when you apparate."

"Dimensions?"

"Basically, you are leaving this world to enter another for a brief moment. Then you return here, but the passageway has taken you to your mind's intended destination."

"Another world? Where?" This all sounds so crazy, yet I was there. I saw these things.

"It is the domain of the Creator, though I highly doubt you would actually see him. Those with this gift say they see colors and lights and shapes such as you did, but nothing beyond that. All of this has been passed down among our people."

I am stunned. A monumental weight has crashed upon me, and waves of heat radiate around in frantic spirals, spinning my thoughts around into chaos once again. Taking a deep breath, I close my eyes and let it out. I cannot keep doing this.

"How do you know your information is still correct? What if details were changed over the years?" Cyndene asks.

Now it is Orlianna who addresses us again. "Of course, there is no way to know for certain, but we have a very balanced society that thrives and works together. There would be no reason for someone to have done that. We see these things for ourselves.

Everything we live through and witness matches the knowledge that we've been given. Beyond that, I cannot answer you. Only the Creator knows for certain, and he has been silent for a very long time.

"But we also know that your ages are not like our own. I knew this before Roghen told me of your conversation with him." She smiles at my apparent scowl, shaking her head. "Do not be mad at him. I suspected for a while, especially after I sensed your feelings, and he was merely eager to know the truth. All of us know of Sephirah. All of us know the stories of the Pure who chose to stay here and the ones they left behind."

"Sephirah?"

A mask of confusion clouds the leaders' faces. They turn to one another yet again, sharing some secret moment that is lost on the rest of us.

"What do you call your village?"

It is Cyndene's turn to look mystified as she mutters, "Nothing. I mean, we don't refer to it as any name. It's the village. Home. We don't leave, so we're always there. There is no name."

"But there is, child. Sephirah is the name of the original colony, your colony. It always has been, even in the days before other colonies existed. I can't understand why they have buried the name as well." Almost to herself, she adds, "Bury the past. Bury it all." She sighs, and I can hear the ghostly whispers of a thousand lifeless spirits mourning mislaid dreams I never even knew I had lost.

A sudden melancholy envelops the room, choking, binding, bleeding us all of the hope we might have felt at knowing the truth. But there are still questions to be answered. Even they do not have all the answers, it seems.

I hang my head in defeat, alert and aware of what needs to be said. "So you don't have knowledge of the tree beyond its existence? You don't know how to help my people?" Sadness turns to anger. "None of this matters if they are all going to die out! What are we supposed to do?" Stinging in the corners of my eyes stops me from continuing. I let it flow, washing away a little of the pain.

"You asked us for supplies. We are more than willing to offer what we can. I do not understand what you are saying. What more do you need?"

They don't know. We never told them about the tree, preferring to protect the secret, keeping it locked away within our tiny group.

Mori clears his throat. "The tree you spoke of still exists. You say it began to diminish in power, but it has served us for generations. Now it is dying, truly dying. And we don't know how to stop it. The Primaries said our lives are becoming shorter and shorter. If that continues, eventually we will all be gone."

Orlianna shakes her head violently. "No! There is a limit to this! We are living proof. Our life spans have remained the same for a very long time. Our ancestors who first came here lived much longer, but that quickly changed. Their children had the same average lifespan as everyone here now. Most of our people, besides those who become severely ill or injured, live to at least seventy years, often eighty or even ninety. It is the natural way of things beyond the reach of the tree. But we gain much as well. Our size, our strength, and our gifts."

So much makes sense now. The Healing Tree, the Jadhenash, and me makes three. But understanding myself and accepting my current predicament are two completely separate processes, the steps for which I cannot even begin to fathom. How does one cope with the daunting thought of a future as a creature exactly like, but yet entirely unlike, yourself?

This needs to be spoken. I don't formulate the words; rather, I feel the words within me, and they leave me without needing any direction. "You are everything you are because they left the tree. They left its power, but they gained their own. So now, we have left its safety, and we are beginning to lose what it gave us in order to gain something entirely different. But why? What is the purpose?"

"There is no purpose, child. Not as far as I know. The Creator does what the Creator does. Maybe there is a reason, but maybe it's just what happens. A choice is made by leaving that tree. I don't know if it's reversible or not. No one ever went back."

"This Creator of yours sounds like he's having a bit of fun at our expense. If not, there has to be a reason."

"The important thing is that you decide what you want. Very soon, you will all change in form and power. You may decide you like these gifts and want to stay. But I imagine that nothing can replace your home and the comfort of what you know. Yet, that is slowly coming to an end. Perhaps not in your lifetime, but it is diminishing, and I have to believe that it will not diminish any further than what we have here. Even still, your choice would be made for you at that time. There would be no tree to save you."

No tree. The words ring hollow inside my head. The truth of that statement is far too harsh to consider. There *must* be a way to stop the tree from dying.

Somewhere there has to be an answer.

Wait. She said gifts. *Gifts*, as in the plural kind. The kind for which you need two hands to point out, or two heads to wrap your...um...head around.

"Did you say gifts? As in, more than one?"

Again with the furtive glances. Enough already. An uncomfortable silence ensues, followed by an even more uncomfortably long silence.

"There is"—Veynor's face contorts with hesitation—"a possibility of something else. Something you seem to be overlooking, but it is not a gift that we can help you with. I'm not sure… it seems likely, but impossible yet still. I don't know." *Get to the point, old man.* "Everyone has a gift. All of us. As will all of you very soon it seems. Exactly one for each person. Some can sense the thoughts of others, such as Orlianna; some can move things with their own thoughts, like me; a very few are able to apparate, such as you; there are interpreters who can decipher ancient and unfamiliar texts and languages; some can even sense the presence of Shadows before anyone else. There are other gifts, but most are similar in kind to those I've mentioned.

"However, there are books—journals—that indicate other gifts that have not manifested during any time known to current or recent generations. We only know from reading, and I'm not even sure we know anything, really. There were one or two of the ones who first came here who possessed the gift of foresight. Not total omniscience. That is only in the hands of the Creator. But an ability to receive visions from the Creator himself, and to see what will be."

Laughter rings out in the room, booming from corner to corner and echoing off into the distance. It continues for a moment until I realize I'm the one laughing. Ceasing abruptly, I look to Bhradon, who has retreated into his own personal silence, shielding out the world and all of what is occurring. If he doesn't hear it, it isn't true. If he doesn't see it, it doesn't exist. I know this game.

Realizing that I must say something at this point, I let myself feel all of what I'm thinking and burn with the emotion. I want to let it out. I want to scream.

"Creator? You want to sit here and talk to me about a Creator that is watching us crumble away and not lifting a finger to help? Who has left us here to die for no apparent reason?"

"We have no way of knowing what his reasons—"

"No! Don't talk to me about what we know and what we don't know. I'll tell you what we know. We know that our tree is dying. We know that our people are dying. Do we even know if this Creator exists?"

"He is the center of every story we have of the First. We didn't come from nothing. No matter how you perceive it, something brought us into existence. The truth is, we do not know for certain whether or not he—or she—exists. But we believe in the truths behind the knowledge we keep. We place our trust in that knowledge, and only time will tell us if that trust is well founded."

"So you choose to sit idly by and wait?"

"Idle? No, of course not, child. We work, we exist. We survive. The Creator's time is not our time. No one can see his purposes or his plan. If we could, perhaps everything would make more sense. But we must wait. We have no other choice."

"Waiting is not an option for my people any longer. Their existence may continue as you say, but at the cost of what makes them who they are."

"I'm sorry. I wish I had the answers you seek. Truly. But you"—tilting her head slightly—"you...there is something else. Perhaps it is you who may find the answers. Maybe there is more to you than we know."

"More as in what?"

"As I said," Veynor interjects, "everyone has a gift. One gift. But there is something…and I believe only time will tell us the true nature of things."

"We don't *have* time!" Mori's sudden outburst startles everyone except for me. I could feel his anger building with mine.

And mine is at its breaking point. "Look at me! Look at how quickly I've changed, how quickly all of us will change. Only a couple of months away from the Healing Tree, and this is what our people have to look forward to. They will not adapt so easily, especially the elderly." *Gani.*

"We will be here to help in any way we can."

"You can't help us. No one can help us. Life on this miserable planet"—my breath ragged and shallow, rasping out the words in a low whisper-scream—"is pointless and serves no other purpose than to provide entertainment for a deity that finally got bored with his toys and left them scattered on the ground while he wandered off like a spoiled child."

I don't even feel the tears flowing. But I know this is too much for me to handle right now.

I have to get out of here.

CHAPTER 43

I run.

I run to force out the images, the feelings, the *anger* boiling inside of me. Anger at the Primaries for their malicious treachery, their sickening lies and ability to fool the entire world, or what *was* the entire world to me just a short time ago. An unapologetic deception that has no place in my reality. Anger at our people for allowing their own sightless ignorance to slowly devour their own existence until now there is nothing left but a hollow shell of wasted tears and empty dreams. Anger at these people, these *kindred* who live as though none of this happened, as if we are all supposed to be happy about our fate. Learn to love an early death, they say. The echoes of the sentiment pulsate within my mind as they eat away at the last shreds of my sanity.

How can they trust in something they've never seen when we can't even trust the ones around us? A being who abandoned us, left us here to die. To go beyond the known. What is there, beyond this life? Do we meet this Creator? Do we get the chance to ask the question that no one wants to voice?

Why have we been left here? What purpose does that serve?

Why give us a tree to sustain us, only to limit its lifespan as well as ours?

So I run.

I run until my lungs burst, until my legs give out, until my heart bleeds with the melted hopes of a thousand and one dying people. A pain I cannot touch—touches me. Fire envelops the void that has overtaken my insides.

Why?

Why is this happening? What is the point of creation for the sole purpose of its slow destruction? Is this some sick game being played by a nameless, faceless deity with countless years of boredom choking its existence, pushing it into whittling down eternity with the tears of a multitude as entertainment?

I cannot block out the pain. I cannot block out the sound of those cries. A dying society silently screaming its impotent opposition, a nonexistent rebellion to a cause they're not even aware of.

Up ahead, the back gates. Never used, never opened. And I need to get out, get away from this place that is suffocating me with every step I take within its confines. It looks as though a massive barricade is being used to keep the gates from being opened. To keep something out or keep something in?

I don't even realize I'm straining with the effort while attempting to lift the obstacle to my freedom, sweat already running down my body in tiny waterways, until I feel my arms being grasped and pulled away from the wall. I spin around as I'm pulled back.

Taernus.

Not of this place, but not of my own. The only one I've gotten close to here who hasn't lied to me. But I know my sense of trust is even further shattered than it was before I arrived here. Struggling to avoid my innate desire to rip free, to run away, to hide myself even from this friendly face. I need an answer that no one seems to have, to a question that no one wants to hear.

How do I save my people?

The concern is evident on his face but mixed with an over-whelming tang of confusion. He lets go of my arms—*my massive arms*—slowly and with purpose, but I don't run. Taernus might be one of them in body, but now so am I. Yet he didn't lie to me. He didn't know who I was and turn a blind eye. Not like these so-called leaders. People they trust to do the right thing. I feel his eyes boring into me, pleading for an end to his anxiety.

There is no good way to begin. "Not so small now, huh?" How enlightening.

"I don't understand. How did this happen?"

"I honestly don't know. She says…" hesitating because I've told him nothing of the Healing Tree until now. "The leaders have suggested that it's something to do with being away from our home for too long. Seems we are the same creatures after all."

"I don't get it, Corinne. What does your village have to do with you growing *overnight*?" He sighs, and adds, "Look, I'm sorry for running off before, but I felt my presence was not exactly helpful."

"What? Because of Bhradon? No, he's just upset like the rest of us over everything that's been happening. Stress levels are pretty high in our group." Pausing, I wait for the right words to find me. "And the thing about our village…it's different. We are different from you in so many ways, but mostly because of…because of our tree."

"Your tree?"

"Yes. It's hard to explain, but we live much longer than you do. Or, at least, we did. We've been slowly dying earlier and earlier over the years. And I guess now I've lost even that. Orlianna and Veynor told me about the gifts. Well, I guess I discovered it myself, but they said everyone has one. Veynor referred to mine as apparition, but all I know is that I suddenly showed up at their dwelling on the other side of town just seconds after having the destination set in my mind. I did it without even realizing what I was doing." I don't even want to think about the *other* thing. I tilt my head accusingly. "You never told me you have these powers."

"And you never told me you have a magic tree."

"It's not magic. Not like the stuff in books. It's just there. Part of nature, as Gani would say."

"Who is Gani?"

"She's my great-mother, the one who raised Mori and me. Our parents were killed by the Shadows, the Evil Ones, when we were little."

"I am sorry to hear that. You never told me this story."

"It isn't something I like to talk about. Mori and I have always had each other, and Gani was always there. My brother and I share a very special bond, mostly because of being twins, I guess. But we are very strongly connected. I can't really explain it."

"It's nice to have someone to connect with. My brothers and I were close, but some of us had a falling out. After that, we were never the same. But I know what you are asking. You want to know what my gift is, don't you?"

"I can't deny my curiosity considering how much time we've spent together, and I've never seen anything."

A sadness enters his eyes. "They told us not to perform them in your presence until they figured out who you were. I'm sorry."

"I thought we were friends, Taernus!"

"We have, indeed, become friends over these weeks. But, in the beginning, none of us knew anything about you. And I just assumed the leaders would bring everything to light before now. Again, I'm sorry. But perhaps I can make it up to you, if only in a small way. Seeing as how you are intent on getting out of here, it seems."

I stare at him quizzically, his eyes shining with mischief as he turns away from me to face the back gates. Just as I begin to formulate the question in my mind, the block of stone barring the exit begins to tremble with an unexplained energy. Nothing else around us moves, and before I have time to decipher what's going on, the stone is in the air, above our heads, floating in just such a way that stone should not be doing.

At least, not in my experience.

Have I finally and officially lost my mind?

"You are seeing this, right? Please tell me you can see it, too."

A deep, throaty chuckle erupts, and as he turns his head slightly to look at me, amusement lights up a sparkle in his eyes. "Yes, of course I see it. You asked about my gift. Well … this is it."

Struggling to comprehend and speak simultaneously, all I initially manage to squeak out are incoherent strings of sound. Then, "You can lift things?"

Laughing again. *Why is this so funny?* "To put it simply, yes. I can lift things, both with my mind and my body. Things no one else, besides those who share the gift, can lift." All I can do is stare, wondering, *is this real? Is all of this actually happening?*

He walks over to the floating block as it lowers to the level of his torso, placing his hands underneath, tilting his body back ever so slightly. Suddenly, the trembling stops and the giant mass of stone begins to fall. But only for a breath. Immediately, Taernus catches the falling object in his hands, the weight gently resting in his palms. He turns around, boulder and all, and grins.

What a show-off.

Yet his mirth is contagious in an odd sort of way. Ironically, I feel a weight lifted from me, if only slightly. The issues I'm facing fade away just enough to allow me to think clearly without the threat of another panic attack.

And my path has been cleared. Literally.

"Taernus, I don't know what to say, but thank you."

He sets the rock down to the side, away from the gates. Leaning against the wall with an air of noncommittal curiosity, he asks, "And why do I deserve your gratitude, my dear?"

"For opening the door, so to speak."

Again, he smiles, but only for a moment. The gesture immediately disintegrates into a frown that could almost be considered a pout.

"And where are you going?"

"Somewhere. I don't know. I just need to get out of here for a while. I need to clear my head."

"That I can understand. But aren't you putting yourself at a bit of a risk leaving the village alone?"

"They don't usually come out during the day too often." *But sometimes they do.*

"You of all people know that's a flimsy argument at best. Didn't you tell me how you were attacked before nightfall? Still sounds risky to me."

"Yes, but it was nearer to dark then. It's barely midday now." I know I'm just making excuses, but I have to get out of this place. A feeling is pulling from deep within me, dragging me away in its insistence. I must leave. Now. I start to move toward the now unbarricaded gates, but he grabs my arm tightly and pulls me closer.

"At least let me go with you. I know the area, and I can show you some places you might find interesting. Maybe you can even find some answers." He looks at the ground and then back up at me, biting his lower lip. "I promise not to speak a word without your consent."

Slowly, I nod my approval, and the grip on my arm disappears instantaneously, the sudden absence of warmth oddly discomforting.

We silently walk to the gates, pushing the doors open easily as a sudden breeze sweeps through, banging them against the inner walls. Stepping out into the wilderness, we pull them back together, and I notice there is no outer handle or pull of any kind. A thought occurs to me.

"What about the barricade? The village would be exposed to an attack until we return."

That smile. A warmth spreads through me, and I feel myself smiling back again. Looking back at the gates, he says, "As long as I know where the object is, I can still move it." As he says this, I hear the telltale reverberation as the barricade lands back in place. "Shall we?" He motions in a semi-vague direction, as good as any, so I begin walking.

As we travel, Taernus says nothing, a fact for which I am grateful. Yet some part of me does want his advice, despite the fact that I don't even know what to ask. The statue that brought us here looms off to the right of my field of vision, but my random course is leading me in a different direction this time. My mind is jumbled, reeling with the surreal nature of all the events that have occurred this day. And it's only midday. Only a few hours since I woke up to this newfound nightmare.

As if the one I was already living wasn't enough.

Walking in silence, I let chance guide me, as it has already decided my doom. Orlianna says the Creator decided all of this. If this deity is so inhumane, what does that say about these people?

Gani always taught us that nature, and whatever entity of creation was behind it, could never do harm. True, there were potent forces of nature that left destruction behind in their wake, causing hurt and injury. But the blind power behind it is merely the hand of creation cleansing the world and wiping away its tears. The rainstorms feed the soil and the plants, including the Healing Tree. Sometimes floods result from an overabundance of these storms, massive deluges that have, on occasion, washed away the life of some poor soul who didn't follow the protocols set in place. But, despite the gravity and sadness of the situation, the loss of life is not the fault of the storms. And those same tempests are our savior when we struggle through the droughts that sometimes plague us, quenching the thirst of the parched shriveled dirt.

Up ahead, the glint of the afternoon sun glides across a surface emitting a blinding kaleidoscopic of color. As I move closer, the scenes depicted before me become more clear, the rainbow surface smooth and, surprisingly, intact.

I see it, and I know.

I've seen this before. What seems like ages ago, a deserted

town, ruins with very little protection and a domain of danger. A Shadow chasing us as we ran for our lives, as we attempted to find shelter from the evil without. Beautiful pictures displayed on the walls, windows of color and hue beyond the dreary scope of what was once my normal life.

"What is this place?" My voice is barely a whisper.

"A chapel. This one is a little larger than the one in town."

"Roghen mentioned something about a chapel. I haven't seen it. Why didn't we visit it on our original tour?"

"I was told to avoid that area for the time being." When he sees the hurt look in my eyes, he adds, "Please understand that we didn't know you at the time. I didn't know you, Rinni."

"So what is it?"

"What? The chapel? You've never seen one?"

"I have, only I didn't know what it was. I recognize the colored windows. The pictures, they... I don't know. I feel something when I look at them. I feel like crying for no reason. How depressing is that?"

"No, not depressing. They are beautiful. And sad, yes, but only because they seem to tell a story. Do you see it?"

I do. But I'm not sure how to explain what I'm feeling, so I don't answer. I merely nod my head and continue up to the open void where the door should be. Walking over the threshold, I'm almost knocked over by an overwhelming dread that fills the small space with a choking finality.

The interior is similar to the one in which we hid from the Shadow. Again, a walkway down the middle with seating on both sides. I stride down the center, oblivious to anything around me. On the dais at the end of my path, there is a book lying open on the floor, scorch marks heavily evident on its weathered exterior.

Picking it up, I see that the front third of the book is almost completely gone, except for a portion of the cover still attached to the spine. And it looks just like my book.

"Have you seen one of these before?"

"I have."

"Are there a lot of them? What are they?

"There are probably a good number of them. I've seen quite a few myself. The chapel in the village has several, but most of them are burnt pretty badly. This one seems somewhat intact by comparison."

Yes, I had noticed. The one I took from the ruins is in decent condition, but portions of it are either scorched or missing. My fixation on this book is strange, I know. But I've always enjoyed the mythology books I managed to find back home. The Primaries tried to remove any books of that nature from the Records Room, but some had escaped that fate. I liked the idea of trying to explain our past, and so many of the stories seemed to do just that, albeit with different answers to the same question. The irony of that thought does not escape me at the moment.

"But what is it? Who wrote it?"

"Who knows? It does have some interesting material, albeit much of it is long and boring. And downright confusing. Have you read any of it?"

I grimace. "Well, I've tried, but like you said it's a bit much to try to understand all in one go. It's made like the ones from the Old World, so I keep wondering if there might be answers in it."

"Indeed, there just might be. Have you read any of the end of the book?"

"Oh, no. I'm nowhere near that far. I keep skimming over

parts, but it's still a lot to take in. Why? Is there anything interesting at the end?"

"Quite a bit, actually." He leans across me to turn the decaying book over and flips it back a few pages. Throwing his weight back onto his elbows, he gestures to the open page and says, "This is where the really fascinating bits are, my dear. Really makes you think. Try starting here." He points.

At his insistence I read aloud, "And I saw an angel come down from heaven, having the key of the bottomless pit and a great chain in his hand. And he laid hold on the dragon, that old serpent, which is the Devil, and Satan, and bound him a thousand years, And cast him into the bottomless pit, and shut him up, and set a seal upon him, that he should deceive the nations no more, till the thousand years should be fulfilled: and after that he must be loosed a little season."

Shaking my head violently, I blurt out, "That's not what I call fascinating. Sounds downright depressing and scary all at the same time. The dragons I've seen in books were huge monsters that breathed fire. I don't think I'd like living in fear of something like that running around loose. Though I do wish I could, maybe just once, see an animal from the Old World. Perhaps just a small one though"—giggling to myself—"and certainly no dragons."

What in the world has gotten into me?

"Corinne, do you really think it's an actual dragon?"

"What do you mean? It says it right there. What other kind of dragon do you know of?"

"You claim to be an avid reader. Tell me, is the dragon always really a dragon?"

Thinking, I look away to glance at the walls of the chapel. "I guess not. I mean, that sounds less scary than an actual dragon."

Smiling, he answers, "Yes, well, there are many things in this world that I'm sure would terrify you, Corinne." I feel a chill in the air at those words, and I shiver involuntarily.

"So what do you think it means, Taernus?"

"First of all, you might find that reading some more will help in your understanding."

"If you know something, just tell me. I'm sick of all the secrets and the lies. Everyone seems to have something to hide, and I can't trust anyone. Why should I believe anything anyone tells me now?"

"You ask me to tell you, yet you admit you wouldn't trust what I say. That is why I'm asking you to read it for yourself. I want you to see rather than just hear it from me." Placing his hand under my chin, he lifts my head and stares directly into my eyes with a look of such deep and shocking sincerity that I find myself nodding obligingly. He's right. I've only been successful lately when I rely on my own instincts and experiences. I need to see this for myself, even if it is just a book. Yet it was also just a book that lead us here on our journey. A journey to find answers, whether we like what we've discovered or not. Perhaps that book was meant to lead us to this one, and to someone who could interpret its meaning.

And when the thousand years are expired, Satan shall be loosed out of his prison, and shall go out to deceive the nations which are in the four quarters of the earth....

"So is Satan the name of the dragon? I still don't understand."

The gleam in his eye seems out of place under these dreary circumstances and surroundings. He looks almost ... pleased. "Do you still insist on referring to him as a dragon?"

"So it's a he? Is he a person?"

"As much as you are, Corinne."

"Then why would the Creator imprison him? Isn't the job of a deity to look after their creation?" My thoughts run immediately to the stolen moments back home, sometimes filled with forbidden stories of ancient mythology and deities, some of whom were very unkind. I guess I just never liked the idea of a being that could create something it did not love enough to protect. So I've always rejected the idea in my head. It runs so contrary to Gani's stories about nature and its harmony.

"I admit it is confusing and complicated, so much more than the words on the page can convey. But I wanted you to see before I tell you the story."

"What story?"

"Our story."

Several moments seem to pass before I respond. "What story would that be?" My voice sounds far more nonchalant than I feel.

"Your story. My story. Our shared history. And misery." I'm shocked at his sudden display of dejectedness, an unaccustomed mask for his usually sunny demeanor.

"Are you saying you know more than the elders do? How is that possible? How would you know more about the past than they do?"

"Because I was there."

CHAPTER 44

I blink.

I blink again.

A pain begins to radiate out from my chest. Suddenly, I realize I've forgotten to breathe. With a quick intake of air, I lean forward, clutching myself around my midsection, gasping for the second and third breaths. I let the physical reactions wash over me in a wave of semi-conscious fluidity.

Until he touches me.

With his hand on my shoulder, a warmth flows through me, rinsing away the ill effects and filling me with a glowing resurgence of energy.

"How...how did you do that? Bhradon's been the only one who could—but you did it so *fast*."

Taernus looks at me strangely at the mention of Bhradon, but answers, "It is an empathetic gift. The ability to know when and how someone is hurting and heal them indirectly. He... Bhradon... has done this before?"

"He always seems to know when I'm having one of my, um, panic attacks. I don't know. He holds me, and I feel better. But you barely touched me." Bhradon always senses when they're coming on, almost before I do.

His gift.

I stumble on my next words in the fearful excitement of discovery. "He can read minds. Or... they said it wasn't like that exactly. I don't know. But he just... can. Is that what you did?" The thought of yet another person in my head is quite unnerving.

"If you are asking me if I can read your thoughts, the answer is no. It is, as I said, an empathetic gift. I can feel your pain, but it is not painful to me. Not in the strictest sense. It is more like a calling to heal you, and I feel it as a pulling sensation. To put it simply, the thoughts in your head reveal themselves as emotions rather than actual thoughts. Your friend is quite lucky to have such a beautiful gift in his life." A heavy, dense bitterness in his tone floods the room at this last statement.

"But you already have a gift. You showed me. Orlianna said everyone has only one gift." Something within my core stops me from revealing my own secret. Perhaps I'm just as much of a hypocrite as everyone else, but the feeling is too strong to ignore. And I'm not even sure what the other thing is.

His luminescent smile returns as glorious as ever but with a hint of mischievousness behind the innocent exterior. I watch as he leans back and lifts himself off the step to pace in front of me. Incomprehensible thoughts flicker across his golden features as he runs his hand through his hair only to have the sections fall back into rivulets of warm brown radiance. I'm once again astounded by his beauty and grace, especially against the backdrop of darkness and destruction by which we are currently surrounded.

"My dear Corinne, you are a rare creature indeed. I had high hopes for you, and you have come through all of this showing far more strength, intelligence, and resolve than I even expected. Yes, it is true that earth-born beings all possess one gift. But the truth is that, while I am almost identical to your people, my gifts—my *powers*—did not derive from this world as yours do." Laughing at the look of shock on my face, he stops to consider his words. "Perhaps I should begin our story, no?" He spins around to look at some spot behind the dais.

Just when I think the silence is never going to end, he speaks. "Long ago, a race of people discovered something they thought would change their lives. And, oh, how it did. A lesson perhaps in messing around with things you don't understand. But no matter. What they sought was the key to immortality. A path to life beyond the scope of their world's limitations." At this, he laughs, the sound a sardonic chuckle that reverberates around the dark and ruined structure, enveloping the room in an ironic sadness. A mockery of the palpable tension filtering through the damp air.

Moisture congregates on my exposed skin, cooling my body temperature and sending sparks of tingling apprehension through vertical patterns, head to toe, in an unending cycle. Yet his bitter mirth seems short-lived when he continues. "They played around with power beyond their comprehension. They were the ones to create their own destruction. They opened a hole into this world."

"Into this world? This world? You mean the people of the Old World? You know what happened to them?"

"What happened to them was of their own doing. The hole

opened up, a portal between their world and ours, the dimension where my brothers and I resided. For so long I had waited for that moment, the moment when I could physically *crush* those vile, self-absorbed creatures. *He* gave everything to them, everything we were denied. He made the mistake of trusting them, and they abused that trust to their final ending.

"Once the portal was opened, we desecrated and demolished them and their world. The Creator should have been grateful to us and considered it a just punishment for directly disobeying his command, a punishment he himself once uttered. Our intentions may have been different, but our results should have been the same. But no. He took pity on them. Then he began to send his warriors out to stop us. Battle raged on for what would seem an eternity to you. Before long, all of their kind were extinguished, an entire species wiped out in a matter of years, but we continued on, fighting a seemingly unending war against his forces.

"In the end, we were beaten and outnumbered. We were always outnumbered. The world was empty and destroyed. Then the object that began the war was stolen away by two of his best guardians, who took on the form of the people who had lived here for so long. For a thousand years, my brothers and I were bound and chained, unable to seek out that object. An object that, once within my possession, would allow me to recreate this world in *my* image instead of his. He has no vision, no sense of the possibilities within that power. But I do. I can make this world better than it has ever been, my dear Corinne."

"I'm not sure I understand. Who are—or were—these people? The people in the village believe in the Creator, but you speak of him as the ruler of a race that died out, as you say. Someone must have survived the Old World for us to be here now, right?"

"He gave up on those people he held so dear. He was angered by our interference, our judgment, yet even still he allowed them to die. Are they with him in his realm now? Perhaps. They were promised an eternity with him, despite their deceit and self-ishness, but he took it from my brothers and me and denied us entrance. That was our home once, the place of our creation. My pathway to that realm was taken from me when he locked us away. I can no longer travel to that place or speak to him. Nevertheless, his realm is not meant for you either, I'm afraid. You may have flashes of it when you apparate, I'm sure, but his promises do not apply to you any more than they do to me. You are the vestiges of a broken race, a species never meant to exist. We are the same, you and I, and all these other poor creatures out in the world."

Distress chokes me, shoving away all necessary air for me to breathe. Struggling with the simple act of taking the air in and letting it out, I focus my attention on his words.

We are not who we thought we were.

Too many thoughts are scrambling inside my head at once, and I'm finding it impossible to sort through them in any meaningful way. I'm not even sure I know how to voice any of them.

Not human.

But what then?

"What am I?" I whisper into the shadows.

Taernus steps forward slightly. "You are the product of something that was never supposed to happen, I'm sure. It took me a long time to piece together all the details from the colonies I've visited and the journals I've found. But it seems that the two guardians that were sent to protect the object ended up falling victim to the natural desires of their human bodies. They developed an attachment for one another, and the inevitable result was the creation of a child. One child became many, families began to form, and generations of these hybrid creatures ensued."

Interrupting, I exclaim, "You're talking about the First aren't you? They were the guardians!"

"Yes, they were the guardians. But they were sent to protect something the Creator wanted hidden from me, not to repopulate the planet. Yet who could blame them? He sent them down in human form and left them here without anything to guide them in the right direction. They had no idea what they were supposed to do or how long they were supposed to wait. Because he abandoned them, just as he abandoned my brothers and me when he chose the humans over us. We were heaven-born, higher than any of the earth-born beings, yet he chose them. Now my kind and your kind, the same yet different, are stuck here, doomed to an eternity with no hope of happiness."

"Yes, but *what am I?*"

"We are angels, you and I. I was born of Heaven, you of Earth. Your initial human form is simply a result of being born from a human likeness. The First were like us, like you as you are now, but obviously far more powerful than your earth-born nature is capable of being. Yet I see *your* power, Corinne. I can feel it flowing through you and around you. You are so much more than the others will ever be. And I know that you are smart enough and determined enough to do whatever is necessary to help your people."

"What can I do? You're telling me that my entire life has been a lie, that I'm the offspring of angels not humans, that the deity who supposedly created all life left us here to suffer, and that some magic object can…"

I can see the brightness in my eyes reflecting back at me from his, our eyes like shining stars within the same constellation, reflecting our mirrored excitement back onto each other.

All this way, and the answer was right where we started.

The Healing Tree.

CHAPTER 45

He needs me to take him home. To my home.

Sensing the sudden comprehension in my eyes, he rushes in. "Take me there, Corinne. Together we can stop the dying, stop the suffering. You and I can do so much for everyone."

Isn't he the one who practically shoved that book down my throat? Is this a joke?

"You seem pretty keen on believing that stuff I read."

"It's a bit more than that, I'm afraid. Maybe you missed the part where I *told* you that I had, in fact, been chained up for a thousand years."

"So you're saying it's true, then?"

"Depends on what you mean by true. The past is always true. It's already happened. Yet much of what you see written there cannot be trusted at face value. It was written by men who blindly worshipped the Creator and sought to control the masses with propaganda. Just look at what your Primaries did. They are the ones who are deceiving everyone, not me. Just like the men who wrote that book. They sought to destroy my name, and now others seek to destroy my cause because they wish to live in the past instead of making our own future. It's the future I'm concerned about. What will be is not always what has to be."

"You've lost me."

"Endings can always be rewritten, my sweet Corinne."

"What do you … what do you mean?"

"I know everything about you, Corinne. I know what your future holds, if only you would open your eyes and see the possibilities. Those words"—pointing to the half-forgotten book lying still open on my lap—"are merely the wretched hopes of someone determined to ostracize everyone trying to help him. My kind and your kind alike."

My kind. The words echo through my head, but the meaning is still caught somewhere between *impossible to believe* and *easy to imagine*. Somehow the idea, as horrific as it is in some ways, seems to settle quite naturally into the grand scope of things. It all makes sense. Yet it doesn't.

I'm rambling.

He continues. "We are currently living in a time between times. The majority of what was recorded in that book has already happened, but this… this tiny fraction remains. This moment when the end of his tyrannical edicts draws near, and we can change the future. Stop the abuse of our brethren. We can rewrite the ending he intends and make the ending we *deserve*." He hesitates only slightly before adding, "All you have to do is show me the way, and we can change everything. Forever."

"How?"

"By using the tree's magic, we'll have the power to reinvent this world, make it our own. And he won't be able to interfere anymore. Let them have their world. This one is ours now. Think about your friends, your Gani, everyone you know. No one will have to suffer anymore. No one will have to experience death. They will be able to live forever, here, with us."

Forever. Mori and Gani. *Bhradon*. We'd be able to stay together. No death. No sickness. No pain. All I have to do is... what exactly?

"What do we have to do? I mean, how does this work?"

"The power can be taken. But not by just anyone. The strength of your earth-born people is limited. My race is pure; therefore, we are equipped to handle objects of heavenly power such as this."

"Are there others of your kind still out there?"

"Of course. We are heaven-born. We cannot be killed, and we cannot die. My brothers are out there. Soon they will join us."

"Why me? Anyone from home could show you the way."

"Corinne. My dear, sweet Corinne." Leaning down with one elbow on his bent knee, he reaches out to swipe a stray hair from my upturned face. "You are so much more than you realize. If I merely needed a guide, I would not have taken the time to show you all of this and open my heart to you. You are special, my dear. Far more than even I suspected. I knew there was something within you from the first moment I saw you. And now I can feel it radiating from your very core. You are strong. Stronger than anyone of your kind should be, not being pure. I'm not sure why this is, or what it means, but I do know that I cannot do this without you. With you by my side, we will have an enormous impact on the world. A new canvas will be open to an infinite number of possibilities, and I look forward to seeing what you do with your new power."

"My new power? I thought *you* had to claim it?"

I can see him squirm slightly, and I wonder what he isn't telling me. His next words are alarming at best. "Yes, that's true. But I want to share it with you. I need a queen for my new realm." He quickly amends, "Our new realm."

Queen?

"You can't be serious? I'm not cut out for that sort of thing. I mean, look at the mess I've already gotten my friends into. And Bhradon is already more than a *friend*. He's my mate. For life."

"You can't really mean you'd give up the chance to save your people over him? You are far more powerful than him or any of them. We belong together, you and I. This is destiny. Don't you see that?"

I can feel the threads beginning to unwind, the possible hopes for a brighter future diminishing. Something is tugging at the back of my mind, threatening to throw me backwards over a precipice behind me that I can neither turn around to see nor escape without reining in my enthusiasm. How do I even know he's being truthful? No one seems capable of being straightforward with me, yet I sense his honesty without knowing why. I don't know what his intentions are, but I can feel that what he says about the Healing Tree is true. It can change our world, and he wants to do so.

And so do I. But at the cost of losing Bhradon? I can't do that.

Am I really so horribly selfish?

There must be another way. He can do this on his own. I will show him to the village. I will help in whatever way I can. But I will not abandon Bhradon.

And there it is again. That tugging sensation. Not pulling me onward, but rather in reverse. I can't put my finger on it, but something doesn't feel right about any of this. I don't know. I need to talk with Bhradon and the others. Mori always knows the right thing to do. He would have a more objective opinion on this than Bhradon would, considering his earlier misgivings about Taernus.

That apparently were well founded, it seems. At least in the sense of Taernus's feelings for me. Queen, indeed.

Begrudgingly, I stand up, lifting my head to stare into the darkness behind his still radiant form. "Promise to help my people, and I will consider showing you the way." At this, the corners of his mouth fly upwards, the obvious delight spreading into his eyes. The joy is short-lived as I continue. "But I cannot be your queen. I love Bhradon with all my heart. And I need to speak with them about this before making a decision. This is far too big for me to decide on my own."

The smile is replaced with a dark look that I cannot quite discern. His voice far more quiet than it was a moment ago, he replies, "This is not their decision, Corinne. I gave it to you. And you will be my queen, or else you will continue to watch as your people suffer and die." With that, he stalks out the door of the ruined structure, leaving me to an ever-growing darkness and even darker thoughts.

I don't know how it got so late so quickly, but I know that getting back to the town is vital right now. The Shadows could already be nearby, and I'm feeling extremely vulnerable as I stand here on my own.

Leaving out that same opening, I head in the direction of the front gate since I can't open the back gate on my own, and I have no idea how far away or in which direction Taernus is. Or if he'd even help me right now.

I never intended to make him so angry with me. He's been nothing but helpful and kind since I got here, and I'm afraid I may have hurt his feelings. But what was I supposed to do? I can't help that I'm already with someone. This whole situation is getting far too out of hand.

A sound, off to my right, barely audible but distinctly unnatural. And entirely familiar.

Not again.

CHAPTER 46

Running for my life has never quite suited me. I mean, I'm in decent shape, especially after weeks and weeks of nothing but running and climbing, made even more tiring by the addition of packs that seemed so very light as we rationed our meager food supply, yet so insufferably heavy as we panted and heaved in the midday heat.

But, come on. Seriously? Haven't we done this already?

All of this flows rapidly through my head, down past my beating heart, and out my feet, driving them to *move move move*. Never before have I felt so utterly alone. Before, even when we were separated, at least I felt the closeness of the group nearby, our combined fear actually, ironically, strengthening me. Right now, I feel my courage deflating under the terrifyingly *real* idea that I might die. Today.

Hearing them getting closer does nothing to speed my body

along. After a certain point, you can only go as fast as you can go. No matter the consequences. I'm still certain I've never ran this fast in my life. My short, inconsequential life. A life I could have used to help everyone, and now I'll never be able to tell them the truth. I'll never be able to save my people, and it's this thought that crushes me to the core.

And I'm staring at Cyndene. *Why am I staring at Cyndene?*

And why is she staring at me like that? She's not moving out of the way. Can't she see the danger?

Before I can further contemplate her sudden appearance in the forest, we tumble together onto the ground as I slam into her at breakneck speed. Struggling to right myself in order to continue fleeing the Shadows, I'm about to shout out a warning to her when I notice two things.

One, she's not in the forest.

Two, neither am I.

It takes a moment before I realize what's happened. I did it again. I apparated without even meaning to. In my panic, it didn't consciously occur to me. Either way, I'm currently thankful for my new-found gift. More so than I can express without bursting into tears.

Which I promptly do.

Luckily, she doesn't try to force me to sit back down. My nerves are raw and pumping, still on alert from my much-needed burst of adrenaline. Cyndene merely stands up beside me, putting her tiny arms around my body in a show of (hopefully) sincere friendliness. Her warmth is comforting, but she doesn't speak at first.

After some time, she gently looks up at my face, now leagues above her miniature frame. "You had us so worried today. We had no idea where you'd gone, and the guards at the gate said they hadn't seen you all day. Bhradon's been losing his mind, especially since Taernus was—" Pulling herself back and tilting her head, she leaves the thought unfinished. "Where were you? And why were you running like that? From the look on your face, you seemed terrified."

"I was. It was the Shadows. I was running, and they were chasing me. Then suddenly I was here, and I thought I was still outside. I couldn't stop running in time." I look at her sheepishly before adding, "Sorry."

Her mouth opens to say something, but Mori comes running into the room with a very frazzled-looking Bhradon right behind him. Both of them rush over to me, embracing me with a fierce emotion.

"Rinni"—Bhradon's voice is a thin rasp that speaks of screaming my name for hours on end—"please don't ever leave like that again. I've lost my mind searching for you. Where have you been all day?"

Desperation covers every inch of him, and I know I must tell them the truth. All of it.

"I needed to think. So I decided to sneak out the back gate. Only there was this huge rock blocking my path, and Taernus—"

Bhradon's growl turns into shouting. "Of course! Taernus! I should have known!"

"Bhradon, I need you to let me finish. This is much bigger than your issues with him." Hesitating, "I know what happened to our ancestors."

Three identical masks of bewilderment stare at me in anticipation. And I don't disappoint. I tell them every detail, every word that I can remember from the conversation, including the part about Taernus wanting me to be his "queen."

Bhradon is seething, shaking from both anger and incredulity. I wrap my arms around him, whispering again my promise to him from the night before. I would never leave him. Not for anything. Not for all the power in the world.

"So, what now?" Mori asks. "Do we take him to the tree?"

Sighing, I say, "I don't think partial commitment was an option. From the look on his face when I turned him down, I got the distinct impression that he wasn't giving me a choice in joining him. And that alone leads me to distrust his intentions. We have to protect our people and the Healing Tree. We can't give up the location until we have a better understanding of everything."

"Agreed."

Suddenly, thoughts of home trigger a violent reaction in my core. A memory opens up, and I can see.

The symbol. The book.

I knew I had seen that symbol before. Up on the high shelf where I found the journal, there was a book with the same symbol imprinted on it. Right where the Primaries apparently kept everything they wanted hidden from us.

They knew.

CHAPTER 47

A decision has to be made. As a light rain falls outside our make-shift home, thoughts of our real home are at the forefront of everyone's mind.

Bhradon, lying on his bedroll with his head in my lap, absently strokes the side of my leg as we all sit in mute contemplation. He's grown a foot since this morning but refuses to acknowledge it.

What is the best course of action? What is the right answer?

Never forget that life is rarely easy, and decisions rarely simple. Thinking of home, Gani's words once again echo in my head. *The right decision isn't always the best decision.*

So which is it? The best decision or the right decision? Is there a difference? If so, I don't see it. Everything points to doing what is necessary to save our people. And everyone else in the process perhaps.

Mori lifts his head up from its perch atop outstretched palms and turns around in his chair. Already his limbs are twisting and tugging at his core, his height nearing my own at an alarming rate. Surprisingly, no pain seems to accompany the changes, which is bewildering on its own. "Can you imagine trying to explain all of this to the village? Telling them about our gifts. Explaining how they too will develop one, and oh, by the way, welcome to an early grave. How will this affect those who are already too old by their standards? Gani…" Unable to finish the thought aloud, I can see him following it through in his head.

Bhradon picks up at his hesitation. "I think you're jumping ahead here, Mori. We don't even know if this will affect all of us"—not an inkling of irony in his voice—"since no one else has developed a…gift."

Violently shaking her head, Cyndene erupts from the chair beside Mori. "Bhradon, stop. Just stop. Mori's changing, I'm starting to change. Even you have grown since yesterday. Why are you fighting this? You already have a power—"

"I do not read minds, Cyndene! I would know if I could. Rinni and I have been together for so long, and we're so close that it isn't unnatural for us to sense one another's feelings. Nothing magical about that."

"I know this is hard for you. It's hard for all of us. But some part of me split in two when I found my brother. I still don't know why they took him, or why we found him so far away from home. But I just knew there was an answer in our future. I just felt it."

Mori grumbles, "Only we still don't know what to do, do we?"

She glares at him. "Rinni has no choice but to accept this because she's experiencing it firsthand. Mori, you have a connection with your sister that none of us can even begin to understand. You told us you believed her because you felt it was right."

Gently sliding out from underneath Bhradon's sprawled form, I walk over to the table. "Yes, of course I believe. That doesn't mean I accept it. I don't accept failure. I don't accept that there is no answer for our people. We have a choice to make. That's all we need to concern—"

I'm thrown back through the air as a jolt of paralyzing agony courses through my veins.

CHAPTER 48

Three fuzzy images block my view of ceiling. Someone starts to pull me up, and, again, I feel an indescribable pain shooting up my arm and through my core. I must have screamed because voices other than my friends suddenly join the chaos of chatter that doesn't actually sound like words. More like muffled yelping.

Someone else tries to help me up, and I stiffen in anticipation of the searing pain once again.

Only it doesn't come. My relief knows no bounds.

As my vision clears, so does my sense of hearing. Questions. They're asking me questions.

"What happened?"

"Is she alright?"

"What was that screaming?"

"Are you in pain?"

Yes, of course I'm in pain. Didn't you hear my scream of agony? Instead, I say, "Not anymore. The pain, I mean. It was excruciating. Like having my insides burned up. But I'm fine now. Truly."

Am I?

What exactly did happen?

I had walked over to the table, speaking to Mori and Cyndene. I was trying to make them see that the rest doesn't matter. Only our village matters. Our people and our tree.

I touched Mori's shoulder.

That's the last thing I did before it happened.

Ushering the Jadhenash out of the hut with promises that I would be just fine, I quickly spin around to my friends.

"I touched your shoulder, Mori."

"Okay, so…what does that mean?"

"It means you have a power. I mean a gift. I think you shocked me. And I think it's happened before. Not like that, obviously. Try it again."

"What?"

"Well, not on me. Just in the air. Or something."

"Rinni, how am I supposed to do something that I didn't consciously do the first time? I have no idea what happened, but if it was me, it wasn't on purpose. And I'm sorry for hurting you."

Waving his apology off with my hand, I continue. "That doesn't matter. The point is that you did it. Try it. Please."

Glaring at me for a moment with his classic patronizing stare, he eventually sticks out his hand and tries to concentrate. I have no idea what he should be doing, but at least he's trying.

And suddenly tiny flares of lightning shoot out from his fingers, as well as his arm and shoulder.

Unbelievable.

I get space traveling and weird dreams, and he gets the elemental forces of nature.

So unfair.

He looks up at the rest of us with a sheepish grin. "Well" is all he says.

Well, indeed.

"So, crazy powers aside, we still have to make a decision. Do we give Taernus the location of the tree and let him decide our fate, or do we hope that the Jadhenash can help us somehow?"

Bhradon scratches his head. "Rinni, I don't think we have a choice. These people don't know anything. Seems this is bigger than all of us, if what…he says is true. About the heaven-born and the Old World and all."

"But divulging the location of our people could be disastrous." Mori's simple statement speaks volumes of truth.

Thinking, I say, "You're right. And we have to tell him that."

"All of us, Rinni. We need a united front on this."

So we head out into the village center, stopping to ask if anyone has seen Taernus. His hut is dark and empty. The night sky is black despite the moonlight, and shadows creep around the edge of every building, making our task seem far more sinister than is necessary. Still, not many are out on the streets at this time of night, and those that are do not know where he might be.

But, suddenly, I do.

"He's at the chapel. The one here in town."

"How do you know that?" Bhradon's impatience is growing again.

"Because he's waiting for me. We can't reach the outer one. They won't let us through the front gate, and the back one is blockaded without his help, but he knows I'll come to this one if I want his help."

We head up the slight incline to the far corner of the village. Stopping when we reach the entrance to the building, all of us look to one another for support. This is it.

Stepping over the threshold is like walking into a painted dream. The interior has been renovated, decorated, and turned into what must be a decent likeness of its former beauty. Books everywhere, but stacked neatly in rows on bookshelves. Colors exploding from every wall, every corner.

And there he is. Lazily sprawled across the large seat at the front of the room, behind the podium. He smiles when he sees me, but I can see the tension in his eyes at noticing the rest of the group.

"Hello, Corinne. I'm so glad you found me. Have you made your decision about joining me to help your people?"

"I have. And I'm afraid I can't just lead a stranger straight to our doorstep."

"Stranger. Why, Corinne, I'm hurt. I thought we were friends."

"We are. But you aren't one of us. You said so yourself."

"Yes, I see you've brought your friends. How nice of them to join us." Irritation edges into his speech, and I do see a look of pain in his eyes.

Then he turns his gaze upon Bhradon. "Ah, the loving mate. How wonderful that our dear sweet Corinne has someone like you to look after her. Someone who can solve all of her problems and save the day." Cocking his head to the side in a pretense of sudden realization, "But you can't, can you? You can't solve her problems, and you certainly can't save your people." He looks at me. "But I can."

"Be that as it may, Taernus, I cannot take you there. I cannot be your queen." I'm surprised that Bhradon hasn't snapped and lunged for the taller angel. He hasn't spoken a word. I turn to look at him, to reassure him of my promise from the other night.

Only he's not moving. At all. I'm not even sure he's breathing. Just as I start to run toward him, I feel—or rather, I don't feel—my legs turn wobbly and refuse to move. Oddly enough, I don't crumple to the ground. I just can't move them.

"What is going on?" I cry, looking around me at a bizarre assortment of frozen facial features on bodies in various stages of movement.

"No worries, my dear. They can breathe normally. They can hear everything we are saying. But no one in here is going to move without my say-so. Including you."

I still seem to have use of my upper body, but little good that does me as I'm running through escape plans in my head. Nothing. There is nothing I can do. Even if I could move my legs, I can't leave the others. They can't even wiggle a finger.

"But why? Why are you doing this?"

"I told you. I want you to be my queen. And I want you to help me build a new world here on this Creator-forsaken planet."

"I told you why I can't do that! There are too many unknowns, for starters. I'm sorry. I just can't."

"Because of him?" He nods in Bhradon's direction. "It seems as though he may be the biggest obstacle in all of this. Let me ask you, Corinne"—his face is close to mine, yet just out of reach, almost whispering—"what would you do to save his life?"

An audible gasp leaves my throat. "No, Taernus. No, please! Why are you doing this?" The panic is rising in my chest.

He suddenly leans back away from me, breathing out with a note of contemplation etched across his forehead.

"Get rid of the competition, so to speak. Hmm? But, no. What's the pleasure in that? I'd only be making him a martyr. I don't wish to compete with a memory for all eternity." Sighing, he turns away. Almost to himself, "Why can't you just see the potential future ahead of us, Corinne? Your people would be free. No death. No pain. No endless worrying."

"Sounds a little too good to be true." I want to spit in his face for threatening Bhradon.

He spins around and walks toward me again, an oily grin spreading across his face. "But isn't that the way of things? One moment, you think everything is grand and glorious, and the next moment you're wondering what happened to your happy little world. Perhaps I've been looking at this all wrong. The mate isn't really the problem, is he? Blood runs thickest, or so they say. Let's watch and see how thick it really is."

Horrified, yet unable to close my now-frozen eyelids, I have the impression of turning around to my right, though the sensation is lost on me, as I can't feel anything from my head to my feet.

There stands my brother, apparently free of the invisible restraints that still bind the rest of us. He looks down at his hands as if he can't believe he's able to move again. Just as slowly, he looks back up. At me.

Sudden chaotic stirrings on the air. Whispers dripping with poisoned words and filthy murmurings. No. Not murmurings. I heard it, before, in the forest. Only I couldn't understand the words then, thinking them nonsense made up by my over-sensitized imagination.

But I understand them now.

I scream at him, watching the scene unfold but unable to stop it. My scream reaches no further than the inside of my head. This is *not happening not happening not happening not happening*—only it *is* and I can't *stop* it and I can't *fix* it and all I can do is *watch* in *terror* and *grief* as my brother—my *twin brother*—continues to move his hand toward the dagger lying casually on the sideboard as if nothing were odd in the least, as if nothing could be more natural or more normal for him to do.

The voices continue coaxing him, encouraging him, as I continue to scream inside my head. As he closes his hand around the hilt, I search pleadingly in his eyes for some recognition that this is *not normal not normal not normal*—but he lifts it up, and without blinking an eye, buries it to the hilt with a sharp jab into his stomach.

CHAPTER 49

His eyes. Now they see, widening in surprised recognition, his confusion evident, lips frozen in a state of perpetual shock and terror. Understanding and agony mixed into one beautifully horrible visage. A lifetime of eternities in a single moment of time.

"As his twin, you should be feeling everything he's feeling, no?" My mind does not register meaning, only words. He continues, "I see that blood does indeed run thick."

The stain on the front of Mori's shirt is spreading rapidly. He collapses to his knees—whether from the shock or from the pain I don't know. All I know is that my world has died. Crushed into a speck of light, snuffed out like a candle in the wind.

My body falls ungracefully forward, landing on hands and knees. Rushing forth, crawling, dragging my shaking form to the one gently convulsing on the floor in front of me. I don't look for the others. None of them matter right now. There is only this.

Half of myself lies bleeding to death on the floor of a chapel, in a village that is not home, with only a quiet sobbing as background noise. I can already see his essence drifting off, dissipating through cracks along the building's stony interior, slipping through my hands before I can grab hold.

There is nothing I can do but hold him as both his shaking and bleeding increase. Wrapping my arms over him, I scream the scream I'd been forced to hold in for so long, with wracking cries of guilt and pain to accompany my grief and misery.

A hand on my head, stroking my hair. I turn in frustration, but it's my brother's hand. He's looking directly into my eyes with such lucidity that for the space of a breath I start to believe he might make it through this. But then I look down at the black-red blotch fanning out at a horridly rapid pace, and I know that is only a dream within my own mind.

His voice is raspy, with a gurgling rattle that unsettles me almost as much as the bloodstain, unraveling my thoughts into disconnected pieces that try to make sense of themselves. I try to stop him from speaking, letting him know that we can just hold each other, and that will be enough. I had felt the dagger entering his body. I could feel the fear and the pain, the sheer terror of knowing you are dying that lit up every synapse within his brain. Part of me is gone. He is leaving me, and I cannot comprehend that future.

But now, there is only calm within him. And I stare in wonder. He looks at me with what could almost be a smile and says, "Don't worry, Rinni. Everything will be okay."

What?

"Okay? How is this okay?" My voice chokes off in sobs.

"Not right now. But it will be." A flash of pain across his face,

gone almost instantly, and he continues, "I wanted to tell you...
tell you that I saw it, too. It was later, after we got here. But I was
scared to say anything. Only now"—a wry smile lifts the corners
of his mouth slightly—"it seems so silly. All of it. We were so
blind, Rinni. And you—"

His voice cuts off suddenly as his eyes widen and glaze over,
and I can feel that this is the end. I scream his name, shaking him
with a violent force. Then, just as suddenly, his eyes return to
normal, and he looks at me with a sense of wonder.

"You have to do it, Rinni. You have to trust him."

Moments pass as I stare at him in disbelief.

"Trust him?" I sputter out between clinched teeth. "He did
this to you, Mori!" My incredulity lessens when I realize he must
be delusional from the blood loss.

Without warning, he reaches out and grabs my forearm. Tiny
flickers of lightning flash across his skin and up my arm. Only this
time, the pain is only minimal.

My vision goes black.

Glimmers of hazy movement, points of light in the far distance
that twinkle out one by one.

And I'm back at home.

Everyone is standing outside near the clearing on the hill. No
one is moving or talking.

Only staring.

My insides go up in flames. Just like the tree.

Ablaze with a fierceness that eclipses the sun's glaring rays, the
Healing Tree is the center of attention.

Or not.

Another violently glowing entity is up in flames but growing
with each passing second. I recognize the entity.

Running toward the crowd, I call out frantically for my loved ones. I see Gani standing off to the side, a somber look on her face.

"Where is Bhradon?"

She points to the far side of the tree. I start to run in that direction, but she grabs my arm and says, "I told you that searching for the truth almost always leads to destruction."

"But I was trying to save us, Gani!"

"I know, child. And you have to decide how far that destruction will go. Striving for what's best is not the same thing as doing what's right."

"I don't understand! Which one is correct? How are they different?"

"It's a choice between knowledge and trust. You know that you want to save us. You found the answers, but the knowledge you've gained shows a path that you loathe to take. Trust sometimes means going against that knowledge. Sometimes we must put our faith in those we feel deserve it the least."

"I can't…none of this makes any sense! Mori said to trust him! How could I possibly do that? He killed my brother!"

She smiles at me in a way that makes my heart ache for home. "You do not yet see. You need more time." And, with that, she disappears.

I need to find Bhradon. I don't ask anyone if they've seen Mori this time. I know he isn't here.

When I approach him, Bhradon looks at me with a sadness that speaks of every hurt I've ever caused him.

"How could you, Rinni? You promised."

"What? I haven't broken my promise. Bhradon, I swear I would never do that."

He turns away from me to stare at the tree. I try to get his attention, but it's as though I'm not even here. Turning to look at the entity in front of the tree, I see that it is growing at an alarming rate. The flames, both on the tree and on the entity, lash out at everything around, licking and burning in an incessant greed to consume it all.

Consume us all.

A blinding light obstructs my vision, replaced by a sudden blackness. When I can finally see, I'm back in the chapel. Looking down at my twin, I stare with mouth agape with wonder and confusion.

"Just found out I could do that. Twin thing, huh?"

"What was that?"

"You have to trust, Rinni. You have to do what's right."

"How is that the right thing to do? I want to see him suffer for this, not give him the power he wants!"

"You need time." Just like Gani in my dream. *Or whatever that was.*

"What was that, Mori?"

"That was you being you. You always had to be the special one, huh?" His teasing smile turns serious. "But I'm glad I got to share in it for a little while."

"Share in what?"

"Twin powers. We could have had a show or something, Rinni. Everyone back home would have loved it at the Gatherings."

"I don't understand any of this. What are you talking about?"

"You just need time. I wish I could be there with you. But you knew all along I wouldn't be, didn't you?"

He's right. I did. Only I didn't want to see it for what it was.

Shakily, I whisper, "It was a vision, wasn't it?"

"Yes. Just like your statue man. I told you I saw him, too. Only after we got here. Guess I was always a step behind you, Rinni. But something had told me even back then that I should believe you. When I had the dream a few weeks ago, I wanted to tell you. But at least I knew I had been right in believing you."

"But they aren't dreams are they?"

"Depends on how you look at it, I guess. Aren't all of our hopes just daydreams we think about when our minds wander to them?"

I know his pain is peaking, and I can feel his anguish. Yet he continues to act as if nothing is wrong. As if he isn't leaving me. A wound to the stomach is a slow, painful way to die.

I lie down next to him on the floor as he cradles my shoulder. With my head on his chest, I can feel his heartbeat slowly, ever so slowly fade away. I know he's gone without looking up into his eyes. A part of me evaporated into the ethereal beyond when he took his last breath only a moment ago. But I don't want to look, don't want to see, don't want to know.

And so I wrap myself closer and continue to hold onto his form, the last vestige of my mirror image. My twin. My brother.

After a while, a hand brushes the back of my shoulder. But I don't want to look up. I don't want to move on. Yet I know I must.

Bhradon's voice is soft and comforting. "Rinni," he starts, "we can take him home. He should be buried with our people. I'm so sorry. I just don't know what to say right now."

"Yes, that would be nice. Thank you." And I lean up to curl in his arms, the sobs returning and echoing off the walls as my cries become louder and louder. Eventually, the sounds begin to attract the attention of neighboring houses. Someone runs to get help.

A large crowd gathers near the entrance of the chapel, gawking at the scene with matching expressions of bewilderment. Through the clustered people march Orlianna and Veynor, their faces full of concern and sorrow.

"What happened here?" Veynor's voice is almost a whisper.

Cyndene's voice is just as quiet, but her tone is strong and authoritative. "The one you call Taernus is a fraud. He threatened Rinni and…killed Mori."

I had forgotten her presence until now. I look over to see her hunched on one of the seating benches near us. Her face is blotchy and tear-stained, the skin around her eyes red and almost swollen shut.

She loved him. I guess I already knew that.

"Was there a struggle? Did he have help?"

I should explain what I know. These people have no idea the evil they have brought into their midst. "He is not one of us. Not entirely. He possesses far more power and strength than any of us. His gifts are numerous, probably far more than what I've seen."

Orlianna flounders beside her mate. "How can that be?"

"He is one of the angels created in Heaven."

"You mean the Creator's realm? But he looks like us!"

I proceed to tell them the story he had told to me a few hours ago. It seems a lifetime has passed. "But I see now that his version of the truth was twisted to his own designs. He is the one the book calls the dragon. And Satan."

The leaders exchange glances. Orlianna says, "Lucifer. *How you have fallen from heaven, morning star, son of the dawn….* He is very deceptive according to the book—I assume you speak of the book with the cross—and has many names."

"Lucifer? That is his name?"

"As I said, he has many. But I believe that was his name before he fell from Heaven."

"So he wasn't kicked out as he said?"

"Well, yes and no. He became selfish and greedy, desiring all the Creator had and more. He started a war amongst the angels. He and his brethren were forced out of the Creator's realm, and so they came here. But their expulsion was their own doing. They chose their fate. All of this is in the book. But, of course, we never knew what to make of those stories."

"He deceived me into believing he was my friend." Tears well up in my eyes once again, and Bhradon's grip on me is tighter. "I don't know why I believed him. I had moments when something felt *wrong*, but I still believed he wanted to help us, even if he was asking too much." Queen. Power. Rule. Realm.

Right. Yes, I should have seen it. Should have known. And now, my brother.... this is *all my fault all my fault all my fault*—

Internal thoughts interrupted by a steady stream of conversation, I slowly stand up, taking a last long look at Mori—*Mori's body*—and head away from the staring eyes, the smothering crowd of the curious and concerned. Bhradon's grip on me returns, pulling me back into the storm, the chaos, the reminder of what I have done—*what have I done?*—but I shrug off his touch. This is my burden to bear.

So which one is better?

I'll leave that up to you to decide.

My decision, Gani had told me.

And I'm going to make the right one.

CHAPTER 50

Murder lurks within me. It oozes from my pores. Swirls within my vision with a mantra of malevolent vengeance, trying desperately to corrupt my entire being.

But it can't. Because I know what I must do.

I see. I understand what Mori meant now. He said to trust him. And it strangles me with distaste, a feeling of bitterness within my core.

My hope is stronger than my rage.

My path has taken me to an inner room within the chapel. The attempts at restoration in the main area obviously did not extend into this enclave. Still, there is an aura of otherworldliness about it, a feeling of being frozen in time. A frozen artifact of the Old World. They came here for comfort. They came here for answers. I have found mine. But where is my comfort?

Just as the thought occurs to me, a slight breeze sweeps

through the room, lifting my hair and leaving a tingling sensation on my neck. Plucky indeed.

Ah, my fearless foe. We meet again.

Only now, I don't imagine fighting unseen forces. Instead, I bask in the relief that it brings. Relief from the past, present, and future. The future I am creating, as well as the one I am throwing away. Where this small comfort came from is a mystery. But I feel strengthened and confident, despite the desperation in my core.

I don't want to do this.

But I must. Because I know how it will play out.

I must take him home. To the Healing Tree. To be his queen.

Bursting out of the inner room with a sudden desire to get this over with, I walk straight past everyone, ignoring Bhradon's call for me and Cyndene's questioning whisper. They will follow. They will all follow because they want to know what I am doing.

They think I'm going to kill him.

But I'm not.

I'm going to let him do that himself.

CHAPTER 51

Visions are only glimpses into a possible future, not necessarily what will be. It all depends on the choices we make. Not our intentions. Our decisions.

My intention is to kill the bastard that murdered my brother.

That would fulfill what's best for me and for my family. To avenge Mori. But also to rid the world of this horrible monster. That is my intention.

But that is not the right decision. The best thing for us, yes. But not what needs to be. What has to be.

Because it's the right thing to do.

I'm going to trust the one being that I have the least confidence in, the least understanding of. Not Taernus or Lucifer or whatever his name is.

The Creator.

Taernus—I mean Lucifer—is sitting peacefully in his hut,

looking for all the world as if he hadn't just murdered my brother in cold blood.

Monster.

Traitor.

The fact that he didn't wield the dagger himself is irrelevant. He made Mori do it. I know he did.

I can sense the others filing in behind me as I stand in his doorway. Finally, he opens his eyes and smiles as if he'd invited me over for tea.

"Well, my dear Corinne. How nice to see you again. And so soon." The smile that used to warm my senses now drips like rotten sludge from his once-beautiful face. I only see evil now.

"I've come with my answer."

"Oh? And what is that?"

Taking a long, shaky breath to steady my nerves and keep me from visibly weeping at my own treachery, I say, "I will take you there. And be your queen."

The uproar behind me doesn't matter. Nothing matters except for the shocked silence that I know is walking slowly away from this disaster. From my betrayal.

Bhradon, I swear that I will never leave you. Ever. I will always be by your side. Even in the midst of disaster.

With disaster at our doorstep, I betrayed him the moment I had the chance. That's how he will see it, anyways.

But I don't have a choice. Taernus—*Lucifer*—must believe that I will fulfill my promises to him. And for that, I must deceive them all. Especially Bhradon.

It hurts like a fire within my core to think about how he's feeling right now. So I don't turn around. I can't watch him leave.

"Well, then. I suggest we head out right away."

"It will take many, many days to get there."

"Oh, but my dear, remember your gift."

I had forgotten. Completely forgotten. But how would that help him? Unless he has that power as well....

He continues, "Never mind. It doesn't matter. I think we shall travel my way, instead. That way, we can all be together for the spectacular beginning of my new realm. Our new realm, my sweet Corinne."

He stands up, taking my hand in his, and the bile rises in my throat. But I don't let it show on my face. I won't smile. He knows I hate him for what he did to Mori. But his ego is big enough to believe that I would begrudgingly accept his offer for the sake of my people. Apparently, he doesn't mind a reluctant mate.

We head toward the front gates, the onlookers gathering more and more by the moment. At the sight of us, the patrol guards eye the crowd in confusion. Lucifer turns around, and with a flourish of his hands, he begins to make a speech to the crowd.

"Dear people. I regret to inform you that I will be taking a leave of absence from you for a while. When I return, it will be in my full glory, and at that time, you may consider paying homage to me, as the savior of your world. Until then, feel free to continue suffering in your mindless attempt at existence. We may be the same species, but you certainly lack the resourcefulness that the heaven-born have always possessed. Even those idiots upstairs had imagination, albeit lacking in a sense of vision."

The people stare at one another in bewilderment, trying to puzzle out what he is talking about. But I know. Orlianna and Veynor know. I wonder what they think of all of this. It doesn't matter, though. Soon, none of this will matter.

I can hear Cyndene sobbing on the left side of the crowd, her arms wrapped around her chest and shoulders sagging with the weight of today's events. I feel so incredibly sorry for her, despite my own pain and sorrow. But that doesn't matter either. None of it does.

He continues, "I will be taking Corinne with me to be my mate and my queen for our glorious new kingdom." Pausing, he adds, "And I think her friends as well. The ones that are left, of course."

No.

I can't bear to see Bhradon right now. I can't watch him look at me with that expression of despair again. I saw it in my dream. My vision. It was heartbreaking. I can't go through that again.

But it was, in fact, in my vision. This is all or nothing, it seems.

I have no idea where he went, but thoughts of him escape my mind as a large looming shadow crosses over the assembled group. I look up. Dozens of figures are floating down into the village, as if from nowhere.

Dark, inky-black figures.

CHAPTER 52

There's nothing like a swarm of Shadows to disperse a nosy group of people.

Not people. *Angels.*

We are not human. We are angels. Earth-born.

The Shadows land with surprising softness and walk straight toward us. My gut instinct is to scream and run. Then I remember my gift. *My power.* I could run from them. I could run from all of this.

But I can't. I have to do the right thing.

So I stay, frozen in fear, but strong enough to face it.

My worst fear. My worst nightmare.

One of them stops in front of Lucifer and speaks.

Speaks. Yeah.

"We have scouted out the area where one of our brothers was wounded, but there is nothing to suggest habitation. He has told us that most of his company was burned as well, but so severely that they were unable to report in due to their injuries. As of right now, they are missing. They were supposed to be exploring the region south of there, and he believes they may have found it. One of the earth-born was taken and questioned, but he refused, even with … extreme persuasive measures."

Cyndene's high-pitched squeal is unmistakable. I look over and realize that she never moved when the creatures landed, either from shock or from some deep-seated obsession to know the truth. From the look on her face, she must have realized the same thing I did.

That earth-born they tortured was probably Winslir.

The creature instantly cocks his head in her direction as some of the others slowly creep toward her.

"Now, now. We don't want to scare the poor girl, do we? Brothers, perhaps it would be best if you tidied yourselves up a bit. Make yourselves presentable. After all, these are our guests. Not to mention friends of my soon-to-be queen."

The entire area is bathed in a rich radiance as the Shadows begin to glow. The inky-black skin and hideous faces with fangs meant to rip apart flesh—all gone.

In their places stand luminescent bodies with human-like features, yet tall and strong like the Jadhenash. Correction: like us, like *him*. Only none of them has quite the same essence as my once-friend. Not as striking or radiant as Lucifer once seemed, they exude a lack of elegance that makes perfect sense.

These are his brothers. *Fallen angels.* And he is their master, whether they see it or not.

All he desires of them is their obedience. He will not share his new kingdom with anyone. Including me. All he desires of me is my powers. He doesn't know about the visions, but my guess is that he doesn't have the ability to apparate.

Those of us still within sight of the surreal spectacle all stare in wonderment. Many start to come out of their hiding places, presumably with some ill-conceived idea that these creatures are harmless, all because of their new exterior. They can't see the ugliness that was there only a moment ago. Same creatures. Same evil hearts. Different facade. Maybe this is their true form. But it doesn't mask their true nature. At least, not for me.

"You see, my brothers prefer their darker nature, and naturally, they are inclined to use a darker form. They seem to like it for some reason. I don't really understand why. Our natural form is so much more pleasing to the eye."

Lucifer sends two off in search of Bhradon, returning promptly with a very solemn-looking version of the man who was my mate. He looks directly at me, and stinging erupts behind my eyes. Trying to force it down, to keep myself from crumbling into pieces, I shut my eyes to the pain. When I open them again, the creatures have both him and a whimpering Cyndene standing in front of us. The dejectedness in his eyes speaks of loss, of lies. Of love.

And I killed it.

It would be best to stop this whole charade and run into his arms. But that isn't the right decision.

With one angel on each side of them, they suddenly take off into the air and fly away. Immediately, I feel myself being lifted up as well. Turning my head, I see that the monster has me wrapped in his arms, a repulsive embrace that reeks of insincerity.

We fly off in the direction of home. His minions said they found the area our village is located in, but they may not know the exact location. From up here, however, it shouldn't be too difficult to discern amongst the towering trees. Maybe they lack the ability to see from afar.

After several hours, the forest clears somewhat, and I can feel home calling to me. We land softly near the edge of the village center. The patrols on the gate must have seen us coming a mile away, yet still people are scattered around in huddled clusters. Pandemonium breaks out as the stragglers run for the nearest open doorway, their fear finally outweighing their curiosity.

I realize that they must really have trouble seeing far away because, instead of heading straight for the Healing Tree, the murderous beast looks at me meaningfully, as if waiting for me to point the way. I'm not sure how else he could have missed the enormous tree, as low as we were flying.

Flying. I was flying. How my life has changed.

I lift my finger to point toward our destination, and he grabs my upper arm in a not-so-gentle manner, dragging me along the path. Bhradon and Cyndene are being moved along in a similar manner.

Gani. I see her in the shadow of a building as she begins to follow us, albeit from afar. This will be the last thing they remember of me. That she remembers of me.

I may throw up.

When we reach the clearing, Lucifer seems to completely forget about me in his ecstasy over finally seeing the object of his desire. The sparkle in his eye is a gleam of pure joy, and I could almost believe for a moment that he isn't a monster.

But he is. And his happiness comes from crushing others. Do I believe for one second that he ever had any intention of helping me or my people?

Of course not. But he doesn't know that I know.

Since he's left me on my own, I scuttle over to Gani despite my aversion to even looking her in the eye right now. I have to tell her that Mori's dead. And that it's all my fault.

And that I'm about to sacrifice everyone to the Devil.

CHAPTER 53

Before I speak a word, she grabs me and hold me in a tight embrace. Pulling back, she looks at me with tears in her eyes.

"We've been ... we thought ... I thought ... I thought you were dead!"

And leaning over beside her, I empty the meager contents of my stomach into the lush grass.

I can't say it. I just can't. If I say it aloud, that makes it final. Not that it matters anymore. None of it matters anymore.

Okay. "Gani, Mori didn't make it."

Fresh tears well up, and it's my turn to hold her tightly, rocking her back and forth, humming my mother's tune.

After a moment, she pushes back and stands up. "Your mother would be so proud of you, Corinne."

Flabbergasted, I exclaim, "What? Why? All of this is my fault, Gani! You don't understand—"

"Yes, I do. I told you to choose carefully. And I see that you've made your choice." She smiles.

"No! You don't know what he's about to do. There's so much I want to tell you, but—"

"But there isn't time, child. It's best this way."

Gaping at her in puzzlement, I walk away as she scoots me along, as if I'd interrupted one of her midday naps.

Mori isn't here. I knew he wouldn't be. That message had been given to me over and over, but I wasn't listening. There is no point in shouting his name. And Bhradon isn't even looking at me. His eyes are focused in the same direction as every other eye in the area. The heat is already beginning.

Lucifer pulls power from the tree, causing it to glow with a white-hot aura. I don't know if he even realizes that he, too, is glowing with heat. Fire blazing all over his slowly enlarging body as the power enters into his being, and he continues to absorb its magic, greedy for every last drop. The more he takes in, the bigger his already enormous form becomes.

All of his hubris, anger, and hatred fused into a roiling mound of immense red-hot power. The smell is not like that of burning flesh. It is a living memorial of our once great communal fire, which now seems a lifetime ago. The fire that existed only because of the power of the Healing Tree. We knew it held magic beyond our understanding, but this … this is like nothing that mere words can describe. In this moment of pure energy incarnate, Lucifer is the closest representation of Heaven's majesty we will ever see in this life. A twisted, corrupted version of what it is and what he should have been. The infusion of the corporeal and ethereal is, nonetheless, breathtakingly beautiful yet terrible in its extremity.

The heat emanating off his massive form is beginning to singe everything in the vicinity. Lucifer, blinded by rage and greed, continues to grow exponentially as the people gaze in shocked and terrified wonder. They understand the reality of the situation. There is nowhere to go. There is no escape from this fate. Neither for him nor for us. Yet I have already seen this. I know what happens next...but not after. I only believe. Trust.

Forgive me, Bhradon.

A flash of light, a sudden silence, and we are no more.

CHAPTER 54

Sound that is not sound.

With a loud blast that pierces the silence, everything around me begins to move as one toward a blazing scene that seems far away, yet close enough to touch.

Fire that is not fire.

In the distance, a muffled cacophony of music and noise greets my senses in a wave of disconnected consciousness. I hear, but I do not see. My mind can envision what my eyes cannot, and I know that this is the end of all things.

Bhradon.

That one word, one thought, breaks me back into a million pieces.

Please forgive me. I had no choice.

But I know that isn't true. I did have a choice. I could have ignored what I had seen, what I knew to be the right future. The right path.

The choice was everything. It was all I had, all that kept me focused on what I knew I had to do. I chose this. I chose our fate, but the Creator knew all along that I would.

All the dreams—pre-visions as I now know them to be—and all the things I *saw* in my mind were a giant piece of the plan. *His plan.* But he allowed me to choose.

What if Mori had been here? What if he had the same vision as I while still alive instead of while dying, with no sense of understanding that comes with death and the afterlife? Would he have chosen as I did? Would he have tried to stop me? Wouldn't *anyone* have tried to stop me had they known? To keep me from destroying our people? He knew that I would choose wisely, but my heart bleeds for the end of everything we know.

*****

A voice carries with it a sense of urgency. The sensation of opening my eyes—of once again *having* eyes—overwhelms my thoughts, and I look around.

White. Everything is completely and utterly white.

Once again, a voice urgently crying out. My name. It's crying out my name. Turning around, I see someone behind me. He almost blends in with the starkness of the background, but he moves around to stand in front of me. Only then do I realize I'm also standing. There is no furniture here, nothing to sit or lay on. How did I get here?

He speaks my name again with the same insistence as before. I open my mouth to answer and suddenly realize that there is also no floor.

I am floating.

"Where am I?"

"It's good to see you awake, my friend. Where do you think you are?"

"I have no idea."

"You have come to the place between places. Where your ancestors came from."

"Heaven." It isn't a question.

"Yes, but don't get too comfortable. You won't be here very long."

Frantically, I stutter over my words, "But why? I thought I did what he wanted! Where are you sending me? Where is everyone else?"

"Corinne, my sister, my wonderful glorious sister, you are not being sent anywhere. But the new realm is being built, and you are back with us, so you will join us when it has been completed."

"Who is us?"

"My family, your family. Our family. We are all angels in our own right, and you are a dear sister to me, Corinne."

"You know my name, but what is yours?"

"Phanuel. I am saddened by the fate of our brother, but I am glad that his treachery is over. He will pay for his actions for all eternity within the fires that he and his followers so feared. He claimed not to believe in the inevitability of it all, that he could change the ending, yet their fear of your fire was for good reason."

"Your brother... Lucifer. I wish it could have been different. He killed my brother."

"He did many, many things that were beyond evil. But that isn't why you followed the path that you did."

"No, I would have tried to kill him myself if it was just about Mori. But I knew—somehow I knew—that this was bigger than that. I just couldn't see how the plan ended."

"Yet still you chose to follow it. That was incredibly brave of you. Not having the luxury of a life spent here, you had no concept of where to place your trust. He knew that. But he also knew that you were smart enough and strong enough to withstand the temptation to follow your own path. Always thinking of your people before yourself. You risked your life to save them."

"But I sacrificed theirs in the process."

"Did you? Is this not better? We will be rejoining the others in the new realm on Earth, so do not be discouraged by the strangeness of your current surroundings." He has a genuine smile full of happiness and purity.

"But the Earth is gone, Phanuel. He destroyed it. And I let him." The loss is overpowering when I think of the magnitude of what was done.

What I did.

"You were not permitted to see what came after, but know that I have been there with you in spirit all along the way, guiding and protecting you as well as I could. The loss of your brother was devastating to you, but some part of you must have believed that death was not the end. Otherwise, your choices might have been different. Don't you see? You are all here because you put your trust in him. You have helped to fulfill his promise to the humans, a place upon the Earth where they may dwell in peace and prosperity. But that door is open to us as well. We are all welcome in the new realm, Corinne. It won't be long before this realm fades away. Never having spent time here, I think you will be much more comfortable once we return to the Earth with our kin."

"Are you saying that Mori is here?"

"Yes, he is here. And he's been anxiously awaiting your arrival. Along with others you may want to see, I'm sure."

"Bhradon. I'm afraid he may not want to see me, though. And…my parents?"

His broad smile only widens. "Come. Let us join the others."

~ DENOUEMENT ~

A realm of peace finally found its home. Home is here on Earth.
For them. For us. For everyone.

For the salvation of my people, I sacrificed them. I threw away
everything I knew and everything I loved simply because I knew
it was right. I put my trust where it needed to be all along, and
I watched my people disappear on the breath of a fiery wind.
A wind that has swept us into the new world, a world of hope.
The world we were meant to be a part of since the beginning of
time. For although it still feels strange to be in such a vastly different form now, it somehow feels like home. Home is within
the heart, and my heart still lies with the ones I love. Nothing
will ever change that. My brother and I still share a bond that no
words can explain. Gani is so much happier now than she ever
was bending over a hot fire to toil and cook all day, every day.

And Bhradon.

There was no reason to fear an unforgiving nature with him. He says he trusted me all along, but I know that isn't true. The look on his face that day will haunt me for all eternity. Plus, I'm certain he was just as frightened as everyone else was when the end came. No one was more afraid than I was. But he will not let me go for all the world, and I have no desire to protest.

My people are safe. They still struggle with the idea that they are not, in fact, people. Not in the human sense, anyways. But they are happy and well protected by the fact that these forms do not, and never will, die. We will not have to endure that again. Never again.

My ancestors, the First, sacrificed themselves for the love of the Creator in order to protect his kingdom. They gave up their former lives, their angelic existence, to travel here to Earth to save a precious piece of the Paradise that he had once built for the people.

The humans. But they fell victim to their own humanity.

As did the First. For the love of him, they came to Earth to protect a sacred, yet dangerous, artifact. For the love of one another, they remained and started a family.

The First built and cultivated a society out of love. Their descendants forged a gathering of those who would fight to keep the memory of our first mother and father alive. The determination and bravery of those people inspired those of us who remained, and we were able to find a personal connection to the importance of our past and what it signified for our future.

For we are the Last.

EXPLORE MORE BOOKS
BY LISA M. GREEN

Discover your next favorite fantasy read at *lisamgreen.com/books*. You can find information and links to retailers for each book.

* * *

ESCAPE TO A NEW WORLD

Sign up to hear about new releases and other updates from Lisa M. Green, and you'll also receive a free preview sampler of *Dawn Rising,* the first book in the Awakened series. This sneak peak contains the first five chapters, so it's longer than the typical "Look Inside" samples and lets you get a good taste of the world and writing before you decide whether or not to dive in headfirst. Go to *lisamgreen.com/dr-preview* for your free copy.

* * *

ENJOYED THE BOOK AND WANT TO
SHOW YOUR SUPPORT?

You are an amazingly awesome person! Thank you! Please take just a moment and post a review of the book on Amazon, Goodreads, Barnes & Noble, or anywhere you normally post reviews.

Once again, THANK YOU!

ACKNOWLEDGMENTS

My gratitude goes out to the following people whose contributions made this book possible:

My cover art and website designer, Jason Green

Contributing artists Chrystan Tucker and Autumn Greer

All of my loyal supporters on Facebook, Twitter, and Goodreads, as well as everyone who followed my journey on the website

The members of various writing forums who have given me some much-needed advice and encouragement

Dr. Darren Crovitz and the whole gang from the 2006 creative writing class—we definitely need a Crovitz reunion!

And to those who believed in me before any of this was possible, a huge thank you to all of my supporters on Kickstarter, especially:

Austin and Victoria Kiddle

Dave Archer

Dianne Fries

John Estes

Becky Estes

Melinda Green

Brandi Belicek

Christopher Valois

Awakened ~ Book One

Once upon a time, a girl was born. A hundred years later, she grew up.

Aurianna must rewrite the past in order to save the future. She was supposed to be the answer to an enigmatic prophecy discovered on the night of her birth. But a terrible curse changed her life forever.

That is, until a mysterious stranger arrives to break the spell. He awakens Aurianna to the truth of her past and the powers she never knew she had.

When he sweeps her back in time, she discovers there is more to her life than she ever imagined. The world she encounters is both strange and familiar. But learning to control her newfound elemental powers will be the least of her problems.

She must race against time to uncover the truth about a catastrophe that will leave the world broken, divided, and at war.

Aurianna just wants answers. But the people need a savior.

For more information about Dawn Rising, as well as other books in the Awakened series, visit lisamgreen.com/dawn-rising.

LISA M. GREEN

DAWN RISING

AWAKENED ~ BOOK ONE

ABOUT THE AUTHOR

Lisa M. Green writes stories of myth and magic, weaving fairy tales into fantasy. She enjoys reading, writing, cooking, traveling, hiking, and playing video games that girls aren't supposed to like.

lisamgreen.com
facebook.com/authorlmgreen
instagram.com/authorlmgreen
@authorlmgreen

Lightning Source UK Ltd.
Milton Keynes UK
UKHW010627220221
379183UK00001B/52